The Kindness of Strangers

by

Tina Cox

© Tina Cox 2013

All rights reserved

Lizzie's Story

Chapter 1

The morning with its leaden grey clouds, which almost seemed low enough to touch, and the freezing temperatures in the shoe box she laughingly called her studio apartment matched Lizzie's mood exactly. There was more ice on the insides of the windows than there was outside, no food in the room – not even the makings of a hot drink, and no cosy duvet to snuggle in. Depression had enfolded her for weeks now, like a blanket, but a blanket like no other as this one gave her neither warmth nor comfort. She had tried so hard to make it on her own, but now with the threat of the re-possession and near starvation - which were the direct result of her redundancy (but the indirect result of so much more) – hanging over her, she had had enough.

'You'll soon be running back to your doting Mummy with your tail between your legs and I'll be here waiting for you,' Pete had sneeringly foretold when she had left home, having also had enough of him. Enough of his lascivious looks, of the weight of his body as he pinned her against walls so that his hands could stray all over her whenever Mum left the room. And more than enough of his 'promises' to make a woman of her as soon as they had the house to themselves.

Ever since he had moved in with her mother, six months before she had been forced to leave, Lizzie had known real fear. This was something which was completely foreign to her in a father figure as her own beloved, and much mourned, father had been kindness itself. She had always felt safe and protected when her Dad was alive and she knew he would have torn Pete apart with his bare hands if he had been around and known what was going on. But then if he had still been around Pete would never have been able to con her mother that he was a decent, honourable guy and would never have been allowed to move in with them.

During those terrifying months, as Pete had got bolder and more threatening, Lizzie had often thought about what Dad would do now if he were able to protect her as he always had; and had managed to draw some comfort from the certainty that he would have defended her.

He wasn't there now however, she only had herself and her own wits for protection. That had led to her stealing the carving knife from the kitchen, and hiding it away at the very back of her bedroom cupboard behind mountains of old books from school and college.

This theft had remained undetected as Pete was more partial to take-away pizzas and burgers than roast dinners meaning that their eating habits as well as the safe happy atmosphere of the house had changed, and not for the better. But the knowledge that she had the means to defend herself was some small comfort.

When her mother's new boyfriend had first moved in, Lizzie had tried to welcome him, even though part of her resented someone else occupying her father's place in the family home, sitting in her father's favourite chair, carelessly mowing the lawn her father had tended so lovingly and sleeping in her father's place in her mother's bed.

    Despite these natural resentments, resentments which most sixteen year old girls would feel, Lizzie had tried to see him as someone who would make her mother happy again after the pain of losing Lizzie's father to sudden and catastrophic cancer.

    It seemed so long ago now since they were a happy self contained unit, although in reality her father had been dead for only eighteen months. Back then Lizzie had been spending every available minute studying hard preparing for her final school exams in just over a year and hoping to get good enough grades to take her to college.

    Her ambition had been to train as a veterinary nurse and, for as long as she could remember, she had used her pocket money to buy any book on the subject she could get her hands on, reading them avidly both out of interest and to give her a head start once she started college.

    These were the very books which had helped to conceal the carving knife when she had lived at home for those last dreadful weeks and months. Now a column of those same books supported a lamp by her bedside in her room, and helped stop the rickety table from wobbling. The lamp was probably as old as she was with a lethally frayed flex and the rickety table was in no better condition. With its worn, almost transparent and ancient 'Formica' topping, from which all trace of pattern and colour had been rubbed away, and legs on which there were a thousand chips in the enamel paint, now grey with age and unmentionable stains.

The books and her mobile phone were the only things Lizzie hadn't been able to sell for food or coins for the voracious electric meter. All her lovely clothes carefully and lovingly bought as presents or received as treats over many years had gone. At the time she had told herself it had been a worthwhile sacrifice if it helped maintain her independence, her safety; and anyway she had reasoned, she only needed a couple of changes – one to wear and one to wash.

Being forced to part with her lovely watch was much harder. It was the watch her parents had given her for her thirteenth birthday – to celebrate becoming a teenager, and she had cried when she had surrendered it to the pawn broker, who had seemed to sympathise with her, his features kind, although not kind enough to give her what the watch was really worth. Her portable television and video recorder, DVD player, stereo and her treasured camera had all gone the same way.

All had gone to the pawn shops she never knew existed until a few weeks ago, but in which she was now on first name terms with the various owners and where she had witnessed many tears similar to her own as treasured possessions were surrendered for hard cash.

The sacrifices had staved off what she was now forced to accept was the inevitable for a few more months as she had sparingly rationed the proceeds on food, but mostly on rent.

Now all she had left were her precious mobile phone and the books with which she couldn't bring herself to part, and which would be worth nothing to anyone else anyway. She had kept the books because they symbolised her ambitions and the hopes which she had held onto that she would be able to follow her dreams. She had kept her phone so that she could still talk to her mother, who unaware of Pete's threats, could not understand why Lizzie had left a seemingly happy home and worried about her constantly.

Her mother found it even harder to understand Lizzie's refusal to tell her where she was living, begging Lizzie to tell her or to come home. Lizzie knew, however, that if her mother ever found out, so would Pete and that must never be allowed to happen. But it grieved her that by withholding such information she was adding to her mother's worries about her and to her hurt and confusion over Lizzie's apparent abandonment of her.

Lizzie had originally thought that when her phone's meagre air time balance finally ran out she would have to somehow find the odd coin to ring her mum from a call box, but just the thought of going out at night after her Mum had got home from work and walking the half mile or so through the scary, run down, gang infested streets terrified her. And where were these coins to come from anyway?

Until three weeks ago Lizzie had really thought she might be able to manage on her own. She wouldn't go as far as saying she was happy about the situation and had reluctantly accepted that her plans for college would have to be put on hold, but it had been better than living with Pete and his threats. She had been employed and had the security of a wage just large enough to pay for rent and food. Now the job was gone, evaporating as effectively as mist in the cold reality of the world wide recession.

It had been a long way from what she had wanted to do, only being a job in a shop, stacking shelves and doing the odd shift on the till, but it had been a job which had given her security as it had brought in the money she needed to exist.

But the store had been forced to cut back on staff and as they explained it was last in, first out. The kindly manager, Mr. Trescott had cushioned the blow as much as he could by telling her that it was a very reluctant decision on his part as he had recognised great potential in her.

'You are a willing worker, always on time for work and always pleasant with the customers – which is more than can be said for a lot of young girls these days in my experience,' he had said. 'Nevertheless I have been under a lot of pressure from head office to cut back and so I'm afraid I am going to have to let you go. If anything should come up in the future I'll be in touch, you can depend on that.'

His words had been good to hear, but they were cold comfort, because kind words would not feed her or keep a roof over her head. Now her rent was due tomorrow and her hard faced, chain smoking landlady would not be swayed by promises or hard luck stories. There would be no kind words from her, nor any sympathy to be found in her cold eyes, and there was no way Lizzie was going back home. Her job, her wage, soon her flat and any hope of security in the future were all gone.

She couldn't even think of her old house as home now; it hadn't been that since Pete had moved in, but what was she going to do? She would not be able to ask her mother for a loan, for even if Pete allowed her to advance the money, her Mum would want to know why Lizzie had felt she had to move out when she seemingly had everything she needed at home. And Lizzie couldn't explain, couldn't tell her Mum what Pete had threatened while hinting that he was just waiting for the opportunity to put his threats into action. Much as she would like to tell her mother what he was really like, part of her wanted to protect her mother from any more hurt; she had been through enough. 'And what if she refused to believe you?' whispered the devil voice in her head. Her mum seemed to be happy with Pete and as she had seen no evidence of a problem, a tiny, minute part of Lizzie worried in case her mother refused to accept the truth.

She was only sixteen though and sometimes when cold, hungry or worried, like she was now, she longed for her Mum - for her loving arms which, when they enfolded you, could block out any and all troubles.

How could she not know what Pete was, Lizzie asked herself for the thousandth time? How could she not see him for the pervert he so obviously was? How could she have missed the subtle innuendoes or the hungry predatory looks he cast in her direction?

Miss them her mum had though and Lizzie could only think that was because her Mum was so happy to have a new, apparently honourable man in her life. To quote the old adage love was indeed blind.

Since losing her job Lizzie had tried everywhere to find work. She had asked in shops, cafes, fish and chip shops, even lying about her age in the hope of finding work in a bar, but she was met with the same answer at each place she tried.

Most people had been sorry, or at least had said they were, but their regret did nothing to improve her situation. As her depression deepened further her head seemed as if it was encased in a steel band and weight pressed down on her making logical or sensible thought impossible.

What was she to do? She couldn't go back to the place she had once called home, she couldn't get a job anywhere and shuddered at the thought of going on the streets to earn a living – that would be as bad as surrendering herself to Pete.

There was only one other option open to her and that was to take enough paracetamol to end her miserable life. She had two pounds seventy-five pence left in her purse, surely if she went from shop to shop buying the two packets which were the limit that most reputable dealers would sell, she could amass enough.

She imagined the scene – her dead on the floor, her landlady complaining about the mess she had made on the carpet and her mother's … no she couldn't bear to think of her mother's reaction when she was told the news. Couldn't even allow herself to consider the pain her actions would cause.

If she went down that road, it would weaken her resolve and she could not allow that to happen. But before she did anything else Lizzie decided to ring her mum using her last few precious minutes of air time.

She would say goodbye to her in a way which, she hoped, would not arouse suspicion, but she had to hear that loving voice once more.

Tears were streaming down her face blurring her vision as Lizzie opened her mobile phone's address book and scrolled down to MUM. She should be at home now as she only worked for a few hours in the evening at the local old people's home so it was a good time for Lizzie to speak to her one last time. She had only enough credit for this last call and even then it would have to be frustratingly short.

Her disappointment and frustration were almost overwhelming as she heard a stranger's voice informing her she had got through to Mulberry Hill veterinary surgery, which had been the place they used to use before their beloved dog had died, shortly after Pete had moved in.

Secretly Lizzie had often wondered if Pete had been responsible for Patch's death, she wouldn't put it past him because when Mum was out poor Patch's life had deteriorated as well. Lizzie had often heard the dog yelp in surprise and anguish after a vicious kick had been delivered. She had tried to defend him but that had only made Pete worse, until one day she had found Patch writhing in agony on the kitchen floor foaming at the mouth.

Lizzie's Mum had been at work and Pete had refused to help, so Lizzie had carried him all the way to the surgery on her own where the vet had seen him immediately. They had tried to save him, had given him something to make him sick while asking if he could have been in contact with any type of poison. But it had been too late and Patch, the best friend of her childhood, and the most loyal pleasant dog anyone could wish for, had died in her arms.

With a voice thick with tears brought on both by memories she would rather forget and frustration at hitting the wrong number in the phones' address book she tried to apologise and was just about to disconnect when she heard the person at the other end speak again.

'No wait!' said a voice which now, in her distress she barely recognised vaguely from previous visits to the surgery. 'Don't hang up you are obviously really upset. Have you rung about a sick animal?'

'No, I ...I'm sorry I rang... I rang the wrong number,' Lizzie managed to stutter through her tears.

'Well something has certainly upset you, I'm on my break at the moment,' continued the first kind voice she had spoken to in what seemed like far too long a time. 'Why don't you tell me what's wrong?'

Lizzie would never be able to understand why she did what the voice asked of her. Perhaps it was the need to unburden herself to tell a sympathetic human about her troubles. Perhaps it was merely a subconscious desire to have someone stop her going through with her plan, but she hesitated just long enough for the voice to continue kindly and gently.

'My name is Sharon,' she said. 'What's yours?'
'Lizzie.'
'Hello Lizzie you sound very upset - what's wrong love,' she asked again.
'I can't go on any longer, it's all too hard.'
'What's too hard, tell me love, I want to help.'
'I had to leave home when my mum got a new partner – he kept threatening to... to ... '
'He was going to attack you?'
'Yes ... So I had to move out.'
'Didn't you tell your mum what was happening?'
'I couldn't - she seems so happy with Pete.'
'So what did you do?'
'I found myself a grotty room with an even grottier landlady who calls it a studio flat.'
'How long have you been there?'
'Just over six months. It was alright at first because I got a job stacking shelves in a supermarket, but they had to cut back on staff and so I had to leave. I can't get another job and now the rent is due at the end of the week, and I can't pay it ... I can't even afford anything to eat. I'm so cold and so hungry... '
'And of course you don't feel as if you can go home ... don't you think you could tell your mum what has been happening?'
'No ... So I've got to... I've got to...
'You aren't thinking about doing anything silly are you love?'

'It's not silly – it's the only thing left that I can do. I've got no choice. Everything's gone wrong. I worked so hard to get good grades in my GCSE's. I was going to go to college, but now...'

'What were you going to study?'

'I wanted to be a veterinary nurse.'

'Oh. Well surely that's something to look forward to.'

'How can I? I've got no money, no job. Soon I won't even have my room. How can I put myself through college?'

'How old are you Lizzie?'

'Nearly seventeen, what's that got to do with anything?'

'Nothing ... no, I just wondered. I thought you sounded young that's all.'

'Too young to know what I'm doing, I suppose you think!'

'Not at all, my daughter is about your age and she is more than capable of making her own decisions believe me – or so she often tells me,' Sharon said with a giggle in her voice. 'So how did you have this number in your phone's address book - do we know you?'

'We used to bring our dog to you... he died not long before I left home... I often wonder if Pete poisoned him... He hated poor Patch.'

'Oh I see, I think I remember him, so your mum would be Mrs. ...?'

'Harrison. Why are you asking me all these questions?'

'I'm sorry I'm just trying to get a picture of you in my head. Call me strange but I like to know who I'm talking to,' Sharon replied suddenly afraid of alienating the girl.

She wanted to ask where she was living, but knew by Lizzie's suspicious tones that any more questions would make her disconnect and she didn't want to risk that so decided to keep the conversation lighter. 'Of course, yes I do remember you now. You asked if it would be possible to do some work experience at the surgery when you were at college.'

'No chance of that now.'

'Look Lizzie will you promise me something.'

'What?'

'I'm still on my lunch break - will you meet me in the park at the back of the surgery in half an hour? If you really have made your mind up, there's nothing I can do to stop you, but at least meet me and talk for a while. If my Katy were in trouble I would want to think someone was there for her.'

'I don't know ...look I've got to go ...I'm nearly out of credit.'

'Okay, but just promise you'll meet me.'

Chapter 2

But the phone call had ended. Sharon was left impotently holding a phone from which only galling silence resonated at the other end.

Frantically worried now about this young girl and what she might feel forced to do in her despair, she dashed through to the vet's consulting room, ignoring all protocol about interrupting a consultation.

Grabbing the vet, Steve's, arm she dragged him into the operating theatre at the back of the consulting room and explained as briefly as she could what had happened. He was both amazed and naturally indignant at her unusual and unprofessional behaviour but this melted as quickly as it had surfaced as he gave her his blessing to leave immediately in the hope of finding this troubled girl.

'If there's anything I can do to help just call me okay,' he said as Sharon dashed for her coat and the door, without even glancing back, but lifting her hand over her shoulder to acknowledge that she had heard him..

Grateful for his understanding, but desperate to get to the park she ran from the surgery still pulling on her coat as she went. How could she help Lizzie? What would she do if the girl failed to show? How could she find out where she lived in the hope of preventing a tragedy if Lizzie didn't show up at the park?

All these questions ran through Sharon's mind as she raced at top speed for the park, her eyes searching for anyone who might be Lizzie as soon as she was through the park's gates.

Scanning every tree and every bench, even the children's swings for a likely candidate, her desperate eyes finally alighted on a girl of about the right age who was shivering in a thin jacket totally inadequate for such a cold late autumn day and who looked as if she hadn't had a decent meal for far too long. Her skin was pinched with cold and grey with tiredness and hunger, but Sharon noticed the satin-like gleam of her hair, wondering how Lizzie had managed, despite everything, to keep herself so obviously clean. She must still have pride in herself for she obviously hasn't let herself go despite all her troubles, thought Sharon and marvelled at the girl's courage and resilience. Perhaps I can use that, Sharon thought, tap into those hidden reserves to show her there is hope, and that another way out of her troubles can be found. What and how Sharon had no idea, but the sight of that gleaming mane of hair had further convinced her that she must try everything to find a way.

Afraid of making her bolt by approaching too hastily Sharon walked as calmly and quietly as she was able to the bench on which the girl, she hoped was Lizzie, sat.

'Lizzie?' she asked tentatively.

Her enquiry met with no response, the girl didn't nod, or look in her direction – there was nothing in her attitude which might suggest Sharon had found the right person or even that the girl was aware of her presence.

'Hi, I'm Sharon,' she continued deciding to presume that this was Lizzie. 'You look really cold, love, here let me put my coat around you.'

Lizzie flinched at the touch of the coat and Sharon's hands as she placed it gently around her trembling shoulders, but she didn't pull away or, worse still run. For what seemed an eternity they sat immobile and silent, but at last as the warmth of the thick jacket began to thaw Lizzie's shivering body she turned to face Sharon.

'We can stay here if you like,' Sharon said at last 'but how about we go to the café and get us both something to eat. I don't know about you but I'm starving and I could do with a nice hot cup of tea as well.'

The only response was a nod so small Sharon wondered if she had imagined it until she rose and Lizzie followed suit holding the edges of Sharon's coat across her chest, desperate for the warmth it gave her.

They walked in silence to the small café which was situated at the far end of the park and was popular with dog walkers, joggers and birdwatchers alike. It was a firm favourite with mums with toddlers or buggies too. Mothers who, having abandoned menial household chores, were out for the afternoon in the vain hope that fresh air and an hour or two running around and playing on the adventure playground would ensure their children slept that night.

It was early in the daily life of the café and Sharon was relieved to find they had the place almost to themselves. The earliness of the hour though did nothing to lessen the smell of chips and all day breakfasts. Having been cooked so regularly over so many years their fragrance seemed to have seeped into every table, every chair and had even into the walls themselves and still hung in the air like a blue fog.

'What would you like to eat Lizzie, don't worry I'm buying. I had to come out to get something for myself anyway and I'd much rather not eat alone,' she said suddenly afraid the girl would view her offer as charity.

Lizzie said nothing, so Sharon went ahead and ordered a sandwich for herself and an all day breakfast with a side order of chips and bread and butter for Lizzie, along with a large mug of tea for each of them. She hoped the sight and smell of the food would be enough to tempt Lizzie to stay and talk to her.

Her hopes proved to be justified as before long a plate laden with three rashers of bacon, two fat juicy sausages, eggs, hash browns, mushrooms, tomatoes and beans was placed before Lizzie, while her chips and bread and butter were placed at her elbow.

'Is this all for me?' Lizzie asked, reacting for the first time as if climbing up from some deep trance-like state.

'It certainly is – I don't think my poor old arteries could stand all that fat. I'm more than happy with my chicken and sweetcorn sandwich – tuck in love. We can talk when you've eaten and then only if you want to.'

Just as Lizzie was starting to demolish the gargantuan meal with surprising speed and obvious relish, Sharon's mobile rang. Looking at the small display screen she saw it was Steve, her boss, and so decided to move away from the table so she could talk more privately, but stationed herself just inside the door in case Lizzie should make a run for it.

'I have to take this call Lizzie, sorry. I won't be long, but it's work, they could have an emergency,' she said but her words produced no response.

Their conversation was brief and to the point, but left Sharon feeling more grateful than she had ever done that she worked for such a wonderfully kind man.

Despite the call lasting less than three minutes Lizzie's plates were completely clean by the time Sharon sat down once more, their surfaces wiped so clean that it was hard to imagine they had held a large amount of food just minutes before.

'My goodness you soon saw that lot off,' said Sharon laughing and was heartened to receive a smile in return.

'That's the first meal I've had in over a week … thanks,' Lizzie replied her hands wrapped around her mug as if soaking up its comforting warmth.

'Right so are there any other reasons you're contemplating doing what I think you are - other than the ones you told me about?'

'Don't you think they're enough?' asked Lizzie with a new hardness to her voice.

'Oh yes, more than enough - don't get me wrong. It's just that all those problems are so easily solvable.'

'You think?' Lizzie replied sarcastically. 'Don't even bother suggesting I go home again. I can't and I won't.

'Fair enough – but what about getting another job?'

'Do you think I haven't tried? There are no jobs to be had – I've looked everywhere, everyone is blaming this recession. So you see there really are no answers to my problems.'

'Well there are if you have a wonderful boss like mine. That was him on the phone just now and we have a proposition to put to you. Please hear me out and let me make it quite clear he is not offering you charity. If you decide to accept his offer you will certainly have to work for it. For months now he has been advertising for someone to live in the small flat above the practice. The flat would be rent free to any tenant who is willing to undertake certain duties at the practice. The tenant would be required to clean the surgeries and operating theatre as well as the waiting room and the staff room every day. In addition they would be required to clean the cages where post-operative patients have to spend the night recovering after surgery and possibly feed them if they are ready to take food, or at least prepare the food under supervision. A nurse is always on duty overnight to monitor them, but cleaning and feeding as well is too much. In addition to this there would be a small wage, just pocket money really if truth were told, and a bursary should the applicant wish to go to college to study any subject connected to veterinary care.'

'You're kidding me!'

'No, believe me it's a very genuine offer. The upstairs flat is small, just a tiny sitting room - cum kitchenette with a bedroom which is only just big enough for a single bed and small wardrobe, I'm afraid. But there is also a shower room so the flat is totally self-contained, it even has its own entrance so the tenant wouldn't have to drag bags of shopping through the practice's rooms. As far as I remember it's fairly clean although nobody has used it for ages and it probably needs a lick of paint everywhere but nothing that can't be easily sorted out.'

'You said something about a wage as well.'

'Well more like pocket money really, as I said, eighty pounds a month Steve says, but that would just be for food. The cost of electricity would be included you see, because the flat runs off the same meter as the rest of the practice. You would be working in the evenings and early mornings, so the days would be your own.'

'And I could get to go to college as well?'

'Yes Steve would pay any fees, and because your days would be free you would be able to fit college in as well. Of course you'd have to get yourself there and buy any books you might need.'

'That's no problem – I bought most of them when I decided I wanted to train as a veterinary nurse – I've read them all as well, loads of times – I almost know them off by heart. I wanted to give myself a head start.'

'My, you are keen aren't you? – it looks as if we might have struck gold with you. You are just what we need to inject some new ideas and enthusiasm into the practice.'

'You are serious – this isn't some kind of cruel joke is it?'

'No love, we wouldn't do anything so mean to anyone. Steve is perfectly serious and so am I. I'm not telling you any lies or winding you up as my daughter would say. As I said Steve has been looking for someone to do this for ages and has advertised the post several times, but to be honest anyone who came for it soon lost interest when he told them he could only offer eighty pounds a month, and when they saw how small and dingy the flat is.'

'Well I'm more than interested. This is a real life saver for me,' said Lizzie.

They caught each other's eye then and both burst out laughing as they realised just how true Lizzie's words had been.

Chapter 3

As they were both keen to capitalise on the agreement it was decided that Lizzie should go back to the surgery with Sharon right away to meet Steve and see the flat.

Of course as soon as she saw him Lizzie realised that Steve had been the kind vet who had tried so hard to save her beloved Patch, so even without his incredible offer he was an instant hit with her. Lizzie remembered how long Steve had worked to save Patch and how genuinely distraught he had been when all his efforts had failed. More surprisingly though, given the number of clients he must see every day, Steve had remembered her and Patch, which made Lizzie both less surprised at his kindness and even happier at the prospect of working for him.

She had wondered about the state of the flat after Sharon's less than complimentary description of it but when she saw it she instantly felt at home. It considerably bigger than her so called studio flat which was, in essence, just a dark dingy room with damp riddled walls and no room to swing a kitten let alone a fully grown cat. This flat by comparison was palatial, having a separate sitting room and bedroom with no damp or ill fitting windows through which gale force draughts regularly blew. Best of all however was the fact that she would no longer be forced to share a communal bathroom with other less than personally fastidious or considerate tenants. Lizzie had lost count of the number of times she had cleaned the bathroom only to find that it was again filthy and littered with the needles and other detritus left by her drug crazed neighbours. She would be able to keep this bathroom clean to her own high standards and already knew she could make the flat really cosy.

'It's fabulous – were all the other applicants mad? How could anyone have turned this down?' Lizzie enthused.

'Well believe me, lots did,' Steve had laughed. 'I know it's no palace and that it will need work, but it's nothing that a few tins of paint and a couple of new carpets won't solve. I'll buy the carpets for you by the way - they'll only be cheap ones but at least they will be new and clean - if you agree to decorate it yourself.'

Lizzie could not believe her luck. She had gone from the very depths of despair and contemplating an overdose as the only way out of her problems to having a home, a job and what she wanted more than anything else in the world – the chance to go to college, all in a matter of hours!'

'And you're serious about paying my college fees as well?' she asked still unable to credit how her life had been turned around in a short time, by one magically misdialled phone call.

'Perfectly serious – there is only one proviso.'

Here it is thought Lizzie - here comes the sting in the tail. Her concern must have shown on her face which suddenly dropped as she saw all her hopes being dashed.

'Don't look so worried, I was just going to say that if you agree to the job and the bursary, I would want you to commit to working here for at least three years after you qualify. I can't afford to train someone up only to have them disappear to a post in a rival practice.'

'Oh that's no problem. I've always wanted to work here ever since you were so good and kind when my dog died.'

'Lizzie's dog was Patch, the poison victim,' said Sharon quietly reminding Steve of that dreadful time, although there had been no need – his memory of that dreadful day was a sharp as it ever had been. He had felt so sorry, so inadequate that he had been unable to save what was obviously a much loved pet. But more than that Steve had been enraged that someone could wilfully poison such a sweet animal. Having cared for Patch during his lifetime, administering annual vaccinations and treating minor problems Steve knew how gentle, well behaved and loyal Patch had been. In his own mind he had always been convinced that the dog had not only been poisoned but that it had been a deliberate act. Being so sure that that had been the case, Steve had often wondered about the circumstances which could have led to it happening.

'I remember it well – it was an awfully sad case,' was all he could say.

There was silence in the small flat as each of them remembered that cold rainy night, until Sharon looking around suddenly gasped bringing her hand to her mouth.

'What about furniture!' she said looking around the bare space. 'I suppose your present place is furnished.'

'If you can call it that, but yes I have no stuff of my own.'

'How about I give you a hundred pounds or so to start you off? There's a place in the High Street that sells good quality second hand furniture. The guy who owns it is not only a client but a good friend of mine. How about I give him a call and tell him to expect you?'

'I can't believe all this, I keep thinking I must be in the middle of some weird but wonderful dream and that soon I'll wake up to find myself starving and cold in my grotty old place.'

'It's no dream believe me, you may think my offer is an answer to your prayers, but believe me the feeling is very mutual. Even with this recession I've been unable to find anyone willing to take the job on. Not being able to fill the post has meant asking the nurses to do all the cleaning tasks in turns and that has not been popular when they've already put in a full day's work – trust me! So more often or not I have had to do the work by myself just to prevent a revolution or a mass walk out. I don't think I could have continued to work all day and most evenings and then be on call as well, without having some kind of breakdown. With you on board I might even get my life back, I might even learn to relax … even sleep again,' he said with an ironic laugh.

* * * * *

The very next day Lizzie, with a cheque for a hundred pounds in her pocket, walked the short distance to the second hand shop. The cheque seemed to be giving off a heat of its own which warmed her hand more effectively than the sad old fire at her studio flat ever had, even when she'd had any coins to feed it's voracious appetite. The warmth the cheque generated was much more effective as she held it protectively all the way to the shop.

Dave the owner was a man of about forty, probably the same sort of age as Steve, and had dark, unruly blond hair and a mega watt smile which brightened both the dark gloomy day and the overcrowded dingy interior of the shop, piled high as it was with the leftovers of so many lives.

'Hi, you must be Lizzie, Steve told me to expect you, he said you were going to take some of this surplus stock off my hands and because of that I intend to treat you like royalty,' he said flashing that smile at her again while holding out his hand in greeting as if she was a real grown up. What Dave didn't mention was that Steve had briefly told him of the circumstances and assured him, in the strictest confidence, that a bit more money would be forthcoming if necessary.

'Come on through love, what do you want to look at first?

'I don't know I've never shopped for anything like this before. I've a whole flat to fill too - where do I start?'

'Well, from what I can remember of the flat it's not exactly a twenty room mansion,' he laughed. 'How about we do it room by room?'

'That would be great ... thank you,' replied Lizzie gratefully.

'Right then, if my memory serves me right there's hardly room for a three piece suite, so how about just a couple of nice cosy arm chairs. I've got two out the back as it happens – I picked them up from a house clearance only last week. They're in good nick and are a nice neutral pale coffee colour.'

Lizzie liked the shape and colour of the chairs which was a warm shade but at the same time serviceable and to her eyes stylish. She then sat in one to try them out and found that they wonderfully comfortable; she loved the colour and the way they seemed to offer her comfort by wrapping themselves around her, almost as if hugging her. Lizzie tried hard to hide her excitement, but in reality she was buzzing with pleasure, soon they would be hers.

Dave tried hard not to smile at her obvious excitement, he knew she was trying to be grown up and sophisticated about it, but her shining eyes reminded him of his own girls on Christmas mornings. He was suddenly filled with the desire to give this girl everything she wanted. He knew only too well that if his own girls were in trouble he would do anything to protect them and although normally an even tempered, gentle man had the sudden urge to rip the guy who had threatened Lizzie limb from limb.

'Can I afford them?' she asked seemingly casual, but she was standing in front of a mirror fronted wardrobe and he smiled as he saw, reflected in it, her fingers crossed behind her back dispelling his recent dark thoughts.

He realised that he'd have to be careful. Steve had confided that although down on her luck it was obvious that Lizzie had her pride and so it was important that any deal was believable and could not be perceived as charity.

'I'm looking for fifteen pounds each or twenty-five pounds for the pair – does that suit? Nobody wants soft furnishing in that kind of colour at the moment, even if it is second hand and it's always harder to shift odd chairs than it is a whole three piece suite, so I'd be stuck with them if you don't want them.'

It more than suited and before the hour was out so did many other deals. By the time she left the shop Lizzie was the very proud owner of not only the chairs but a single bed with a pristine mattress, a dented but warm coloured pine wardrobe with a matching bedside cabinet, a sweet little kitchen table with flaps which could be raised to extend its surface area and two almost matching stools. Dave also had some electrical items which were, he said, difficult, if not impossible, to shift and let her have a tiny table top cooker with two hotplates and the smallest, sweetest oven she had ever seen along with a fridge which looked just big enough to fit in the corner of the kitchenette.

'All this must be worth a lot more than the hundred pounds Steve gave me surely,' she said worried now that some of her treasures might be taken from her.

'Well I can't charge you anything for the fridge or the cooker. There are so many safety regulations on second hand electrical items these days, that it makes it nearly impossible to sell them on. To be honest you would be doing me a favour by taking them off my hands. So yes I reckon a hundred will about cover the rest.

Grateful, very un-grown up tears threatened to spill from her eyes as she handed over the cheque arranging delivery for the next day before she left.

Lizzie had arranged to go back to the surgery after her shopping spree to meet the rest of the staff and hoped she would be able to take another look at the flat which was to be her home.

Sharon greeted her warmly as she walked through the door before taking her to the staff room to meet the nurses and receptionists who were taking their lunch break. Everyone was friendly and several of the girls told her how glad they were to be finally relieved of the cleaning duties. They gave her coffee and biscuits and before long she felt as if she was already part of the team.

Sharon had yet another surprise for her as she said she had hunted through her garage the evening before and found several tins of part used paint which might be enough to decorate the limited walls of the flat. There were old but serviceable paintbrushes as well which made Lizzie long to start straight away, and made the others smile at her obvious enthusiasm.

'Well I suppose it would be sensible to do it before the new carpets are fitted,' said Sharon. 'I just hope you like the colours.'

Lizzie spent the rest of the day painting - finding the colours almost what she would have chosen herself. There was nearly a full tin of warm cream and a small amount of a rich milk chocolate colour, which would tone beautifully with her lovely chairs. Before long three walls of the sitting room were painted in the warm cream and she was just starting to paint the last wall in the chocolate colour when Sharon appeared at the door with another mug of coffee and yet more biscuits.

'Wow, that looks amazing. Those colours really complement one another. I can see this place will look really smart by the time you've finished with it. What colour carpet will you want?'

'You mean I get to choose?'

'Of course, as Steve said it will have to be cheapish quality, but no reason why you can't have a say about colour.'

'What about one the same shade as this feature wall then?'

'Good choice, warm not overpoweringly dark and a good serviceable colour as well. Have you found anything amongst the paints you would like for the bedroom?'

'I really like the green, my bedroom at home was green so I thought that would be nice.'

'That would look good, the paint is a little bit dark for such a small room but you could always lighten it up by adding a bit of this white paint to it. I often play around with colours when I decorate which is perhaps why I have so many bits and bobs left over,' Sharon laughed. 'And if you were thinking of getting a cream carpet for the bedroom that would also lighten it up a bit. You don't want anything in here too dark I suppose because it's such a small room. But listen to me telling you what to do; sorry love, my Katy would be ripping in to me something dreadful if I was offering her advice.'

'No you're right. I would never have thought of mixing the paint - that's a really good idea and I was thinking about a fairly light cream carpet anyway. I really don't know how to thank you and Steve. Yesterday I was as low as it is possible for anyone to get and now my life has turned around completely and I'm having such fun! If it hadn't been for you both I don't know what I would have done. Well I do of course ... you saved me, and I can't understand why you bothered when nobody else did.'

'Think of it as the "Kindness of Strangers" love. My dear old Mum always told me we are put on this earth to help one another and as I said to you when we first met I would like to think someone would help my Katy if ever she was in trouble. Kindnesses should be passed around and one day I hope you will be able to do something for someone else who really needs help.'

* * * * *

Another six months had passed since Lizzie's crisis and during that time her life had completely turned around. She loved working at the surgery, loved the quietness and peace of her night time shifts, loved being able to talk to the animals who were recovering from surgery and were often stressed in unfamiliar surroundings. Sometimes she would gently stroke them as well and she hoped that her gentle touch, soft voice and kind words soothed them, even perhaps helped in some small way with their recovery. She would also ask Steve or one of the nurses what had been the matter with the animals and would then research their complaints or injuries, and their treatment. Once Steve realised what she was doing he always tried to find the time to talk to her about each of the animals who passed thought the surgery, occasionally testing her on their symptoms, diagnosis and treatment.

Steve had worked with many dedicated vets and veterinary nurses, but he had never met anyone like Lizzie who had researched and read so extensively on the subject ever since she was a very small girl. At first it had been his way of encouraging her, bit it wasn't long before, amazed at her knowledge he found himself discussing cases with her as if she was fully qualified and even seeking her opinion on occasion.

The flat was now her cosy sanctuary; painted and carpeted and with the furniture she had bought from Dave it had been transformed. She still saw Dave regularly as he often popped in with a lamp, a vase, a set of pans or even a pretty little occasional table or some other small item he 'couldn't shift.'

Lizzie didn't believe him, but had learned that kindnesses meant as much to the giver as they did the receiver. She knew now that they were to be passed around as Sharon had said, and hoped one day to be able to do as Sharon had suggested and help someone else in need, as she had been.

She was also two terms through her course at the college and to her own surprise as much as anyone else's she was a star pupil. Her dedication and enthusiasm made her willing to work as hard as she could and Steve often joked that he would be glad when she had qualified as he couldn't wait for her to begin work at the practice.

She discovered that she was able to live quite well on the small wage she received. With very careful management she had partly replenished her wardrobe with good quality charity shop clothes, had enough to eat, a small amount of credit on her phone and, over several months, had even managed to save up enough to redeem her beloved watch from the pawn brokers.

But the biggest surprise had been unexpectedly running into her Mum in the supermarket one day. Tearfully her mother had told her how she had received visits from several worried and irate neighbours complaining that Pete was trying to molest their daughters.

She had swiftly and unceremoniously thrown him out, but not before telephoning the police to report him. Pete was now in custody awaiting trial.

'Did he try it on with you – was that why you felt you had to leave?'

Lizzie had told her mother everything then, they had gone back to Lizzie's flat where they had hugged, made gallons of tea and cried together. Her mother had wanted her to come home, but Lizzie explained that she was committed to the surgery not only because of the bursary but also because of Steve and Sharon's kindness.

Her mother had been disappointed at first but ultimately she understood. She was just relieved that she had her daughter back. Now they met up regularly at Lizzie's old home where her Mum cooked her huge, delicious meals, often sending her away with another meal ' just to save her cooking' the following day. In short her Mum was intent on spoiling her rotten. It was she who had bought two sets of beautiful bedding for Lizzie's flat along with a pretty set of china and some easy to maintain pot plants which gave the small flat an even cosier feel.

Lizzie had so much to be grateful for and she never forgot that for a second. Her last thought at night as she lay in her warm cosy and safe bedroom was to remember Sharon's words. 'Think of it as the Kindness of Strangers' she had said.

Sharon's Story

Chapter 1

Sharon was tired. No - more than tired if she told the truth – she was exhausted after an incredibly busy day at the surgery. It seemed as if everyone in the town with pets had been through the doors at one time or another. At one stage the waiting room had been so full that some clients had been forced to wait outside in the rain. Waiting times, of usually only fifteen minutes, had been extended to over an hour and tempers had become frayed – and not just among the human pet owners.

A bad tempered cat, one with such a bad reputation in the practice that the nurses would go to great lengths to avoid handling it, had somehow managed to escape from its basket. It had then gone on the rampage hissing and growling in its search of a victim, until finally singling out a small terrified Yorkshire terrier on which to vent its anger, inflicting a painful scratch on his nose in the process. The dog's owner had naturally been very annoyed and a huge argument had ensued, only to be solved by the owner, who was terrified and shaking as much as her poor pet, being allowed to jump the queue, before she fainted from the shock of it all. This in turn caused more friction and annoyance amongst the other pet owners who had been waiting a long time, which only added to the general mayhem.

Two other dogs, already on edge, as many are when they have to visit the vet had decided to have a scrap and Rosie, one of the veterinary nurses, had been forced to throw a bucket of water over them to separate them, unfortunately soaking the already irate owners as well as their dogs The water had then to be cleaned up of course, as well as several doggy 'accidents' brought on by stress or the excitement of the unscheduled entertainment.

The telephone had rung constantly, forcing Sharon to answer it while concurrently trying to take payments, find client files, book new appointments, dispense repeat prescription medication, and calm frazzled nerves. Before even the morning was over everyone was tired grumpy and exhausted.

The problem had been that the junior trainee vet had developed a vicious case of flu and was unable to do her shift and the locum Sharon had booked had failed to turn up, meaning Steve was trying to cover surgery by himself thereby valiantly trying to do the work of two. By the end of surgery Steve looked so incredibly worn out, even before his post-surgery operating schedule had begun, that Sharon was worried about him.

She wished the surgery could afford another permanent fully qualified vet to ease his load but it could not - so in the spirit of compromise Sharon determined to approach the colleges yet again in the hope of finding a student who would work part time for nothing more than the experience it would give them.

If nothing else such a student would be able to give regular booster vaccinations, deal with ear infections, infected wounds and other minor ailments thereby taking some of the pressure off Steve.

At long last the day had ended – or at least the working day. Now Sharon had to go home and start all over again, there she would have to face beds which needed to be changed, a sink full of dishes to wash and the floors to be vacuumed before she could even think about making the evening meal for herself and her two children.

They were both in their late teens and although Katy was still at school Adam had left some time ago, but had yet to find a job. In her darker, more suspicious moments Sharon sometimes wondered if he had even tried, but all he said was, "It's the recession Mum – get off my back." Despite time hanging on their hands, neither of the children showed any inclination to help to ease her own work load. She had repeatedly asked, no begged, them to at least take some of the load off her by helping around the house, but every time she tried her pleas landed on deaf, uncaring ears, and not even simple tasks like bed making or dish washing were attempted. They were, however, only too willing to take advantage of the benefits of her working - with free bed and board and regular demands for hand outs to go to the pub or cinema.

When Jeff had walked out six years ago for his floozy of a secretary who was less than half his age, and who spent enough on clothes and make-up annually to clear the debt of a small third world country, Sharon had thought it would blow over. She had truly believed that Jeff would realise his actions were the result of some kind of male menopause, that he would see the adverse effect his desertion was having on his children, and would eventually come home.

Her hopes had been groundless, however and they had been divorced for four years. Rather than laying the blame for the break up of their marriage squarely, where it belonged, on his shoulders Adam and Katy had irrationally blamed her for the departure of their beloved father and were punishing her every day.

Since then they had treated her as an unpaid servant most of the time and their home as a hotel. Katy, if she was honest, had begun to come through the teenage years of angst and the distress her parents' split had caused, but Adam remained cold and distant to the point of downright rudeness, even aggression.

It would be mostly his dirty dishes which awaited her in the sink, his washing which overflowed from the laundry basket – that's if he had bothered to pick it up from his bedroom floor where he would have carelessly dropped it. It would be his attitude too which would hurt her the most.

Sharon had tried everything to mend their relationship, talking to him, shouting at him, even threatening to throw him out – although the very thought of him alone on the streets somewhere, getting involved with God knew what, terrified her.

She wished his problems could be sorted out with the comparative ease with which they had solved Lizzie's. Sharon had been so pleased to be able to help the girl – she couldn't take all the credit of course, Steve had been wonderful; but then he always was.

And that was a whole other problem. Sharon had never looked at another man since she and Jeff went on their very first date. Even after he had left her she had resisted any and all attempts by well meaning friends to match-make. Apart from the fact that she had had her fingers severely burned by Jeff's desertion, she'd had no time or energy for anything other that bringing up her children and earning enough money to put food on the table and keep a roof over their heads.

After the divorce had been finalised, Sharon had been forced to find work, especially since the alimony cheques, even when they did arrive, usually fell woefully short of the amount agreed by their solicitors for the maintenance of the children. No amount of badgering or phone calls improved the financial situation and despite the difficulties it caused, Jeff merely said he had no more to give. In rare moments of bitterness Sharon thought that this was because all of his money now went on the floozy, but she had never told her children any of this, not wanting them to become embroiled in disputes or to force them to take sides.

Like many stay-at-home mums she hadn't worked since she was pregnant and any skills she had once had were long out of date, overtaken in the headlong race towards technological improvement. So well paid work in her old field of computing was simply not an option.

At first she worked in a supermarket, first weighing cold meats and cheese on the delicatessen counter and then on the check-out. After that things improved for her as she managed to find a job working for a doctor as his receptionist for just over a year. Then he selfishly decided to retire devoting his days to improving his golf handicap and the new doctor, who was a real mover and shaker, insisted on bringing his own team with him.

Sharon realised from the day she had first met him that she wouldn't have wanted to work for him anyway, because he seemed far more interested in expanding his personal bank balance than caring for his patients. She was therefore somewhat relieved when he showed no compunction about sacking her.

Then by a stroke of pure luck she had seen the advertisement for a receptionist at Mulberry Hill Veterinary Practice and after an interview, which was more like a friendly chat between old friends, rather than a formal meeting between prospective employer and employee, she had been given the job and had fallen in love for the first time in her life and not only with the work!

Never before had she been hit by such a bolt of pure lightning as the first time she laid eyes on Steve. Jeff had been an old school friend whose parents were in turn established friends of her parents and, looking back, she now realised they had just drifted into marriage because it had been expected of them.

She had loved him in a way and had certainly been loyal to him, but it had been a more comfortable kind of relationship, a bit like wearing familiar cosy slippers - until they had disintegrated when Jeff discovered he preferred his women in six inch killer heels. Now Sharon knew that whatever it was she had felt for Jeff it hadn't been love or at least if it was then it was a watered down, sad imitation of the real thing.

Steve though, in those few seconds, had made her feel things she never had before, her stomach had flipped almost making her feel as if it was about to pop out of her throat. Her heart had raced and her palms had been embarrassingly moist when he had shaken her hand. To this day she didn't know how she had managed to hold a sane sensible conversation with him when her body felt as if it was taking part in some weird frenetic dance.

Since coming to work at the veterinary surgery she had discovered that he had never married, indeed some of the other girls surmised that he might be gay, but he had told her once after a long day when she had stayed behind to help him clean the surgery, that he had once been engaged. He had thought his fiancée was the only girl he would ever love until she had left him standing at the altar holding a note which had told him, brutally, it would never work, that she loved his brother instead and was going away with him.

Nothing had ever happened between them in the two and a half years Sharon had worked at the practice, other than that they had become close friends ... but she still had her hopes. He was one of the reasons she loved her job, looked forward to going every day. It was more than worth the tiredness, the constant pressure, the occasional distress when a client's beloved pet had to be put to sleep, just to see his smile each day.

Another reason she loved her work of course, was that she viewed her job as an escape from the tension at home and knew that without those hours of not constantly feeling as if she was walking on broken glass she would surely go mad.

Sometimes when she was at her lowest she wondered what she had done to deserve such treatment – why her husband had deserted her for the office bimbo, why he had then gone to any lengths to avoid paying them maintenance and by so doing had kept them in poverty; and why her children had blamed her so unreasonably that they still continued to treat her appallingly.

Sharon was constantly bemused by their open hostility or their arctic coldness, and was more hurt by their attitude then she could explain to anyone. She had always been the sort of person to put other people first, always ready to help out, to listen to their tales of woe for what seemed like hours on end. She was kind, considerate and caring - everyone said so – well everyone except Adam and often Katy. So how was it that they could be so hateful to her? How could they fail to see the truth of what had happened between their father and her and lay the blame squarely where it belonged?

Over the last few weeks Sharon had become more and more tired, not just physically, but emotionally, tired of always being the one to make an effort, tired of trying to win her children's affection once again. Most of all she was tired of being taken for granted, tired of being there for others when nobody seemed to be there for her, on the occasions when she needed support and understanding.

As she pulled on her ten year old coat, wondering if or when she would ever be able to afford a new one, images of her surly, ungrateful children flashed into her mind. She dreaded to imagine what her reception tonight would be – what she would have to face when she got home and wondered how long she would be able to find the energy to cope with her situation.

It was almost the depth of winter now, the clocks had gone back making the dark mornings and evenings start much earlier and last longer. She hated this time of year when the walk home from the surgery was as black as her mood, not to mention both cold and lonely.

The quickest way home for Sharon was across the park behind the surgery and, although the night was as black as pitch and the park boasted no lamps of any description she had never been frightened or worried by her journey through the avenues of now bare trees and passed the children's playground with its eerily squeaking swings where the ghosts of long grown up children still seemed to play.

One of the reasons Sharon had never been concerned was that she invariably had the park to herself at that time of night as the dog walkers and other park users were long gone – back to their warm and cosy homes - or so she imagined. Its gates always closed only minutes after she had reached the far side where Joe, the park keeper stood, keeping an eye out for her as she made her way along the winding paths. When she reached the gates on the far side he was always there waiting, raising his cap with old fashioned courtesy and wishing her a cheery good night before locking the gates behind her.

Tonight was no different – or so she thought at first. The park was deserted as usual, but less than half way across she was aware of a different atmosphere as the trees overhead bent low and the branches rustled and creaked above her head.

On edge for the first time since she had taken this route home she wondered, fancifully if the trees were trying to warn her about something.

Fanciful or not - only seconds later - out of nowhere, she felt herself being slammed against a massive old oak tree with enough force not only to wind her, but to make her crumple to the ground. The push had been so vicious that Sharon felt her back already bruising where his hands had made contact with her body. Her chest where it had hit the tree felt as if something had broken.

Then the real nightmare began. As she lay on the ground and despite raising her arms in an attempt to defend herself, fists beat into her face repeatedly until she thought her eyes would explode. Feet kicked her ribs and lower back and one of her hands was viciously stamped on making her release the handbag she had been clutching protectively. Her handbag was then wrenched from her injured hand, tearing her coat in the process, before her attacker disappeared into the dark.

The whole attack could not have lasted much more than a minute or two, but they had been the worst minutes of her life, worse even than the night Jeff had callously told her he was fed up with living with an old bag like her and was leaving her for someone who had a bit of life in them.

Absurdly, until she tried to move, Sharon's main worry was her torn coat, wondering if it would be repairable and if not how she would be able to afford a replacement. But then she tried to stand.

Pain seared through her whole body, her ribs felt as if they were on fire, her face felt as if some evil little troll was sticking a thousand knives in it and she was crying. At least she thought the wetness running in torrents down her face was tears until she put a hand up to it and was horrified to see her hand instantly reddened by her own blood.

For what must have been five minutes she repeatedly tried to stand, but every movement produced pain so excruciating that she was forced to give up trying. She tried to call out hoping that Joe, who was probably waiting for her at the far gates by now, would hear but she was unable to force any sound through her cracked and already swollen lips.

Her only hope was to sit quietly and hope that Joe would realise she was late and come looking for her – but why should he, she thought with alarm. Although this was her normal route home there were occasions when she would take another, if she had to pick up shopping on the way home, for example.

Tears really did flow then merging with and diluting the blood pouring from her brow and eye. Was she to die here cold, alone and injured and if she did how would her children feel then?

Hearing the sound of heavy footsteps and cheerful, though tuneless, whistling Sharon was paralysed with fear once more, thinking her attacker was coming back for some more fun at her expense – then common sense took over.

Attackers weren't famous for announcing their presence by whistling and surely they would wear soft soled shoes and, whoever was approaching was wearing shoes which made the comforting clopping sound of hard soles on tarmac.

After all she thought, she hadn't heard anyone approaching the first time so surely her assailant must have been wearing trainers so as not to give away his presence until the last moment. Whoever her attacker had been he had wanted to keep his advantage by ensuring that it was a surprise. It had worked and it had been the suddenness of the attack which had added to the shock she was now experiencing.

The whistling was getting louder and the footsteps were drawing closer until suddenly they came to a halt.

'Oh my God what's happened to you?'

Sharon tried to tell him although part of her - the part which was usually able to find humour in most circumstances wanted to say that she would have thought it was obvious.

'Stay there!' commanded the voice – as if she was capable of doing anything else. 'I'll be back in a minute I'm just going for help.'

"Help" - what a wonderful word, thought Sharon, I like to help people, I helped Lizzie, and I've helped lots of folk in the past – help is good, very good especially if it's coming my way now. I really need it, she thought vaguely, before wondering if she was getting delirious – thinking such silly things at a time like this. But she had no time to think anything else because the man had returned with Joe limping along behind him on his old arthritic legs.

'Lie still,' the man said, again making Sharon wonder why he always stated the obvious. 'I'm just going to put my coat over you are shaking badly.'

"Am I? That's funny I don't feel cold," Sharon wanted to say

'We've rung for an ambulance it will be here in a little while,' he continued, saying what - in Sharon's opinion, were his first sensible words.

It seemed an eternity before she was aware of sirens piercing the still cold night air, but it was then only seconds before two paramedics came racing along the path. One carried a large bag over his shoulder and the other a stretcher covered by a deep red blanket.

"That's good," thought Sharon ridiculously. "I'm glad it's red it won't show the blood."

'Alright love we're here now, can you speak? My name's John what's yours?'

'Daron,' she managed through painfully swollen lips.

'Darren! That's a strange name for a lovely lady like yourself!'

'She means Sharon,' replied Joe speaking for the first time,

'She works as a receptionist at the Mulberry Hill Vets.'

'Okay then Sharon,' said the man called John. We'll just check you over a bit and then we'll take you to A&E for a more thorough check up. Where do you hurt? If you can't talk try pointing - just to give us a clue.'

Sharon managed to raise her arm just enough to point to her sides and her face.

'That's very good Sharon now just lie still until I've checked your ribs over, then I'll give you something for the pain. It will soon kick in and you'll begin to feel much better after that.

'Are you her husband?' asked the other paramedic, who had introduced himself as Paul.

'No, replied her rescuer. 'I was just walking through the park when I found her.'

'A lot would have just walked on – well done mate.'

'How could anyone walk on and leave someone in trouble!'

'You'd be surprised mate,' said Paul. A lot of folk would have walked past thinking she was either drunk or high on drugs, or perhaps that the mugger was still around waiting for another victim. You can go now if you like, but you will need to leave me your name and address for the police, they are sure to have some questions for you.'

'No, I'll stay with her. I'll come to the hospital with her if that's alright.'

'Fine by me, better in some ways because it will mean the police will be able to talk to you straight away.'

While this conversation had been taking place, John had been tending to Sharon's injuries. He had shone a tiny light in her eyes, before wiping away a lot of the blood from her face, but Sharon could still feel its wetness so knew the bleeding had not stopped. He had felt her neck before putting a neck brace on while telling her it was just a precaution then felt all over her rib cage and gently manipulated her arms and legs before finally pronouncing her fit to be moved. Then both men had gently placed her on the stretcher before turning to Joe.

'Can you open both of the gates again? John asked. 'That way we'll be able to drive the ambulance straight in. it will be easier for her that way.

Chapter 2

The drive to the hospital was bumpy with every bump or pothole bought fresh agonies in their wake, but it was mercifully short. The man who had rescued her sat beside her all the way talking about silly things in a soft, calm voice and holding her hand as if they were bosom friends. She was grateful for his soothing presence because even though John had given her some pain relief she was still in agony and even though she hoped the worst of her ordeal was surely over, she was very scared.

Never having ridden in an ambulance before she found the experience terrifying, especially when the emergency sirens and lights were switched on; the sound and the whirling blue light making her wonder just how bad her injuries really were.

It was too early in the evening for the regular stream of drunks who poured into A&E most nights after the local pubs shut, so Sharon was whisked into an emergency room immediately. A doctor, who looked no older that her Adam, and a team of nurses surrounded her bed as soon as she was put there then they began cutting away her clothes, even though Sharon tried to protest, before examining her all over.

They checked her eyes again using a little light, just as John had, placed a mask over her sore face and checked everywhere for bruises and breaks before sending her to x-ray for what seemed like a never ending stream of films.

By the time she was back in the A&E department again and had received several dozen stitches to her eyes, cheeks and lips, a policeman was hovering waiting to ask her all manner of questions. But just as it had been when she had first been attacked, speech was impossible through her cracked and swollen lips. So the policeman handed her a piece of paper and a pen asking her to write down her name and address, place of work and details of next of kin.

The man who had rescued her introduced himself as Sam, before telling the police officer what little he knew – but he was unable to say he saw the attacker. Sharon managed with the aid of the pen and paper to tell them that unfortunately she had not seen her attacker either. Explaining that he had suddenly rammed into her from behind and that from then on all she saw was a hooded jacket and a ski mask, but that yes, there had only been one assailant.

She gave details of the contents of her stolen handbag. Apart from the usual hair brush, basic make-up and other feminine necessities there was a purse containing about thirty pounds she told them, no credit cards, but one Visa debit card.

There were her house keys, but as far as she could remember nothing with her personal details on. No address which might enable the thief to make use of the keys by breaking into her home, there wasn't even a driver's licence; that was at home in a drawer because she could no longer afford to run a car.

Having got a statement from Sam who had sat beside her bed throughout her interview with the policeman, nursing a cup of insipid machine coffee, the policeman then turned to the doctor asking for a statement about her injuries and then he was gone.

She tried to tell Sam that she would be fine now, that he could leave and return to his own life, but words were still too difficult and painful.

He seemed to sense what she was trying to say though.

'It's fine I'll stay with you until your children get here,' he assured her. 'You've been through enough for one night without being left alone in this alien environment.'

The doctor talked about keeping her in hospital over night for observation but in the end she persuaded them she would be fine at home.

'We'll compromise and wait until your family arrive - in the meantime we'll keep a close eye on you,' he said.

And still Sam stayed, he asked if she was sure it was a good idea to go home – perhaps she should stay and if that was the case could he go to her house and collect anything she might need.

To each suggestion she shook her head slowly, the pain increasing with each effort, despite the medication she had been given. She tried to tell him that Adam and Katy would arrive soon, although in her heart she was concerned. Looking at the hands of the stark utilitarian clock on the wall opposite her bed, as they crept round and round counting off the hours steadily, she wondered why her children hadn't appeared.

The policeman had said he would telephone the house to tell Adam and Katy where she was and if he failed to get a reply to his call he would go to the house personally. Surely, Sharon tried to convince herself, he would have kept his promise; surely they should have arrived by now.

Ironically she was now worried about them. Where were they, she asked herself again? Were they alright? Had something happened to them?

Eventually the doctor, with some reluctance pronounced her fit enough to leave but not before making her promise to come back or visit her G.P. the following day if she experienced any of the symptoms listed on the sheet he gave her. But still no children came.

'How are you going to get home if your family don't come?' asked Sam with real concern.

Sharon shook her head but soon stopped as the motion made her feel queasy, her eyes seeming to rattle around in their sockets; it was far worse than nodding had been.

'I could get a taxi and take you myself,' he offered. 'I wouldn't be at all happy about letting you go by yourself. Sharon's only answer was to rub her fingers and thumb together in the classic hand gesture which signified "money."

'I'll pay,' he assured her understanding her hand signal. 'I'll leave you my address and you can pay me back later If it makes you feel better.'

Having no other choice Sharon reluctantly agreed so he went off to call a taxi. Before long he was back saying a taxi was waiting by the admissions entrance, handing her a slip of paper as he came with his full name address and telephone number written on it.

It was a slow, painful journey to the main exit where the taxi waited for them and many times through it Sharon wished she had accepted the nurses' offer of a wheelchair to take her the short distance.

Once Sam had helped settle her into the taxi she managed with some difficulty to tell the driver her address and in less than half an hour they were pulling up outside her house. Even there Sam refused to relinquish his care of her and insisted on walking her to the door after dismissing the taxi.

As soon as the door opened, she heard Adam's voice thick with anger and irritation.

'Bloody Hell, Mum, where have you been, I'm starving. Why are you so late? You knew I wanted to go to that new club tonight and there might not be enough time now – I just hope you remembered to go to the bank on your way home – I need a loan.'

He didn't appear though, the sound of his voice merely echoing from the sitting room over the background noises issuing from the permanently blaring television.

Even though Sharon hardly knew Sam, she felt him tense and glancing at him she could see indignation and anger etched on his face.

Adam sprang to his feet as they entered the small room, staring with overt hostility at Sam.

'And just who the hell are you and what are you doing in my house?' Adam demanded.

But by the time his words were uttered he had caught sight of Sharon's damaged face and stiff painful gait.

'Did you do that?' he demanded again losing none of his hostility.

'Yes of course I did you idiot! I beat your poor mother to a pulp before escorting her safely to her door. And if we're throwing accusations around, where were you when the police were trying to contact you?'

'I was at a friend's if you must know.'

'Well at least you're here now and if you are any kind of son you will turn off that television, forget all about your empty stomach and that club you mentioned to stay in to take care of your mother. I may only just have met you but it only takes a few seconds to see how you take her for granted.'

'And just who the hell are you to tell me off?'

'A passing stranger, but one who can see the lay of the land in this family only too clearly. I will probably never set eyes on you again and to be honest I wouldn't want to, so I shall say my piece before I leave. You clearly don't have a job although you are certainly big enough and capable enough to get one. It strikes me that you are a lazy good for nothing, who not only lets your mother go out to work without attempting to help her in any way, but one who also takes her for granted and bleeds her for money at the same time. In my opinion you are also a son who needs to learn some manners and learn how to speak to his mother with the respect she deserves.'

Sharon had been listening to this tirade with growing apprehension, almost expecting Adam to take a swing at Sam, so his reaction took her breath away.

Taking her arm Adam led her to a comfortable chair and knelt beside her after she was settled.

Chapter 3

Sam left shortly afterwards squeezing Sharon's hand gently and wishing her well. Adam saw him to the door and Sharon was amazed to hear him thanking Sam for all his kindness.

As he passed the bottom of the stairs he shouted up to Katy to come down. Sharon could just imagine the scene and understood now why the police had been unable to reach her children. Adam had been out at a friend's house, probably Ryan's, and Katy must have been upstairs having one of her marathon bath sessions, most likely with her portable radio blaring to the limit of its batteries.

Soon they were both there though, demanding - in stereo, the answers to questions she couldn't answer, asking her if she wanted anything to eat (were they joking.) She did however manage to signal that a cup of tea would be wonderful.

Surprisingly it was Adam who went to make the tea – something Sharon didn't even know he was capable of. Even more surprising was that when it came, it was delicious although rather sweet for her taste. If she could, Sharon would have smiled at the thought that he must have heard somewhere that hot, sweet tea was good for shock; but most shocking of all was that he had searched the kitchen drawers for a straw to make drinking it easier for her to drink it.

Signalling for a pen and paper after she had finished her tea, Sharon managed to explain what had happened by writing the answers to their seemingly endless list of questions. She also told them that her handbag had been stolen and that the house keys, her debit card and phone were in it.

Katy was on the case almost before the words were written. She asked where the insurance and bank details were kept then rushed out to report the loss of her mother's property. After only a few minutes she was back to tell Sharon that her bank card had been stopped, the insurance company notified and on their advice a locksmith was coming to change all their locks.

Sharon hadn't known her children could be so capable, so efficient, but was glad to discover it now. She was suddenly and utterly exhausted and wrote that she wanted to go to bed, also asking one of them to phone Steve to tell him what had happened and explain that most likely she would not be able to get to work the following day.

The attack had happened on a Friday night which meant there was only the Saturday morning emergency surgery to cover the next day, but Sharon realised that there was no way she would be able to make that. She would have to be feeling considerably better if she was even able to go into work on Monday, and she wanted to give Steve time to organise a temporary receptionist.

Katy was really kind and solicitous. Adam helped her to climb the stairs which was a slow and painful process. Then Katy gently helped her out of her ruined clothes, bathed her face with warm water to remove the worst of the congealed blood, smoothed Arnica on her already bruising skin, then helped her into a clean nightdress and into bed.

Sharon had thankfully managed to go to the bathroom on her own, wanting to avoid the indignity of having her daughter help her to the loo. She had closed her swollen already half closed eyes as she washed her hands not wanting to see the damage inflicted on her body by her attacker, reflected as it would be in the mirror above the sink.

She wasn't strong enough for that tonight – tomorrow she might feel more able; tomorrow, after she had had a good night's sleep.

Sharon was to be denied the luxury of sleep though as it was impossible for her to get comfortable. She tried lying on both sides, tried lying on her back, which she normally hated – but every position brought more and more pain.

Katy had put the painkillers the hospital had provided on the bedside table with a glass of water, considerately within her reach, but Sharon wasn't able to pull herself up to take them. She tried not to cry out in pain each time she moved, but she must have for Katy came through in the middle of the night wearing only an old T-shirt even though, with the heating off Sharon thought the house was positively arctic.

'You alright Mum?' she asked. 'Are you in pain?'

'Did I wake you love?' Sharon wrote on her pad. *'I'm sorry, I just can't get comfortable enough to sleep. Every time I try to move it's agony.'*

'Haven't you taken any of your pills?'

'I couldn't reach them, I can't even pull myself upright.'

'Here let me help you,' Katy said doing just that as she spoke.

Between the two of them and some painful and inelegant shuffling Sharon was soon sitting up in bed which felt much better. There seemed to be less pressure on her ribs in a sitting position, although her legs, where her assailant had landed vicious kicks still hurt - merely from contact with the duvet.

Katy fetched an old shawl which she put carefully around her mother's shoulders to protect her from the worst of the cold night air. She then took two tablets from the bottle and helped Sharon to sip enough water to swallow them.

'Anything else I can do?' she asked.

'No love not unless you can find some way of suspending the duvet from the ceiling – the weight of it is really hurting my legs!!!'

'Don't go anywhere!' Katy said with a rare smile, 'I'll be back in a minute.'

True to her word she was soon back carrying an old metal tray with legs which unfolded so that it could be placed over someone in bed. Although not as wide as it might be for total comfort ,when placed midway between her knees and her ankles it supported the weight of the duvet enough for it to be a vast improvement. So at last Sharon slept.

In the morning after two more painkillers she did feel a little better. Katy insisted on her staying in bed for at least most of the morning though. Katy was wonderful - she was up and down the stairs every half hour like a human version of a mountain goat, with little treats to tempt her mother – a tiny portion of scrambled egg and tea with the straw comprised her breakfast.

Until Sharon managed to eat something she hadn't realised how hungry she was, so she persevered until all the egg had gone. A short time later not too hot chicken soup arrived – complete with another straw. This was offered and accepted gladly. After that came mousses and yoghurts in various flavours and with just enough time elapsed between each offering to make Sharon able to eat it.

Katy had even rummaged around at the back of the cutlery drawer to find the tiniest of spoons so that her mother would not have to open her mouth too far to eat her offerings.

Sharon was amazed at her daughter's solicitude. It was as if the recently surly, resentful Katy had been replaced by the Katy she had loved and been so proud of before the divorce. The Katy who was sunny, kind and loving and Sharon was more than glad to see her back.

After a while Sharon begged to be allowed downstairs for a little while, but was told that Katy would help her into a bath first. Although getting her battered and bruised body into the bath was not only difficult, but excruciatingly painful – even with Katy's help - the warm scented bubble bath soothed he aches and pains wonderfully. Then Katy gently patted her mother's ravaged body dry before helping her into a clean nightdress and her dressing gown. This achieved Katy shouted for Adam, who had been conspicuous by his absence until then, to help her down the stairs.

At long last she was settled in her comfortable chair again with pillows propping her up and her legs raised on an old footstool. Throughout the process Sharon noticed Adam had been unable to look her in the eye.

Katy had thoughtfully brought down her pad and pen, so Sharon wrote *What's wrong?*

Adam and Katy exchanged a glance, then Adam sat down beside her and took her hand. 'Katy and I had a long talk last night Mum after you had gone to bed,' he said. 'We realise now what pigs we have been. We always blamed you for the divorce but God knows why when it was Dad who ran off with that Silicone Sal. I suppose it was because you were still here so we see you more, and that made you an easy target. It's hard to be nasty to someone you hardly ever see. But we know it wasn't your fault Mum and we're both really sorry. We've been horrible to you and this has been a real wake up call for us – not to mention those few home truths the guy who brought you home fired at me. I'm sorry Mum, really sorry – we both are.'

Sharon reached for her children's hands and smiled at them both – it was agony, but it was worth it.

Just then the doorbell rang and Katy fled to answer it, dashing away tears with the cuff of her jumper as she went. Sharon didn't really want to see anyone. While in the bathroom that morning, she had taken a quick fearful look at her reflection in the mirror and what she saw was worse than even her fears or expectations had imagined.

Her eyes were both so heavily swollen that they were only partly open, her lips and eyebrows were split in several places, with a multitude of stitches running like railway tracks across every surface of her features. And over all her face there was a riot of already multi-coloured bruising. It had not been a pretty sight and certainly not one she wished to share with the world at large.

She was relieved to see Sam stroll into her sitting room a few seconds later. The sight of her face would hold neither shock nor surprise to him – he'd seen it all before. But what was a surprise was the way Adam sprang to his feet greeting him politely, shaking his hand and thanking him profusely for his help the previous evening.

'Would you like a cup of tea?' Adam enquired adding to Sharon's surprise.

Sam refused but giving Adam the beautiful bunch of flowers he carried, he suggested Adam should go off to find a vase for them, raising an eyebrow in amusement as he glanced towards Sharon.

'Don't you dare make me laugh,' Sharon wrote on the pad which now seemed to be part of her life.

'Sorry, but he seems somewhat different – perhaps all this had been a wake up call,' he said unaware that he was echoing Adam's own words of only a few moments ago. 'I won't stay, I'm sure you don't need visitors when you are feeling as bad as you must be – I just wanted to make sure you were alright.'

The doorbell rang again then, but whoever was waiting on their doorstep seemed more urgent - more impatient than Sam had been. Their finger on the doorbell was insistent and, although Sharon didn't know how it could happen that a bell could take on human emotion, it sounded both frantic and worried.

It was Steve who rushed in stopping short only when he saw the devastation the attack had wreaked on Sharon's face, his own face blanching at the sight of what the attack had done to her.

'Oh my God, just look at the state of you,' he said. 'When Katy rang to say you wouldn't be in today I had no idea what had happened. I didn't get the full story and I just presumed you had a bad cold or a tummy bug. It was only after surgery had finished this morning when I walked across the park on my way here that I saw Joe and he told me about the attack. Are you alright love? Well no that's a stupid thing to say I can see you're not alright but ...'

'Better this morning,' Sharon said making a supreme effort to speak in the hope that it might allay Steve's fears a little though at the same time being careful not to open her mouth to far.

'Hey you can speak again – well that is an improvement on last night,' Sam said delightedly.

It was only then that Steve seemed to realise the other man's presence.

'Steve, this is Sam, he came to my rescue last night. I don't know what I'd have done if he hadn't helped,'

Sharon wrote afraid to risk any more pain by talking again.

'Hey I just happened to be in the right place at the right time that's all. Anyone would have done the same – I couldn't leave you collapsed in a heap on the freezing cold ground now could I? Anyway I'll get off. I just wanted to make sure you were okay and on the mend.'

'I still owe you for the taxi.'

'You mean to say you didn't nip out to the bank before I came this morning - how remiss of you!' Sam joked. 'Don't worry about it you've got my address - any time will do.'

But Steve was already reaching for his wallet. 'Let me,' he said. 'How much was it - will twenty do?'

'It was only eight fifty actually.'

'Well take this ten pound note with my thanks. I will never be able to forgive myself that I wasn't there for Sharon.'

Sam came over to say goodbye after pocketing the note with his thanks. 'Now you take care of yourself, perhaps we'll bump into each other again one day, but in happier circumstances I hope.'

'Thanks again Sam I mean it I don't know what I'd have done....'

'Forget it please. My dear old Mum always says what goes around comes around. It was just my turn to be able to do the favour.'

'The Kindness of Strangers,' Sharon managed to say in a dreamy voice remembering speaking those very words to Lizzie only a short time ago.

'That pretty much says it – goodbye Sharon get well, keep well.' Sam said, then he was gone.

It wasn't until Sam had gone that Sharon realised Steve had been holding her hand nearly all the time since he had entered the room.

Suddenly they both became aware of it at the same time, and an embarrassed smile played across Steve's lips, but still he held it - his thumb gently caressing the back of her hand as if trying to rub away the bruises .

'I was so scared,' he said. 'When Joe told me about the attack I was afraid to think how easily I could have lost you without even being able to tell you how I feel. Perhaps until that moment I didn't know it myself, I certainly wouldn't admit it – even to myself, but I think I've been in love with you since the moment you walked into the surgery asking for a job.'

Sharon could not have been more amazed. She couldn't help but smile at the unlikely scene unfolding in her sitting room. Here was Steve, the man she too had loved since that first day, declaring his own feelings. The irony of the situation would have made her smile on any other day because he was not telling her he loved her when she had made a real effort with her appearance hoping to attract his attention, as she had on their regular staff outings to celebrate Christmas and birthdays. Instead he was doing it when she was battered and bruised and certainly not at her most attractive!

None of that mattered now though and ironically she found herself thinking more kindly of her assailant – almost thanking him in fact, because if the attack hadn't happened perhaps neither of them would have either recognised or admitted to how they felt about one another.

The attack had been a catalyst in other ways too as it seemed in an instant to have given her back her children.

Sharon had heard the saying "You never know what you've got till it's gone" many times before and now she recognised the wisdom of those words. Thankfully Sharon had not been lost to them, but she might have been, and they had become aware of how precious she was to them as a result of the attack.

Perhaps now, because of it, they could all move forward to happier times.

Sam's Story

Chapter 1

All Sam's life he had carried a secret around with him. A secret he had kept hidden from everyone except his mother, who knew and understood the reasons behind his need for secrecy, and who loved him far too much to reveal it to anyone else.

Even Sam's wife Lisa and his daughter Emily had no idea of the burden he carried. All that might be about to change, however, as Sam was forced to contemplate the likelihood of his carefully guarded shame being exposed to the world.

As a small child Sam's health had been poor, he had suffered badly with asthma and had been forced to carry inhalers with him wherever he went in case of an attack. Attacks could come at any time. Often several could occur in the space of a few days too, severely curtailing what he was able to do and where he was able to go. More often than not plans which had been made, for even the simplest of trips, had to be cancelled or postponed. A really bad attack could often necessitate a stay in hospital, leaving him still gasping and breathless for up to a week afterwards meaning that attending school was regularly impossible.

Because of his health problems, and the fact that he was unable to take part in normal games, he had been the main target of the bullies who terrorised the playground and his route home. They even found ways to ridicule and humiliate him in the classroom given the chance, when an unsuspecting or inexperienced teacher's back had been turned. This meant that school had been a nightmare for him. It was a place he took every opportunity to avoid and, as a result, his education had suffered badly.

By the time he went to senior school aged eleven, he had missed so much schooling that he could hardly read or write, having learned barely enough to be able to sign his name. The move to secondary school only exacerbated his problems because he was placed in what his unsympathetic peers had labelled the "dummies" class. This meant that the bullying took on new levels of terror and humiliation – so he became so terrified by their persecution of him that again he stayed away whenever he could. He invented all manner of illnesses to cover his absences from the inspired strained back which gave him nearly two weeks freedom to the more mundane and regular tummy bugs, sore throats or migraines. Each time his kind, understanding mother wrote a note on his return, but Sam had the distinct impression that the school and everyone in it neither noticed nor cared if he was there or not. If he had been missed at all, he was certain that it was only by his peers who had been forced to seek out a new target for their campaign of abuse and victimisation.

Now aged thirty-three he still was unable to read, and this was the secret he carried with him every day. With a cunning built on the foundations of all his imaginary illnesses he had become clever at hiding it though, developing strategies for covering up his inability. A prime example of this had been guessing the contents the note Sharon had written to him after the attack she had suffered in the park. After all, he reasoned what else was it likely to say other than 'thank you' and he could bluff his way out of that situation as he had so many others in the past.

As a small boy he had used some of his "at home" time to memorise the streets around his home. He had wandered around the immediate vicinity of his house whenever his breathing permitted it, asking anyone he met the name of the street he was on - as if he had been lost. In this way he had drawn a mental map of the area to which he could always refer. And now all these years later, although still unable to read street names, he could find his way anywhere within a five mile radius of the house he still lived in.

Just before he and Lisa had married - his mother, Carol, had suffered the first of the minor strokes which were to become a regular occurrence in her life. Although all these strokes had all left her relatively unscathed in themselves, each one left her more incapacitated as the effects accumulated. This meant that living alone was both difficult and frightening for her. The successive strokes had affected her right leg which was permanently weakened and on which she now limped badly, but it was her hands which had been the worst affected. Any small movement, doing up buttons, brushing her hair, peeling vegetables, opening jars or tins was almost impossible for her.

Like Sam, she had managed to find ways to overcome most of her difficulties, wearing jumpers rather than cardigans and buying a coat with a zip, which she could usually manage to do up herself for example. Sadly there were a lot of tasks around the house which were now impossible for her though.

Because his mother and Lisa got on so well together it seemed the most sensible thing to move in with her after their wedding – and they had been there ever since.

The situation had been beneficial in many ways because even after Emily had been born it meant that Lisa could still continue to work part time. Carol had offered to baby sit and had managed with time and effort to find strategies to enable her to feed, wind and change the new baby. Money had always been in short supply for them as, without any qualifications, Sam had been unable to find well paid work or, at times, any work at all. Lisa's wage was therefore vitally important.

Even though Emily was at school and no longer needed her grandmother's constant care, Carol's help was still invaluable. She was able to help around the house, doing some light housework and even preparing the evening meal if Lisa or Sam had done the fiddly jobs, like peeling and chopping the vegetables for her. But with typical stoicism his ever positive mother had found a way of embracing her newly limited life style feeling blessed that Sam and Lisa had chosen to support her. The arrangement worked well for all of them in many practical ways and the small carer's allowance which had been granted to them eased their financial situation considerably.

For months Sam had been able to conceal his problem from his boss at the cash and carry warehouse where he had been employed. But one day new Health and Safety regulations had been brought in, copies of which were given to all staff to read and sign. As soon as it had become obvious that Sam was unable to do this he was sacked – on the spot. Yet another long spell of unemployment had followed until finally Sam had secured a new job for himself and one he really loved.

He was a lollipop man, or a crossing patrol officer to give his job its fancy name, at the local school. Thankfully there was no day to day paperwork involved and Sam had much of the day free to help his mother around the house. He loved seeing all the eager, friendly faces of the children each morning and was glad, if not a little jealous, that these children seemed happy to go to school each day apparently free from worry or the threat of bullying.

He knew every child by name, and often the names of their baby brothers and sisters and parents as well. He was interested in their lives and knew when any child had been ill, always enquiring after them or saying how glad he was to see them better when they returned to school - healthy and well.

There was too the added bonus that Sam was able to take Emily to school each day and see her safely into the playground. The wages were small of course, but with Lisa's part time earnings, Carol's carer's allowance and the part of her pension which she put into the financial pot, they managed well enough.

At long last Sam had relaxed, feeling safe and secure in his job for the first time in years, and had foolishly thought nothing could threaten his secret – until last week.

Then the head teacher of the school had called all available parents to a meeting at the beginning of the day. As Lisa started work early each morning and as Sam was on site anyway it had seemed sensible that he should attend. Once as many of the parents who could attend, were gathered in the hall after morning assembly, the head teacher, Mr. Cartwright, had told them about a new reading initiative which the school was anxious to start.

Sam had felt his palms begin to prickle and sweat and his heart to race as the head teacher explained that they were going to ask parents to come into school to read to the children on a rota basis. It would have to be under the supervision of one of the class teachers, Mr. Cartwright went on to explain, because in this day and age it was not acceptable to have anyone in school who had not undergone a police security check, working with the children, unsupervised.

The aim, he had continued, was to encourage the children to read more and become excited about the worlds of mystery, adventure and imagination which could be found in books. He had gone on to explain to them that by their very nature early-learner readers needed to be repetitive in order for the children to learn, recognise, and remember words. This however often made them stilted and boring as only a few words at a time could be used. Sam felt he could identify with that only too well.

In order to bring some magic into the world of books for them, Mr. Cartwright had come up with the idea of asking parents to read a chapter apiece from books the children would love to hear but were not yet, in many cases, able to read for themselves. And he also considered that even those with the ability to read such material for themselves would enjoy and benefit from the experience of being read to.

'We thought we would start by using the Harry Potter series,' he had said. 'All children and, let's face it most adults. love both the books, and the films which have been made from them and there is enough material in the series of books to last the children throughout most of their life at this school. We are hoping these sessions will have other benefits too, like helping to calm the children before, and even during, lunchtimes which can only be a good thing. Lunchtimes and playtimes are the most challenging for many children and, often for staff, as the children can easily become over excited and this can lead to arguments, even accidents. In addition, although we have a very strict and active no-bullying policy, it is virtually impossible to police these less well supervised times fully. It is hoped therefore that the children will love the stories so much that they will talk about that rather than spend their time making mischief, or causing trouble. We hope that many parents will join this initiative with each parent being asked to read one chapter at the end of each of the school's morning sessions,' he had explained.

Sam's heart sank even further to hear this - he had been hoping that he would be able to persuade Lisa to take on the task, but as she worked every day until one o'clock that was out of the question.

The panic he was now feeling was threatening to consume Sam, making his breathing so laboured and painful that he was afraid he was about to have one of his now very rare asthma attacks. Just as the panic was reaching unbearable proportions though, the head teacher ended the meeting and he was able to escape, racing from the room in a credible imitation of an Olympic sprinter leaving the blocks.

His ordeal wasn't over yet though because, after he had performed his lunchtime patrol duties Mr. Cartwright came out to see him.

'I was hoping to catch you after this morning's meeting Sam,' he said. 'We are hoping to start these reading sessions after half term, which as you know is in just two weeks so it doesn't seem worth starting before then. I was wondering if you would do the first chapter of the first book for us. You seem an ideal person to start the project off with as you know all the children and they know you. What do you say?'

What did he say – what could he say? There was no way he could learn to read, making up for a lifetime of inability in three short weeks, so mumbling an excuse about having to get home to his mother who was not well, he once again fled.

As he walked home slowly his head hanging in misery he wondered if it might just be possible to learn enough in that time. He knew he was neither the 'thicko' nor 'dummy' he had been labelled at school. He had a good memory and could hold well reasoned and logical conversations with people, and had an innate understanding of all thing mathematical - it was just reading he couldn't do. But reading was such an integral part of life these days, after all the written text was everywhere, so not being able to do something so basic had left him with little self-confidence along with many restrictions in his life.

The task was probably beyond him in the time he had available, but in order to make an informed decision he had to look at the first chapter of the first book in the Harry Potter series to assess the level of the mountain he needed to climb.

Deciding to take the bull by the horns he turned towards the square where he knew the library was situated. It was not a place he had ever set foot in before, but thanks to his inbuilt map he knew where it was.

When he entered the cool silent building he experienced a sense of pure panic merely by being surrounded by so many volumes, by hundreds and thousands, probably even tens of millions of words that were completely unintelligible to him. He was intimidated too by the casualness, the sheer ease with which others inside the building, the accepted ones ... the ones who had a right to be there, seemed to go about choosing their books or just sat reading quietly at the tables provided.

All at once even the obstacle of finding the right book seemed too much for him. It was such a small thing for anyone who had the ability to read, but how was he even going to find the one book he needed amongst so many thousands of others.

He was just about to turn and flee when a kind voice whispered in his ear.

'Hello there, you look a bit lost,' said the voice which belonged to a middle aged lady with shining brown hair and a warm smile. 'Can I help you at all?'

'I n... need to f... find the first Harry P... Potter book,' he stammered.

'Oh that's easy – I was afraid for a moment you were going to ask me something really difficult,' she said sweetly. 'Come with me.'

'It might be easy for you,' he churlishly muttered under his breath but nevertheless followed her when she turned to smile warmly and encouragingly at him. She led him to a section of the library where the books were much more brightly coloured than in other places and he guessed that this must be the children's section, and that the books were so coloured to attract the attention of small children.

'Here we are: "Harry Potter and the Philosopher's Stone," she whispered drawing him away to the shelter of a tall bookcase so they wouldn't disturb any of the other library users. 'I remember this setting the world of books alight when it was first released. As I'm sure you know, it was written primarily for children but many adults are now as addicted to them as the youngsters. Do you remember the news stories about the queues which formed to get the latest volume and how shops sold out, often in less than an hour. Or how there were even television programmes speculating about what would happen as the story unfolded? Nobody in the book world had ever known anything like it, but I must say everyone thought it was a wonderful thing. If only because it sparked so many children's interest in reading and surely that must be a wonderful thing. Do you want to take it out?'

'Take it out?' Even the concept was foreign to Sam.

'Yes you know, borrow it to take home – you have got a library card haven't you?'

'No.' So there it was - his plan had been scuppered even before he had the chance to put it into action.

'Have you a family member with one?'

'My mother has one although she hasn't been able to come in for a while she has had several strokes you see.'

'What's her name?'

'Carol, Carol Adams.'

'Oh yes I know Carol, we have missed seeing her, she was one of our regulars – so you must be Sam.'

Sam just nodded.

'How is Carol? We were so sorry to hear of her troubles.'

'Not too bad in herself, all things considered. She has recovered most of the use in her arms and legs, although she limps quite badly, but her hands are the worst - they still let her down. She used to love reading, but she wouldn't be able to turn the pages of the books now you see.'

'Well you tell her Trish said hello and sends her best wishes. Now let's see about putting this Harry Potter on your Mum's card shall we, I'm sure we can bend the rules just a little on this occasion.'

Almost before he knew what was happening, Sam was striding out of the library eager to leave its, to him, claustrophobic atmosphere behind him ... the book clutched firmly in his hand. Even the weight and the shiny almost slippery cover felt alien to him, but somehow just carrying it made him feel a little taller, more confident, accepted - more of a man somehow. It was as if he was wearing a brightly coloured badge which told the world he was now one of them, no longer different or substandard. Just by holding it he felt as if he had left the world of his tormentors and his failures behind him, and he realised, possibly for the very first time how much he had missed by being denied the simple pleasure of reading.

Sam didn't want to go home just yet, he wanted to find somewhere quiet where he could be alone to evaluate the task ahead of him so pulling his mobile phone from his pocket he prepared to ring home.

As he looked at the small display screen he was again grateful for his gift of being able to remember anything mathematical. His directory numbers were not stored by name or destination, like 'home' or 'doctor' but was simply a list of numbers 1-12. He could tell you instantly what each number referred to. 1 was the home landline number, 2 was Lisa's mobile, 3 the doctor, 4 his friend Mark and so on. He rang number 1.

Having told his Mum he would be home later than usual and asked if she would be alright, he made his first ever stop at a shop which sold sandwiches and coffee in cardboard cups. Sam was immediately fascinated by the cups because, not only did they have little plastic lids to avoid spillage, but also clever little cardboard handles which pulled out, unfolding like the wings of a butterfly, ensuring that you didn't burn you fingers as you held the cup.

Sam had been surprised to find that he was hungry until he looked at his watch and found that it was after one o'clock – the trip to the library had taken longer than he thought it would. So for once he was going to treat himself to lunch in the park.

Sam hadn't been back to the park since he had found Sharon beaten, shivering and terrified that awful night. He had been amazed when Paul the paramedic had shown surprise that anyone would stop to help. What sort of world are we living in, he had wondered? What has happened to make mankind so self-centred or so afraid that they have lost all desire, the motivation to help one another in times of trouble?

Sharon had been so frightened and who could wonder at that. Sam wondered about the state of some people's minds and how they could willingly and happily inflict such injuries on another human being. What in someone's background could turn them into such thugs? Sometimes he wondered what had happened to those evil and vicious kids who had bullied him, and others, so unmercifully throughout his school days. Had they grown up to become honest upstanding citizens, even respected pillars of society, or had they become the muggers and drug dealers which plagued their small town just as others of their kind did in any similar town or city the world over.

Sharon had seemed such a good kind soul and, although a lot younger than his own much loved mother, had reminded him of her in a number of ways. Perhaps it had been the fact that she was bringing up her children alone or perhaps it was the stoicism and bravery she had shown throughout her ordeal.

The truth was he had been glad to help. Something in him had responded to her situation - and being the one in control, the one to take charge had boosted his self-esteem. That wasn't why he had stopped to help of course, that had been an instinctive desire to help someone in trouble, but the boost it had given him had been a welcome by-product.

Perhaps it had been the boost in his confidence which had made him even consider the possibility of learning to read the first chapter of the book he now held. Before that he would probably never even have considered it.

Chapter 2

So far Sam hadn't even opened the book, he had just been slumped on the park bench deep in thought, remembering horrors from his own past and the horrors wreaked on Sharon that night. And still he sat - turning the book over and over in his hands as if trying to familiarise himself with something alien and frightening, which of course to him it was.

Opening it to the first page he studied it as if assessing the extent of the marathon task before him. It was worse than he had feared, far worse. Eleven pages of closely typed words made up the first chapter. Scanning the first two pages more thoroughly his mathematical skill assessed there to be somewhere between three hundred and eighty and four hundred and forty words on every page, that made approximately four thousand, five hundred words in the chapter.

Hopeless, the task was completely hopeless, he had failed even before donning running shoes, let alone at the first hurdle. His rare treat of a chicken and salad sandwich sat untouched beside him and his coffee cooled in its cardboard prison, as he sank into a deep depression. Approaching him as he sat on the bench, the very picture of misery and despair, his shoulders hunched and his head hanging low, braced between his hands was something the faint hearted would not have attempted. Trish was a resolute soul though and a kindly one, and she was pleased to see him again so soon. Here was a man in the depths of despair – everything about his posture and body language shouted it. Trish could no more have ignored him than Sam himself could have walked by Sharon after her attack.

Trish had decided to take advantage of the benevolent sunshine to eat her lunch in the park – something she often did when the weather was fine. She enjoyed the peace and relaxation it gave her as she looked at the children walking or playing with their mothers and it recharged her batteries for the rest of the day. Watching those youngsters as they played and laughed also brought back welcome, glorious memories of when her own children had been young and the of the fun and games they had enjoyed then.

Glancing across to where Sam was sitting she was unsure how to reach out to him. Something about his body language as he had stood unsure and, yes afraid, in the library that morning had not only caught her eye, but touched her heart. There stands a very unhappy man Trish had thought and was instantly moved to reassure him - to reach out and help him with whatever trouble he found himself in.

Now as she looked across to the bench where his hunched figure sat Trish felt the same emotions rush through her, along with the same desire to help. She hadn't expected to see him again and certainly not so soon, but she was delighted that her decision to take her home made picnic to the park had facilitated another meeting.

'Sam, how lovely to see you again so soon. May I join you?' she asked, deciding that a jolly confident approach might be the best option to starting a conversation.

Sam was not feeling sociable but, not wanting to give offence didn't know how to ask her to leave him alone, so he just nodded.

'I was thinking about Carol after you left, do you have a tape recorder at home?'

'Well, yes we do, but why do you ask?'

'It's just that we have a stock of books on tape, "Hearing Books" we call them, which might be of use to your Mum. We have a scheme at the library where kind people record a book onto tape so that members who can't read books in the normal way are still able to enjoy books by listening to their favourites and even find new titles to enjoy. The scheme is very popular with blind members for instance and those like your Mum who are now unable to read in the conventional way for whatever reason.'

'I'm sure she would like that.'

'Of course the other way to bring books back into her life would be for you to read them to her, a lot of members have someone in their family willing to take on that task.' Trish watched Sam closely as she spoke these words looking for a clue that her hunch might be right.

Sam said nothing, but the way his face had set in an expression of pure misery told Trish that her suspicions had been confirmed.

'Look, I don't want to be rude or force you to confide in me, but am I right in thinking that you have some difficulty with reading?'

Sam stared at her, fury at her unwanted intrusion into his personal life boiling inside him. He was at a loss to find anything to say so rose to leave. She was more persistent than he had given her credit for though, so his only hope of avoiding her interference was to go. She too rose and put out a restraining arm gently pulling him back onto their bench.

'Look I'm sorry if I offended you, let's just eat our lunches and then you can tell me all about it if you want to. I am good at keeping secrets you know. You have to be in my job – members of the public often tell us things they would usually only tell their priest, their therapist, or in some cases a barman when they have drunk enough to remove their inhibitions.'

As Sam was now really hungry and it was obvious this woman was not about to leave him in peace he reluctantly opened his packet of sandwiches and began to eat them slowly keeping his face averted from her all too searching gaze.

'One of my children was diagnosed with dyslexia when he was at school,' she said suddenly. 'He had struggled with reading all through his primary school, but at that time little was known about the condition and so it wasn't picked up. He suffered badly at school often being picked on and bullied because the other children considered him backward. It wasn't until he went to secondary school where there was a teacher who had studied the condition that his problem was recognised. After that he became one of the fortunate ones. He received specialist help and encouragement. Not long ago he finished studying for his degree in conservation at university. He got a first too, can you believe it! Does anything I've said seem familiar to you?'

Sam stopped eating at the same time that he inexplicably decided to stop pretending. He had suddenly become weary of all the lying, the finding excuses and the very strain of it all. It seemed pointless anyway as this kindly stranger seemed to had penetrated all his defences and already know his secret.

'It was asthma with me,' he admitted. 'I lost so much schooling that it was impossible for me to catch up.'

'And were you bullied?'

'Oh yes I was bullied, enough to put me off going to school ever again if I could avoid it, which I did as often as I could come up with new and interesting aliments,' he said with a flash of his normal humour.'

'How much can you read?'

'I can't.'

'But how do you manage? How do you find your way around, read letters or fill in forms. The world demands so much paper work from all of us these days after all.'

'I don't do letters or forms - Mum has always done that for me. Because we still live with her I told my wife when we married that Mum enjoyed that side of life and thankfully Lisa has never questioned it. As to finding my way around I made myself learn the layout of the town from a very early age and now it's as if I have an inbuilt map in my head.'

'That's incredible, does no-one other than your mother know?'

'No, neither my wife nor my daughter realise. People I have worked for over the years sometimes found out when it was discovered that I was unable to read the things I needed to. I lost my last job because I couldn't read the new Health and Safety legislation which was being brought in, nor of course sign to confirm that I had read it.'

'So what do you do now?'

'I work as a crossing patrol officer at the local primary school, and up to today I thought my secret would be safe. There is hardly any paperwork connected to my present job you see and so I had just begun to relax. I have always kept myself to myself as well. I make it a point not to get too involved with other people because of my problem. Strangers are so much easier to fool.'

'How do you go about fooling them.'

Sam thought again about the night he had found Sharon in the park, deciding it would be a good an example to explain the lengths he had to go to, the stories he had been forced to concoct to protect his secret by telling Trish about that night.

'A little while back I found a lady here in the park one night who had been mugged and badly beaten. I stayed with her and called an ambulance before going to the hospital with her. A policeman wanted my name and address in case I had to give a statement – well that was easy because he wrote it down. When she was being discharged though, I offered to get a taxi to take her home. She had no money of course, because her handbag had been stolen and so I offered to pay for it. She asked for my name and address so that she would be able to reimburse me. I got around that by telling one of the nurses on duty that I had sprained my wrist when I was helping her and asked the nurse to write the information down for me. You get clever at covering your tracks you see. Deviousness and inventiveness become second nature. You get cunning you see, that night I deliberately chose a nurse who was rushed off her feet so she would not have time to think about the strangeness of my request which otherwise might have aroused her suspicions. She just wanted me gone, so didn't question why I was asking her to do such a simple thing.'

'You poor man it must have limited your life so much, but I'm sure you don't want my sympathy. What other ways have you found to cover your tracks as you put it.'

'A good one is to pretend I can't see very well and have lost my glasses – on occasion I have even pretended to be blind, but I don't like to do that. It seems unfair, and insulting somehow, to genuinely blind people. I had often pretended to be foreign though and have perfected quite a few passable accents in my time, that can be quite fun!'

Sam looked at Trish for the first time when he said these words, a rare smile playing on his lips.

She smiled back pleased and grateful that she had won his trust.

'Just now you said that you had thought your secret was safe among those you work with now – until today. What happened today to threaten your security?'

Picking up the Harry Potter book which until then had lain between them on the bench he turned it over and over in his hands as if trying to weigh up how he was to continue.

'This ...' he said simply. 'This has proved to be my nemesis.' Then taking a deep breath he began telling her the events of the morning and how they had brought about this crisis in him.

'If I had longer to try and learn to read, if I was to be one of the last parents to take my turn, it might be alright,' he said at the end of his story. 'The head teacher wants me to be the first though because the children already know me.'

'Well from his point of view that must make perfect sense I suppose, and of course you don't feel able to confide in him.'

'Never!' exclaimed Sam. 'It's such a shameful thing in this day and age you see. Everywhere you turn you are confronted by the written word and not being able to read makes you a second class citizen in many ways. I don't want to refuse to do it anyway as I don't want to let Emily down. She's my daughter and I love her too much to want her to be affected by the shame of my inability to read.'

'That's twice you've used the word shame now, and although I can understand how you feel, you really have nothing to feel ashamed about you know. From what you have told me you are a loving son, husband and father, which in today's world is something you should take real pride in. You are also the kind of person who is willing to help others as you did when Sharon was attacked. You have taken any and every job you have been able to in order to support your family – what exactly do you have to feel ashamed about?'

'I've never looked at it like that,' he replied meeting her eyes for only the second time in their conversation. 'I thank you for saying that, it means a lot to me, but it doesn't help solve my current problem though does it?'

'No, but I think I can find a way to do just that if you're willing to trust me. Meet me here tomorrow at around the same time and well talk some more. I will need to borrow back the Harry Potter book, but I'll return that tomorrow as well. How's your memory by the way?'

'My memory! What a strange question. But since you have asked, I have an excellent memory. I've had to have to live without being able to read and fool everyone around me, without an excellent memory I would never have been able to remember the street plan of the town for example.'

Chapter 3

Sam told his mother all about the events of the day when he went to sit with her after she was settled in bed. This was something he did every night and was something they both looked forward to.

Maybe because his father had left them both when Sam was only young or maybe because of his recurrent illnesses, his problem and the way his Mum had always covered for him, they were incredibly close.

Carol had confided in him once that when his romance with Lisa was obviously becoming serious, she had feared they would lose their close bond. Lisa however had turned out to be a wonderful caring girl and Carol couldn't love her more if she had been her own flesh and blood. When Carol had had her first minor stroke only months before the wedding it had been Lisa who had shyly suggested that they should move in to share her old, but large house.

Carol had always been grateful for Lisa's kindnesses which continued to this day. She had proved herself to be loving, sensitive and considerate and if she was to be honest with herself Carol had never been able to understand Sam's reluctance to confide in his wife because she was sure that Lisa would understand and support him. Never one to interfere though she had kept silent until now.

'Perhaps the time has come to tell Lisa that you have a few little problems with reading,' she suggested.

"Bless you Mum," thought Sam never once had she used the "cannot" word in connection to his reading

problem and it had become known between the two of them as Sam's "little difficulty."

He smiled and reached for her old stroke weakened hand, raising it to his lips as he did. He went on then to tell her about meeting Trish, how the librarian had sent her warmest wishes to Carol and told Sam that they missed seeing her at the library. He told her too about meeting Trish later in the park and the mysterious way she had hinted that she might have the answer to his problems – or at least the most immediate one of reading to the children at school.

'Trish is a good woman,' Carol said with obvious warmth and approval. 'She always has time for everyone even the infamous time wasters who just come in to get out of the rain while they are waiting for their bus. She would help anyone would Trish, if she were able. You can trust her you know Sam – if she can sort out this little problem she will, believe me.'

* * * * *

Although his talk with his mother had cheered him a little Sam spent a restless night. Whenever he did manage to sleep a little, words leapt from the pages of giant books took on the forms of surreal, monstrous two dimensional beasts who threatened to devour him and he was more than a little relieved when he finally saw daylight filtering through their bedroom curtains.

As he dressed for work and ate his breakfast he recognised that his most immediate problem was to avoid meeting Mr. Cartwright the head teacher at the school. Sam needed to see Trish again before he felt ready to give Mr. Cartwright an answer about reading to the children.

He was distracted - and impatient for the morning patrol to be over, but still managed to give the children the cheery greetings they had come to expect from him. At long last all the children even the habitual stragglers were safely inside the school building.

As he walked towards the school office where he habitually left his "lollipop" propped against the wall when off duty, he could see the secretary already busy at her computer typing away urgently. He was relieved too, to see Mr. Cartwright busy on the phone, he looked up raising a hand as he did so, as if asking Sam to wait so he might talk to him. Sam deliberately misunderstood the gesture, raising his own hand as if in farewell before quickly making his way to the school gates.

He had been given some breathing space and was grateful for it. Now he had about three hours to kill before it was time to meet Trish again. He decided to spend some of the time looking around the two toy shops in town trying to find a suitable present for his daughter Emily, whose eighth birthday was in a couple of weeks.

Sam had told his mother about arranging to meet Trish again explaining that he would not be home until after his lunchtime duties were completed, so now he had some time to think. He wondered what Trish had in mind and what she thought she could do to help him. Teaching him to read well enough to cope with the dreaded eleven pages of the Harry Potter book would be such a gargantuan task that it was surely impossible in such a limited amount of time, so how did she think she could help?

On his way to the first of their town's toy shops Sam passed several other shops offering a wide range of commodities for sale. One of these was a pet shop and he stopped to look in the window at the seemingly endless variety of pet toys, bowls, beds, cages and other pet essentials.

Emily had never been a girl who wanted dolls or frilly "Barbie" pink bedrooms, but she had always yearned for a puppy. Wondering for the first time if it would be possible to give her what she wanted most in the world. He wondered too if his mother would be able to cope with a dog in the house but he paused anyway. He stepped forward to look at the various notices which he assumed were detailing animal shelters, along with puppies for sale from local breeders which liberally decorated the windows of the pet shop. He could, of course not read what they said, but some of the posters sported pictures of cute appealing puppies and others of rescue dogs of all shapes sizes and ages.

More than anything else Sam suddenly wanted to make Emily's dream come true. If he was to be honest with himself he had to recognise this as a way he might be able to make it up to her if he failed and disappointed her in other ways by not being able to read at the school.

One of the worst thing about Mr. Cartwright's proposal was that his family would discover his shortcomings if he failed. He dreaded seeing shock, disappointment even contempt in their eyes when they discovered that the man they had both loved and previously respected was unable to do what any normal eight year old could do. Perhaps a puppy would go some way to raising him in their esteem once more.

After seeing the children, who went home for their lunch, safely delivered to their waiting mothers, fathers or child minders, Sam knew he had an hour before he would be needed to guide them back into school. He knew that the time would speed by and so he had no time to lose.

Sam made his way to the sandwich shop for the second time in two days and only the second time in his life. Today he chose a cheese and tomato sandwich and asked for another cardboard encased coffee, before making his way to the park.

There was still almost half an hour to kill before Trish was due to make an appearance, so he strolled down to the lake to watch the ducks and geese as they went about their business. The quacking ducks sounded almost as if they were Halloween witches cackling and laughing manically as they demanded the bread thoughtfully brought by mothers of toddlers in their buggies. Their antics amused Sam and lifted his spirits if only for a few minutes. Glancing up he realised that the half hour had passed as he saw Trish sitting on the same bench they had used yesterday, already unwrapping her lunch and looking around as if hoping for a sight of him. Her body language told him that she was already wondering if he would show up and so he hurried toward the bench where she waited.

'Oh there you are Sam, I was beginning to wonder if you were coming,' Trish said, her words confirming his thoughts.

'I felt I had to, after all – and I'm sorry to sound blunt - but you're my only hope of getting through this nightmare,' he replied opening his sandwich after taking a warming sip of his coffee.

'Well let's hope my cunning plan works and that the nightmare becomes a benign dream,' she said smiling at him kindly.

For a while they sat in silence eating their lunches. Trish chatted away about her family and her job at the library, but Sam was too tense to contribute much. His mother had been right, he thought, she was a kind lady. Just from what she was telling him now he could tell she had always put her family and friends first in her life. She seemed to be one of those people who attract folk who are in need of a shoulder to cry on, or someone in their life to see them through a crisis – a bit like him he thought with a wry smile. He just hoped that if ever she needed a helping hand someone would be there for her. And his instincts about her proved to be uncannily accurate when she had finished her lunch and finally revealed her plan.

'What I have done is to record the first chapter of the book onto a cassette for you,' she told him. 'If you go through it gradually you will probably be able to learn it off by rote, a bit like the way dyslexic actors do who use the same method to learn lines for plays or shows. I know you have told me that you aren't dyslexic but surely the principle is the same.'

'But that must have taken you ages.'

'Only a couple of hours. It would have taken less time, but I made a few mistakes and had to start all over again. If you hold the book while you are reading nobody will be any the wiser.'

'But surely I'll give the game away by not turning the pages, or at least not turning them in the right places.'

'Ah, there I think I have been quite clever and I hope you will feel the same,' she giggled girlishly. 'I must say I'm rather proud of myself for coming up with the idea. What I have done is to mark the bottom of each page you will have to turn with a tiny picture of a bell. When I reached that place in the story I rang a bell onto the tape to show you where to turn the page. I must say though that I was rather ashamed to be defacing library property, but as I only used pencil I will at least be able to rub it out afterwards.'

'I cannot believe that you went to all that trouble for me,' Sam said his amazement showing in every word.

'It was no trouble at all, in fact it was a real pleasure. I am one of those strange people who enjoy helping others and you seemed so lost and sad, I knew I had to do something to help, or at least try to.'

'And you really think I will be able to learn it in the three weeks I've got?'

'Oh yes, I'm more than confident that you can do it. You really must learn to have more confidence in yourself Sam.'

'But ...'

'Before you say that you are too stupid to learn these words let me tell you something about yourself. All your life you have confused not being able to read with being unintelligent. You had a very bad experience at school and that is the reason, *the only reason* why you can't read. I can tell just by talking to you that you have a really good head on your shoulders. You are bright and clever Sam, but you have one small disability. Unlike someone who has become partially deaf or blind however your disability is remediable.'

'So you think I might be able to learn to read properly – even at thirty four?'

'Without a doubt you could. What you need to do first is to keep telling yourself that you are intelligent. You have informed and considered opinions on politics, the environment, and all manner of other things, that much even I know from our few conversations. You have a great deal to offer Sam, all you have to do is believe in yourself.'

'Nobody except my mother has ever said that to me before,'
said Sam his eyes unexpectedly filling with tears of gratitude.

'Well there you are then, I always knew Carol to be an intelligent, discerning woman. You should listen to her.'

'How can I ever thank you?'

'Well there are two things I would like you to do for me. The first is to come into the library when you have read to the children to tell me all about it – I will be longing to hear about your triumph. The second is to join an adult literacy group after you have done your reading at the school. There is an excellent one held at our library every Wednesday evening. It is run by a very good and kind lady and is attended by all kinds of people like yourself. There is no embarrassment because everyone is in the same position and Janice, the tutor has had some fantastic results. Two of her pupils are now attending universities, and one of them is nearly eighty!'

'Really ... that's amazing!'

'It is and even those who haven't wanted to go that far have improved their lives dramatically. Every one of them has grown in confidence and been able to prove that by bettering themselves in the jobs they are able to do.'

'I promise I'll come and see you when I've done the reading and I will seriously think about the group – I really will.'

'Great. And if, in the meantime, you need any extra help with it you know where to find me.'

Sam had never considered himself to be a demonstrative man, but he was moved to envelop her in a huge bear hug, as well as planting a kiss on her cheek as they parted.

Sam tried thanking her again but she brushed aside his words.

'I don't need thanks,' she had told him. 'I shall look on this as my "Good Samaritan" experience for this week. I am the kindly stranger passing by and you are the poor man in need of help. It's relatively easy to help one's friends, and I have always tried to do just that, but it's more challenging to help a stranger. I really think it has done me good.'

Sam was amazed at her generosity. She had done him the most enormous favour, not only by taking the time to find out how he needed help - but then to give him the very help he needed in order to save face. What was more amazing still was that she had cared enough in the first place to sense both his need and his pain; and be moved to do something about it when so many would have thought it best not to become involved. Not only had she done all that but she had somehow turned it around, making out that it was Sam doing her the favours in order to save his pride.

After all his pain and distress had not been obvious as Sharon's had been. Anyone walking by would have seen how badly she had been injured and just how much she needed help. It had taken someone with much greater sensitivity and awareness to see the pain he had carried all his life though and be moved to do something about it.

Sam couldn't wait for his afternoon duty to finish so that he could rush home to tell his mother about the plan Trish had devised for him. All the time he was seeing those dear little ones across the road his hand kept straying to his pocket to reassure himself that the book and the precious, tiny cassette was safe. It seemed to him that it was a lifeline, and that is exactly what it turned out to be.

* * * * *

Carol was as delighted with Trish's plan as Sam had been.

'I really think that will work, how clever of her to think of it,' she said. 'I told you she was a warm, caring person didn't I? What's more we can practise it together before Lisa or Emily get home. Trust me you will be word perfect long before the three weeks are up.'

So every spare minute Sam and his mother went over the script. They had decided to pretend he was learning lines for a West End play just to make it more amusing. They began by taking it paragraph by paragraph, moving on only when Sam was word perfect with each section. Sam could not believe how easy he found it and before even two weeks were over he was indeed word perfect. The next stage was to use Trish's symbols to learn when to convincingly turn the pages, and that too proved no match for Sam's determination. Before long he was inventing different voices for all the characters and, by visualising them in his mind, he managed to invent little gestures to go along with the voices he had created.

There was one surprising development however. Both Carol and Sam had become so engrossed in the story even after only one chapter that they both wanted to know how the story continued.

So Sam was filled with a new determination to do as Trish had asked him and sign up for the adult literacy course. It was not just for himself or to save face with his family now - it was a small token of love and a partial repayment of the debt he felt he owed his mother for her life long devotion and understanding.

'When I can read properly Mum,' he promised her, 'I'll not only read you this first book, but we'll read the whole series - and if that doesn't give me the incentive to learn I don't know what will.'

The days and weeks sped by and rather than dreading the experience Sam found he was looking forward to reading to the children, confident now that he was word perfect. And that is exactly how it turned out.

It was only a small school, and although he knew every one of the pupils individually by name it was nevertheless a daunting sight as he sat down, with the book on his knee and gazed out over the sea of excited, expectant faces. For a moment his nerve failed him until he spotted one very familiar and dear face in the crowd, love and pride written there for all to see.

Emily was positively glowing with pride as she sat crossed legged on the floor of the assembly hall that morning and it was just what he needed to boost his confidence for the task ahead. So remembering how his mother had encouraged him to think of himself as an actor learning his lines, he stepped out of his body into that of other characters, just as he had understood that actors did, and smiling at the expectant faces before him he opened the book to the first page

It went perfectly, every word was spoken in the right place with the correct intonation, and every page turned in the right place. Sam even remembered to use his different voices for each of the characters, which proved to be very popular with the children and brought the text to life even more for them.

The first place Sam went on leaving the school after the reading was to the library to see Trish, That had been Carol's idea. 'I can wait until you get home to hear how it went love,' she had said. 'I already know you will be brilliant anyway, but Trish deserves to be the first one you tell.'

Carrying an oversized bouquet, Sam walked into the library with none of the reluctance or hesitancy which had marked his first visit. He appeared to be taller and more confident, making more than a few heads turn to watch his progress as he marched towards the desk. More hugs were given and received in the library that day than the old building had ever witnessed before, astounding many regulars, some of whom were overheard to say they had never seen such a thing in a public building before – but Sam and Trish didn't care.

He signed up there and then for the adult literacy course and once again Trish's words proved prophetic. With a confidence which was growing every day Sam found he took to reading under Janice's tutelage like he had seen the ducks in the park proverbially take to water.

He also made several new friends in the group, but maybe that had been partly because of his very first words to them which had broken the ice by making them all laugh.

'I would like each one of you to introduce yourself and share your reasons for wanting to learn to read with the whole group?' Janice had said at the beginning of their first session.

When it had been Sam's turn to state his reasons he had made them all laugh by saying, 'Hello everyone, my name is Sam and I want to learn so that I will be able to read Harry Potter to my Mum.'

Trish's Story

Chapter 1

Trish needed her job at the library for more reasons than the money it brought into her home. She had brought her children up almost single handedly as Gerry's job on the oil rigs meant he was away from home more than he was there, often for many months at a time.

There had been compensations though, because then the money he had sent home had been plentiful enough for Trish not to have to work while the children were at home. Gerry had wanted her to be a stay at home mother and Trish had gone along with his wishes believing she was doing the right thing by concentrating on the children while they needed her most.

Now they didn't need her any more and they had flown the nest both literally and figuratively – Neil, their eldest, having secured himself a job earning mega money in Hong Kong even before the ink on his degree scroll had been dry. He had never even stopped long enough to thank her for supporting him both emotionally and financially during his four years at university, not to mention during the rest of his life. He just took off without even a backward glance or a wave when she had driven him to the airport where she had stood, nose almost pressed against the glass of the observation lounge, watching and sobbing until his plane was a mere silver speck in the sky.

She hadn't wanted thanks really – that was not what being a mother was about for her, and not for most other mothers either, if truth be told. She certainly hadn't wanted any recompense, but in her darkest, loneliest moments she had to recognise that she had certain feelings of resentment. Her eldest child, who could ... should have taken over the role of man of the house after his father's accident had done nothing at all to support her. Instead he had taken everything she had done for him for granted, casually, as if it was his right and due. Before discarding her, and all she stood for, in the blink of one of his self-absorbed eyes as soon as her usefulness to him was exhausted.

He had merely walked or rather flown away with neither backward glance nor trace of regret leaving her to cope with his father and grandmother alone.

It wasn't his fault, of course, that Gerry had had such a bad accident at work falling nearly a hundred feet onto the North Sea Oil rig's platform and breaking his back in the process. It had been an accident which could so easily have killed him, all the specialists had told her, and she had been eternally grateful that it had not. *Then*.

It wasn't Neil's fault either that Trish's mother had been diagnosed with early onset Alzheimer's in her middle sixties, just after Gerry's accident. Gerry had been just forty eight when he had been injured, Trish had been only forty six, her mother sixty four and Neil had been twenty two. But just as she had been in hope of finding something positive to come out of her empty nest, fate had decreed otherwise.

Always a positive person, whose bottle was invariably at least half full, Trish been cultivating ways to help her look forward to aspects of her life as her nest began to empty rapidly as each of her children left home. She had been envisaging the possibility of days out, new and exciting hobbies and even exotic holidays abroad but it had all be taken away from her as if in the single blink of an eye.

Reluctantly Trish had been forced to recognise that her beloved eldest child was indeed the most selfish of men – spoiled and insensitive without an altruistic bone in his body. Neil had no intention of his own life's plan being hampered or the meteoric career he had envisaged for himself being put on hold for something as insignificant as family problems – which he considered neither his concern or responsibility.

He had his own life, Trish knew that and wanted him to enjoy every opportunity which came his way, as she had with her two other children, of course she did. She never even heard from him these days however, unless she called him, and even then he never seemed to have the time or inclination to talk to her - telling her he was busy and that it was not a convenient time for him. And it hurt, she tried so hard to understand, but oh how it hurt!. He never even remembered her birthday these days and his Christmas card was professionally printed without even the warmth and personal touch of a signature, let alone the scratched symbol of a kiss. Even the envelopes were type written. Trish often wondered if the card was the work of a well manicured and even better paid secretary who was handed a list and funds to buy and post these Christmas greetings to colleagues and family. In her more bitter moments Trish even wondered where on the list she might be; probably towards the end she accepted sadly. Those who could be of use to Neil on the meteoric rise his career was taking would be nearer the top of the list.

Trish's other two children had already left home before the accident happened and her mother had been diagnosed.
Neil had only stayed as long as he had while he was studying for the two successive degrees he had now achieved. It had been cheaper for him then to live at home and much more convenient as he had not had to concern himself with inconvenient tasks like housework, washing, ironing or feeding himself.

Her youngest child Karen had gone to Australia for her gap year, had met a blond and tanned Adonis clutching a state of the art surf board and had married him without ever coming home. She had, appropriately enough, married him on a beach with neither of her parents in attendance and now lived in Melbourne with him and their two children - neither of whom Trish had ever seen except as two dimensional images on the photographs or video films Karen sometimes sent. It was wonderful to see these images of course it was, but, in some strange masochistic way, it made her long to hug them more and to hear the gift of their tinkling childish laughter.

Trish's other child, the environmentally aware and campaigning Matt had been born between the other two and not long before he too left home, had finally told Trish that he had felt insecure about his place in the family. He was not the first born nor the baby and had, for some reason, decided that he wasn't as important as his siblings while he was growing up.

When he had first revealed this to Trish, she had been horrified and devastated in equal measure, having always loved her children equally and truly believing that she had treated them all the same. Consumed by guilt that she might have neglected him, been too busy to see his need, even failed to demonstrate that she loved him as much as his siblings She had tried desperately to convince Matt that he was mistaken, but to this day was never sure that she had succeeded.

Matt had followed his dream and his passion to work in the area of conservation and was now deeply involved in a Whale and Dolphin protection project in the very north of Scotland.

At least Karen and Matt took the trouble to ring her regularly and she took comfort from that. They both told her often that they loved her and Matt visited as often as his hectic life would allow – but at least never a birthday, Christmas or Mothering Sunday went by without them recognising her importance in their lives.

Trish had even bought a laptop computer with a webcam so that she was able to see Karen and her family on the other side of the world, which was a great improvement on the inanimate images she had been used to seeing – and at least she could hear their dear voices and catch up on their news. Sometimes though she longed to have them there with her, their physical presence would be such solace.

It had been very hard for Trish after they had all left home within such a short space of time of one another, especially after Gerry's accident. Before the accident had happened Trish had been looking forward to having some time to herself, to do the things she had always wanted to do and had put on hold while she was caring for her children. She and Gerry had made many wonderful plans too, there were a hundred and one things they had talked about doing after the children had left home, during his long rest periods from the oil rig. Truth be told, it was only thinking about these things which had kept her sane as the children had left home one by one.

All her hopes and dreams had come crashing down around her when Gerry had finally been brought home from Stoke Mandeville hospital though. He had been air-lifted from the rig after his accident and flown straight to the hospital, which specialised in spinal injuries. There he was assessed and stabilised, but given no hope of recovery.

Trish had managed to visit the hospital several times after he had been admitted although the journey was long and tortuous, the situation depressing and the news always grim. There she had been told that as he had fractured his back at the C5 vertebra, which meant that he was able to breathe for himself and had some, very limited, movement in his arms although had no feeling or use in his hands. There was certainly no hope that he would ever walk again – worse still because the spinal cord was completely severed, the little or no function he had achieved in his arms was all the movement he could realistically hope to gain and so he would need constant nursing.

Finally after six months at the hospital where he had been given physiotherapy and taught to make the best of the extremely limited movement he had – and would ever have – he had been sent home. The six months respite at the hospital and the compensation he had received from the oil company who owned the rig had, after the accident, given Trish time and money to convert their one time garage into a room full of aids and equipment for Gerry's return home.

When completed it had boasted a special bed which raised and lowered at the touch of a button, hoists over it to lift or lower Gerry as well as a specially designed wet room with more hoists and levers. Trish thought it looked more like something out of "Star Trek" than a bedroom, but had been afraid to say anything to Gerry, who along with losing most of his movement had – perhaps understandably – lost all sense of humour, and positivity as well. He saw no hope for the future, no possible reason for staying alive.

'I wish they had taught me how to take my own tablets at that place,' he had told her bitterly. 'If they had I'd have taken the lot months ago, then I would be free of this useless wasted body and you'd be free of me. That's what we both really want after all.'

'Now you don't mean that Gerry,' she had said shocked to the core.

'How do you know what I mean, woman? What do you know about how a man feels when he has to rely on some woman to do everything for him. I can't even go to the toilet without help ... you know what that feels like do you? I don't think so ... just get out and leave me alone.'

Their lives seemed to be punctuated by this kind of bitter hurtful exchange these days, and so in her usual no-nonsense way Trish tried to concentrate on doing the things she could as well as she was able. So she had learned not only how to operate all these gadgets and tend to every need of Gerry's but how to keep a fixed, cheerful smile on her face. She soon learned not to show her hurt and anguish during the many times Gerry had vented his anger and frustration on her. Everyone at the hospital had warned Trish that such a cataclysmic trauma would leave Gerry changed in other than merely physical ways. But this man she now spent the large part of her life caring for was not a changed version of her once beloved husband. He was a completely new person, one she would never have dreamed of marrying – one she didn't even like very much. He was bitter, ungrateful, morose and with a vicious tongue – one part of him which unfortunately, she sometimes felt guiltily, still worked perfectly. Both their lives had become hell.

They had just reached a plateau of acceptance and competence with the hard physical routine - although not with the permanence of the situation or Gerry's lack of acceptance over it - when another devastating blow had struck and Trish's mother Fiona had been diagnosed with Alzheimer's.

Trish had been at an all time low in the days and weeks after that diagnosis, there had seemed no way she could carry all these burdens alone, but with her usual optimism she had, after weeks of serious thought formulated a plan, She recognised that with the demands of Gerry's care she would never be able to support her mother if she were to stay in her own home which was on the other side of town.

At the time Fiona, her mother, was merely extremely forgetful, but Trish was constantly plagued by the spectre of left-on cookers, overflowing baths or kettles left to boil dry. It had come to a head when Trish had gone round one day to find her that her mother had been trying to lay sticks in the grate which already contained an out dated, mock log-effect electric fire which Gerry had put in years ago to save Fiona having to light and clean out a real coal fire. By the time Trish had arrived the plastic log effect was melted and the air was filled with acrid smoke and lumps of, still smouldering, molten plastic were adorning the singed and smoking hearth rug. While the smoke alarm, which Trish had insisted her mother had fitted, was screaming in impotent anger and disbelief that it was being ignored.

After that near disaster there seemed no alternative, so Trish had moved her mother, along with as many of her possessions as could be accommodated, into her own home where she took up residence in two of the bedrooms the children had vacated. Trish fitted out the smaller of the two as a cosy bedroom, while the larger one became as close a facsimile of her mother's sitting room as it was possible to recreate. But without the hazardous temptations of a log-effect fire or open grate. At least Trish argued to herself, it would be comfortingly familiar to her mother and she might remember where things should belong.

At first when Fiona's illness was mild she had been encouraged to think the move was to benefit Trish and that she, Fiona, was there to help with the demands of nursing a bad tempered, virtual quadriplegic. It had seemed kinder to let her mother think she was a huge help rather than an extra concern and to be fair at first she had been.

They had coped in this way for over two years until Gerry, whose breathing too had been severely affected by his accident had developed a chest infection. Although mostly able to breathe on his own the physical effort of drawing breath was often too much for him as the muscles in his chest had atrophied, and at these times he needed an almost constant supplies of oxygen. The last chest infection had turned into pneumonia before the end of the day however, despite all Trish's precautions, so he had been rushed into hospital for intensive treatment, but had died before the week was out.

Trish had been shocked and had grieved, but was also relieved in a way, because the man who had been returned to her after the accident had not been the man she had known, loved and promised to spend the rest of her life with, but a surly, foul mouthed, aggressive stranger who treated her as if she were of no more importance than a fly. Her Gerry, the man she had married and promised to love for all of the days of her life, had effectively died on the day he had fallen. But nevertheless she grieved for the man she had just buried, greatly saddened that anyone should have to endure such ignominy and pain.

After his death his hi-tech room with all its super expensive specialist equipment had been left redundant. The compensation Gerry had received after the accident, which they had used to equip the room, was long gone - eaten up by things nobody now needed or wanted. Trish had tried to give the equipment away to a hospital or charity which dealt with similar accident victims, but had been told that they were unable to accept second hand equipment. This seemed ridiculous to Trish but she had to accept it as an illustration of how this crazy world had become terrified of being held responsible for accidents and of running the risk of any subsequent litigation.

Since she had moved in with them Trish's mother, Fiona, had deteriorated quite rapidly, as the doctor's had warned Trish she might. A normal conversation was now beyond her as she repeated herself constantly, forgetting what she had said only minutes before. So saying the same thing over and over again became the norm, although she still seeming to expect a response from Trish as if it was the first time her daughter had heard it. These conversational loops produced all manner of emotions in Trish. They were frustrating, annoying, irritating but, most of all heartbreakingly sad.

Every day brought more of these emotions piling in on one another until Trish thought her head would explode from the strain of it all. She desperately tried to be patient, but it was hard, so very, very hard.

Sometimes Trish thought her own sanity was at risk from the tension she lived under constantly. But the doctor had kindly suggested, on one of her increasingly regular visits to him, that it might be time to think about extra care for Fiona.

'I really don't want to put her in a home,' she had said trying the stem the tears which had begun to flow at the very thought.

'There may come a time when that becomes necessary – in fact it would be best to prepare yourself for that eventuality. That time is not right now however. There are many things we can do, strategies and care packages we can put in place before we do have to take that drastic step.'

'Like what? For the first time in years I have felt that I wanted – needed to work outside the home. In fact I have just got myself a part time job – should I give it up?'

'Well initially I would suggest we get the local mental health team to organise a carer to look after your mother each weekday morning. In that way you could still do your job – which I think will be vital for you. There is, in fact, no way you should give that up as it will provide you with a short breathing space each day.'

At first Trish had refused to even think about having a carer, thinking she was failing her mother for not being able to care for her herself.

Life had certainly improved for a while though since Janice had come to sit with Fiona during the mornings, helping her to bathe and dress before giving her breakfast and even doing a little light housework.

These free mornings had meant that Trish was able to work for the first time since she'd had the children. She had been a librarian then too and, almost as soon as she had begun applying for jobs, she had been fortunate to quickly find part-time work at the local library. For Trish it wasn't about the money - although that in itself was very welcome as it meant they could have the odd little treat. It was her lifeline, the only thing which kept her sane. It was her respite from the sheer wretchedness and strain of her life at home.

While at the library she could relax and be herself for a few hours - she was able to have normal conversations with the people who came and went and, just as importantly, was able to enjoy periods of deep quiet which recharged her. She was able to offer advice and assistance and even have a bit of fun with her regulars who knew her weakness for a good joke. Having learned of her wicked sense of humour, many clients' first words to her, when they came to exchange their books, were "have you heard the one about the ..."

Any irritations at work were short lived and much easier to deal with, than those she needed to face at home, but behind her smile and the fun she had in the library was the all pervading sadness of knowing that her mother was getting worse each day and the constant fear of what awaited on her home. But every morning, as she walked to the library, Trish thanked God for her work and the release it gave her.

It was as if her work in the library and contact with the outside world recharged her batteries sufficiently to go home and face the difficulties, the horrors of life with Alzheimer's once again. But there were still times, very occasional times, when Trish felt sorry for herself and the stupidest things could plunge her into unfamiliar depression.

Last evening when her mother had been in bed and Trish had been watching the news, while enjoying a rare glass of wine, a story had come on about a soldier who had been decorated for a lifetime of selfless service.

Where's my medal? Trish had suddenly thought, with uncharacteristic selfishness and self-pity. My life seems to have been nothing other than selfless services ; kids, husband, mother - but there's no medal for the likes of me, just uncaring rejection and unrelenting service with no end in sight.

These dark moods never lasted long thankfully, as Trish had always been the kind of person able to see the positive in most situations. It often took a lot of hard work and effort for her to remain positive, but usually something happened to give her the boost she needed – that night it had been an unscheduled and unexpected call from Karen.

Josh her older boy was about to start school and had wanted to call to show English Gran his school uniform. As he had stood, beaming from ear to ear, in front of the camera proudly wearing his pristine, if slightly large, uniform and as the image had been bounced across thousands of miles Trish's self- pity had evaporated.

'We'd love you to come over Mum,' Karen said, as she did every time they spoke. 'You're looking more tired every time I speak to you.'

'I'd love it too, nothing would give me more pleasure, but how can I with Gran?'

'I know it's hard, but isn't there a home she could go into just temporarily? Just to give you a break.'

'We'll see,' Trish said as she said every time.

It wasn't just the thought of putting Fiona into a home that made Trish hesitate though, but the thought of undertaking such a long journey on her own. She had never travelled much, there had been little opportunity with the children coming along in quick succession and then Gerry's accident.

They had had the odd family holiday in Portugal or France which had been wonderful, but Gerry had been there then to take care of all the details and to hold her hand when the terrifying roar of the aircraft's engines had lifted them into the sky. Trish hated flying anyway, never being able to understand how a heavy metal contraption was able to resist just falling out of the sky.

Everyone told her that research proved it was the safest form of travel, but Trish was neither convinced nor reassured and the few flights she had taken had done nothing to convince her otherwise.

If she had a friend who would undertake the journey with her it might be different, but those she had once considered her friends had evaporated like morning mist after Gerry's accident. They had, as one, turned their backs on her, conveniently forgetting the countless times they had, in the past, asked her for help or support ... and invariably received it. Sometimes she felt horribly alone.

Even with all her troubles she was still the kind of person who loved to help others though and so it had been with Sam. Just the sight of him as he stood lost and afraid in the library that morning, so many months ago, had melted her heart and made her want to hug him - to take away his pain. He had seemed such a kind man and his problem, although insurmountable and huge to him, had, to Trish, seemed something which could so easily be rectified.

Speaking to him had done nothing to alter her initial impression of him. He was kind, his actions when Sharon had been mugged had proved that as well as his devotion to his own sick and elderly mother.

Perhaps it had been this common denominator in their lives which had made her warm to him even more, determining to help him if she could. And she had.

It had been comparatively easy for her to look dispassionately on Sam's problem to "think outside the box" as Neil would say. To her the solution had been obvious and simple. It had taken her only a couple of hours to record the first chapter of "Harry Potter and The Philosopher's Stone" onto tape, and what were two hours when it meant that she had been able to help someone out of their difficulties?

She had been particularly pleased with the ingenious way she had found to mark the pages and cue the tape in order for Sam to turn the pages in the right places thereby keeping secret the fact that he was unable to read.

It had given Trish enormous pleasure, some weeks later, to know that the reading had gone so well and that Sam had subsequently signed up for the adult literacy classes. But it was the way he had grown in confidence in the few weeks she had known him which was the most gratifying.

She was sure that his lack of reading ability was no reflection on his intelligence, but just the result of his intermittent education as a child. He had promised to keep her up to date with his progress but she had no doubt that he would succeed.

Trish was just about to leave the library at the end of her morning shift when her mobile phone had rung. It was Janice and the very name as it flashed onto the small display screen was enough to fill her with foreboding. "What now?" she thought as she pressed the button to answer the call.

Janice only rang if there was a problem at home. Trish had been hoping to get to the supermarket to do the weekly shop before she went home, but before she even heard Janice's voice she now knew that would be out of the question.

'Sorry Trish,' said the panic filled voice at the other end of the line. 'She's gone walk about again!'

Chapter 2

It was the very worst news – well probably not *the* worst, but it was bad enough. For some time now Fiona had become fixated about finding her baby. She was convinced that somewhere out there her tiny, vulnerable baby was alone spirited away by God knew what.

So real was the past for Fiona, so entrenched she was in the events of her own past - so convinced that this past was the present - that she lived this nightmare scenario every day. Nothing could change Fiona's mind – nothing could convince her that the baby, Trish, was now a grown woman. Not just a woman even, but a widow with grown children and grandchildren of her own. It was fixed as reality in Fiona's mind - even though Trish had tried to explain it over and over again. She had even spent hours making a collage of pictures of herself from babyhood to the present day to represent the passage of time showing Fiona how her baby had evolved through various stages to become the woman she was now.

It hadn't worked though, nothing ever did.

At any, and every, opportunity Fiona would sneak out of the house on surprisingly swift and agile legs to go in search of her child. Today the news was even worse than usual as Janice had reported that Fiona had made her escape while still in her dressing gown and slippers.

That had been more than an hour ago and Janice had said she had searched everywhere for her, wanting to avoid worrying Trish if she could help it – hoping to find her before she needed to call.

A hotchpotch of emotions hit Trish with the force of a force nine gale. Worry obviously, at the thought of her confused, vulnerable mother wandering the streets of their town and hot impotent anger at this bloody awful illness. Guilt too, for leaving her also played its part in the Molotov cocktail of feelings raging through Trish's body, as well as almost overwhelming sadness. A sadness born of the knowledge that her once strong and capable mother had been reduced to her present state by the merciless cruelty of this insidious illness. Sometimes Trish felt as if her mother had been stolen from her by the relentless progress of her illness.

'Where have you looked?' she asked urgently.

'Everywhere I can think of, I've been wandering the streets around here for ages, I've even got the car out to look for her but she seems to have completely disappeared. I was really hoping to be able to find her myself without having to worry you. I'm so sorry Trish.'

'Thanks Janice, for letting me know and for looking for her. You get off home now, I'll take over and if I can't find her in the next hour or so, I'll ring the police.'

Ringing the police was something Trish avoided if at all possible but sadly on several occasions in the last few months she'd had to do it. Each of those times Fiona had been found and brought home safely by kindly officers in a police car. If it was possible, this had confused her mother all the more as she fretted and wondered why she had been in a police car and what she had done wrong. Or on even less lucid days where the handsome young men were taking her – were they going to the beach or on a picnic – oblivious even that they were officers of the law and that she was riding in a police car.

'I'm so sorry Trish,' Janice said again. 'I don't know how she managed to slip out, I'd only just nipped to the loo for a minute.'

'Don't worry about it, it's not your fault,' Trish reassured her. 'She can be very cunning when she wants to be, and she can still move pretty quickly too! You do a wonderful job with her, I don't know how I would ever manage without you, and let's face it you can't watch her every second. Please try not to worry, I'm sure she will turn up safe and sound. I'll call you when I know anything.'

Where could she look? Janice had obviously looked in the most likely places nearest the house, so where could her mother be? She could have travelled a long way in the time she had been missing, so where on earth could she have got to?

Suddenly inspiration struck, making Trish think about the park. When she had been little her mother had often taken her there to play on the swings and slide in the playground and to feed the ever hungry ducks. Surely it was worth a try. If Fiona was looking for the child Trish had been, she might well head for the places they went to regularly when Trish had been very young, although caution told her that Janice must already have looked there.

Hardly waiting to pull on her coat she shouted combined apologies and goodbyes to the other staff, who accepted that sometimes Trish had to rush away at a moments notice. Then she dashed out grateful, as ever, for the understanding and patience of her colleagues. The cool late Autumn air hit her as soon as she was outside making Trish even more concerned for her mother wandering around, as she was, in just her nightdress and dressing gown on such a cool day.

Running now, her sixty something, slightly overweight body protesting at the unaccustomed exercise with each passing step, she heading for the nearby park. The playground was her first port of call but there was nothing to suggest her mother had been there.

She stopped to ask several mothers with their toddlers if they had seen a elderly woman wandering around in her night clothes, but her enquiries were met by only negative responses, sympathetic glances or bemused stares.

Almost breathless with panic she now headed for the duck pond and the nearby café where she was met by a strange but oh so welcome sight.

Her mother was dressed as Janice had described, but now with a thick padded jacket which, as it was several times too big for her, wrapped around her now frail form with ease. She was sitting holding hands with a young man at a table of the al fresco park café , chatting away as if neither of then had a care in the world. They seemed oblivious too, of both the strange sight they created and the small crowd which had gathered curiously around them. The crowd were, however, keeping a discreet distance Trish noted.

The pair of them did indeed present a strange picture to the world. An elderly, totally inappropriately dressed, woman and a young man with skin as black and shiny as highly polished ebony and, what appeared to be, a permanent megawatt smile. His hair was as remarkable as his skin as he had dreadlocks which would have reached down to his waist if they had not been tied back at the nape of his neck by a jaunty red and white spotted handkerchief. They were both sipping hot drinks from the large mugs the café was famous for, and the remains of two plates of toast sat on the table before them.

'Mum, oh Mum, I've been so worried, what are you doing here?'

'I've been talking to this nice young man, he has been helping me look for my baby – he's going to be my boyfriend aren't you?'

'Too right love, I mean who could pass up the offer to be with such a gorgeous girl,' he replied smiling at Fiona and Trish in turn. 'As my new girlfriend says she was looking for her baby – I presume that's you,' said the young man with a cheeky expression on his face and a twinkle in his eyes.

'I'm afraid it is, she doesn't seem to understand that I've grown up, she still thinks of me as a baby you see. It's her illness – she has ...'

'No need to explain, my Granddad had the same thing. It's a bugger of an illness isn't it?'

'That just about sums it up,' Trish said in greeting dredging up a smile from somewhere in response to his own. 'Well it's very kind of you to help her out, most people would probably be too embarrassed or afraid to approach her.'

'No trouble at all - she seems a sweet old lady. I've just been telling her that she must have been a real looker in her day and had all the guys chasing her. My name's Patrick by the way, Fiona and I introduced ourselves before didn't we Fi love?'

'I'm Trish,' she replied suddenly aware that the shock and then the sudden relief had made her tremble from head to toe.

'Here sit down, you look as if you could do with a cup of tea as well. I'll just nip in and get you one,' Patrick said, rising to his feet without waiting for her to reply.

Trish had been going to refuse, but was suddenly aware that she needed a cup of tea more than anything else she could think of. Having reassured herself that her mother had come to no harm from her unscheduled excursion, Trish took the opportunity to ring Janice to tell her that all was well - although in her heart she had to admit it was anything but. This was a temporary reprieve ... a lucky escape, nothing more.

How could everything be alright when her mother was in the grip of an illness so cruel that it scrambled her brain, making her walk the streets in her night clothes looking for a baby aged sixty something?

She had just finished the call when Patrick appeared carrying a tray on which were three mugs of tea and three jam doughnuts.

'Sweet tea and empty calories, just what the doctor ordered,' he had said with the same basso profundo chuckle she had heard when she had first met him. 'Nothing to beat it for shock.' Trish had heard of male voices being described and dark chocolate and felt she now knew what the phrase meant. Almost everything about Patrick was the colour of dark chocolate from his skin and eyes to his hair and now also his voice. Only his smile which revealed teeth of a startling white added another dimension to the palette. His smile was one of the most amazing things Trish had ever seen, not just because of the whiteness of his teeth, but because it drew you to him as if pulled by a powerful magnet. It was a smile full of warmth, kindness and love.

They spent another hour together, with Fiona now immune to the cold, wrapped as she was in Patrick's all enveloping coat - during which time Patrick also seemed immune to the curious glances they were attracting.

'How do you manage with things?' he had asked after their doughnuts had been eaten, inclining his head in Fiona's direction.

'I have a lady who comes to sit with Mum during the mornings and on some days through to the early afternoon, while I'm at work,' Trish explained. 'I suppose I should give my job up really, but I love it and to be honest it …'

'Keeps you sane,' he finished for her, showing complete understanding of her situation. 'I think giving it up is the last thing you should do to be honest. Have you thought about respite though?'

'Well the doctor suggested I should put Mum into a home for a couple of weeks to give me a complete break, but I don't think I could. I'm afraid she would become even more confused in strange surroundings.'

'What about day care? Have you ever considered that?'

'What do you mean?'

'There are centres which people like your Mum can attend on a daily basis. It might be worth considering. From what you have told me, although your carer at home seems very good, your Mum might need a higher level of care.'

'You sound as if you know what you are talking about. Did you use one for your Granddad?'

'We did and it was great. The centre organised all kinds of things to amuse and occupy the old people. They had sing-a-long sessions with all the tunes from the old days. Granddad used to have a great old time "rolling out the barrel" and "hanging out his washing on the Siegfried line" with the rest of them. As you know only too well, people with this illness usually remember things from long ago. It's the present and yesterday they have problems with. Granddad and his chums played cards, chess or draughts if they were able and there was often visiting entertainment like magicians or hand bell ringers. The helpers even organised old fashioned tea dances. The centre he went to closed down, but there is another one locally.'

'It sounds great. Do you know how often Mum would be able to go, could it be once a week?'

'Perhaps, some of the oldies go more often if it is deemed they need a higher level of care, some even attend every day.'

'It sounds as if it would be fantastic, for me as well as for Mum. How would I go about finding such a place?'

'You already have,' he relied enigmatically. 'I manage one at the local health centre and I model it on the one my own Granddad used. I became interested in respite centres when he was diagnosed so I trained in geriatric nursing and now run the respite centre there. It's a lively place,' he said with another of his dark brown chuckles.

'And you would be willing to take Mum?'

'Well as I said she would need to be assessed properly by Social Services and we'd need a referral from her G.P. but from what I have seen today of her mental state and the fact that she has taken to roaming the streets, I would say any assessment granting her a place, would be a foregone conclusion.'

And so it turned out to be, with Patrick's input the assessment was made swiftly and without complication. Both Janice and Trish were asked to give their opinions regarding Fiona's state of mind. Their G.P. was also consulted as Patrick had predicted and, as it was Patrick himself whose intervention that day had prevented a possible tragedy, he was also asked for his own assessment.

Before the month was up Fiona was attending the centre on a daily basis. A volunteer driver collected her each morning and brought her home each evening.

For the first time since before Gerry's accident Trish had time for herself. She now worked longer hours in the library, which relieved their financial constraints further, as well as even having time to visit the hairdresser or to shop in the knowledge that her mother was being well cared for and was safe.

Chapter 3

Looking back on the day Fiona had gone walk about and had met up with Patrick, Trish was filled with gratitude for the kindness of the young man who had so fortuitously come the her mother's rescue.

If Fiona had not met Patrick so coincidentally – if Patrick had left the park by the time her mother got there, if Patrick had been the sort of man to ignore the plight of an old, mentally frail woman or if Fiona had decided to go somewhere else in her search for her baby, their lives might never have improved as they had. What, too, might have been the outcome, if Patrick hadn't had the experience of seeing his own Grandfather with the same illness and had chosen another career path.

It was no good thinking like that Trish knew, but still at the back of her mind she couldn't help wondering if fate or the Gods had lent them a hand that day.

It could have ended so differently if not for him. Fiona could have fallen, or been in an accident crossing the road, which was a constant worry. She had no road sense left at all, and had been known to walk down the middle of the road following the white lines as if they were guiding her to where she needed to go.

Worse still she might have fallen prey to heartless or vicious individuals who might have tormented her or, God forbid, even harmed her, but thankfully none of that had happened - it had been Patrick who had found her and had turned their lives around.

After the day centre had proved to be such a success, Patrick had even suggested that Fiona might benefit from visiting the residential centre to which the day centre was affiliated.

'Just for the odd weekend at first,' he had suggested. 'That way the centre and the staff will be less strange for her if you need to get away for a longer break at any time. You must remember that, as her primary carer, you need time out. If it becomes too much for you and you become ill or worn out – what would happen to Fiona. I don't want to add to your burden, but if that happened she might well end up in a home permanently. You really need to look after yourself just as well as, or even better, than you look after her. We do our bit here but, as I said, you are her primary carer and nobody should underestimate the toll living with this takes, day in day out for years. Alright Fiona may not remember much about the residential centre at first, but you might be surprised at how much she could take on board by visiting regularly. At least faces and surroundings would eventually become familiar just like they are at home.'

Trish was almost terrified to hope that this might be the case, because if it was, there might be just the smallest, the remotest, chance that she might be able to visit Karen and her family in the not too distant future.

One step at a time she chastised herself. But she went to visit the centre to see it for herself and was surprised to find it so bright and lively. Her first impression had been the laughter which had met her as she had walked through the door with more than a little trepidation.

Where were the smells of stale urine and boiled-to-death cabbage always so strongly associated with both schools and old people's homes, she had wondered? Where were the poor old dears propped in chairs staring blankly at mindless rubbish on the television screen which constantly blared from the corner of the room?

Where too was the patronising tone with which the staff spoke to their charges and which most old people hated and found degrading? There was certainly no evidence of any of those things here. The staff treated each old person with respect and when Trish had remarked on this was told that Patrick would allow nothing else. 'He'd be furious if he heard any disrespect or patronage,' one carer had told her. 'He constantly reminds us that the old people in our care are some of those who fought the war in order to secure our freedom. So for that, as well as a hundred other reasons, they deserve our respect and gratitude. After all they have earned it by putting their lives at risk for us. Anyone treating our clients with disrespect or patronage would not keep their job here for long.'

In fact none of the horrors associated with the common perception of old people's homes were in evidence here. All the residents seemed happy, well occupied and the staff bright and cheerful. The staffing ratio too gave an air of confidence as carers were plentiful enough to allow them to spend quality time with their clients. No impatience due to overwork was in evidence here. And even the fact that the patients were referred to as clients spoke of the level of care and respect they were afforded.

Having been asked to stay for lunch, Trish was also able to declare the food to be both plentiful and of excellent quality. In short the home in which her mother might spend some respite time, had appeared faultless. In reality it was more like a four star hotel than an old people's home, so she had agreed for her mother to come for a weekend's trial.

Fiona's first weekend residential visit was to be the coming weekend and to make it even easier for Fiona, Patrick himself was coming to collect her. This would mean that Fiona would go with him willingly and happily. Patrick had already prepared her by saying that he was taking her for a little holiday and Fiona, as far as she was able, was looking forward to it.

Patrick, with typical thoughtfulness, had suggested that Fiona and Trish mark off the days leading up to her visit on their calendar thus adding to the sense of anticipation and excitement rather than dread.

Fiona may be unaware of much which occurred in the here and now and was likely to forget even more of it, but strangely, she had never forgotten Patrick. He seemed to be etched into her consciousness like nothing else which had happened to her in recent years. She still referred to him as her gorgeous boyfriend or her toy boy going all doe-eyed and soppy whenever she saw him.

He, bless him, played along with her, even presenting her with a bunch of flowers from his garden occasionally, a tiny bar of chocolate or some other small but thoughtful gift sometimes; but always giving her an all-enveloping hug and a huge lip smacking kiss when they met up again.

Trish decided that Patrick was an angel, or at least the nearest she had ever come to meeting one. Nothing was too much trouble for him and having witnessed the attention and love he gave the old folk at the day centre on more than one occasion, she marvelled at his patience and dedication to all these poor lost souls.

She had tried thanking him once, not long after Fiona had first joined the regulars at the day centre, but he had brushed it away as one might an annoying fly.

'Don't mention it babe,' he had said. 'Granddad used to tell me that you get out of life what you put in. I have always tried to remember that and live my life by it, although sometimes I wish Granddad had got a better deal out of it than he appeared to. I'm quite sure though that if I'd said that to him he would have told me that God never gives you a heavier burden than your shoulders can carry. He was a great man was my Granddad. He had more wisdom in his little finger than most people have in their entire body. Another homily of his was that the world is made up of strangers, but that strangers are only strangers until you get to know and help them.'

'He sounds wonderful – I wish I'd had the chance to meet him.'

'Wonderful just about sums him up and he'd have loved you, he always had a keen eye for a pretty face not to mention a great pair of legs,' he had said with one of his infectious chuckles.

No wonder Fiona is completely under his spell Trish thought more than once almost every day. Even though her memory was so poor her mother always brought back some snippet of memory relating to an event or an entertainment at the day centre and her conversation was often liberally splattered with remarks like Patrick says ... or do you know what Patrick did today?

This absorption and hero worship of Patrick reminded Trish of when her own children were small and had just stared school. Their reaction to the teachers then had been very like Fiona's with Patrick – her children's conversations then had been just as liberally scattered with remarks like "Mrs. James says" ... or "no Mummy, that's wrong Mrs. Brown say you should do it this way".

At first it had been a little hard for Trish to come to terms with the fact that although she had still been one of the most important people in her child's life, there had been another rival for the crown. Now though she was only too glad that her mother had developed such a close bond with and affection for Patrick and felt no jealousy - only a deep abiding gratitude.

Another typically thoughtful Patrick innovation was to give each of his "oldies" a notebook in which details of the day's events could be recorded. The old people wrote in it like a diary if they were able or if they were not, a staff member did it for them. Then the book was then illustrated by pictures cut from magazines or sometimes drawn in. The pictures or phrases illustrated what the activities had been at the centre that day, there were pictures of singing, dancing, playing cards, throwing and catching balls, knitting and many more in Fiona's notepad.

In this way Patrick explained the old people's memory of days' events might be jogged enough to enable them to talk to their relatives about their day. Even if this didn't happen at least their primary carers were aware of what went on and could talk about each days events with their relatives, even if they received no response.

Another totally unexpected, but welcome benefit had been the improvement in Fiona's appetite. For months Trish had been concerned that her mother was not eating properly. Mealtimes were a constant battle as she refused almost all the food offered to her. There was always a reason – she was too tired, had a bad tummy ache, didn't like the food offered to her, or just couldn't be bothered to go through the motions of eating it. It was just as hard to coax her to drink and if anything that worried Trish even more as she knew how dehydration could be deadly to the old and already mentally frail.

At the centre however Fiona was amongst others, who too needed coaxing to eat and drink, and anyway if Patrick said she should eat – or have another cup of tea then she, always eager to please him, obediently did as he asked.

As a result Fiona's weight, which had dropped to an alarmingly low level, leaving her almost skeletal slowly started to climb back up to something approaching normal.

But the most dramatic development had been that for the first time almost since the diagnosis was first made, Fiona seemed happier, and because of this Trish was understandably happier too.

In short Trish had much to be grateful to Patrick for, that chance meeting with the stranger he had then been, then had proved to be almost miraculous in the many ways it had improved both their lives.

Trish didn't know what the future would hold for them, but whatever it was she was certain that it would be made easier, more bearable by her meeting with this wonderful inspirational stranger.

Just under twelve months later Fiona was booked to go into long term respite care for a whole month. As Patrick had suggested she enjoyed going to the centre, after a little initial anxiety, and had become a regular going every two or three months for a week or two. It was as if it had become a second home for her and Trish even noticed some improvement in her mother sometimes after a stay – due perhaps to the stimulating activities the residents took part in. The improvement was only minimal and very transitory, but Trish was sure she didn't imagine it - it was there and she was grateful for it.

This was the first time Fiona would be staying at the respite centre for so long, but as the staff assured Trish, her mother had little or no concept of time passing and would be as content and happy as she had been on other occasions A whole month meant that Trish would, for the first time, be able to visit her family in Australia so her ticket was booked and paid for and she had invested in a whole new wardrobe of clothes which would be suitable for the hot Australian summer. She had been nervous about travelling such a long way on her own until she confided this to a colleague at the library, who then told her that her sister was going to Australia to visit her own family at about the same time.

 A small amount of re-scheduling and a few telephone calls were enough to re-arrange their flights so that they could travel together on the same plane for almost all of their journey. Trish had met Wendy for coffee on several occasions now and they had hit it off straight away. Today they were meeting for lunch for the first time and Trish was looking forward to it immensely.

 Trish had been studying books on Australia during her coffee breaks at the library, and she had discovered that Melbourne, where her family lived was right on the coast with beaches and beautiful scenery aplenty – not to mention many fascinating places to visit. So Trish was ready for her big adventure safe in the knowledge that her beloved mother would be safe and well cared for while she was away. She would be able to totally relax and enjoy this other branch of her family whom she was desperate to get to know, and all because of the kindness of a man who was once a stranger and was now counted among her most valued friends.

Patrick's Story

Chapter 1

Apart from the fact that he missed his Granddad more with every passing day, Patrick had never been happier – but he still didn't feel complete.

He had a wonderful wife, Marie who was as fair as he was dark and a daughter Saskia who, in his totally unbiased opinion was the most intelligent, talented and beautiful girl ever! He lived in a comfortable house and had a rich fulfilling job which he loved almost as much as he loved his wife and daughter. But for as long as he could remember there had been a nagging, gaping hole in him. He had been brought up by his grandparents, although his beloved Gran had died when he was only ten. Although lost and grieving now himself, Patrick's Granddad had continued caring for him alone, unselfish an unswerving in his devotion. He had been a wonderful man who had dealt with each and every adversity life had thrown at him with a gentle faith, quiet determination and massive amounts of courage.

Patrick had had everything his Grandfather had been able to give him, not necessarily in financial terms but in opportunities and example. His wisdom had been as boundless as his love of life and the people he shared it with. And his inner circle, as he called his group of close friends, had been likeminded souls, as generous and kind as he was himself. Granddad had brought laughter and fun to the entire household or whichever circle of friends or acquaintances he happened to be with at the time - and he had been the primary influence in Patrick's life.

When he thought of his childhood Patrick predominantly remembered laughter and the gentle guidance with which to make informed choices, along with the freedom to make those choices without duress. The only questions his grandfather had asked revolved around others and how Patrick's actions would affect them. In this way Patrick had grown up able to make his life choices confidently, but to be considerate of others while doing so.

School had been very hard for a kid with coal black skin and a Jamaican accent which was only slightly diluted by living in semi-rural England. There he had repeatedly been bullied, ridiculed and mimicked but with his Grandfather's help and guidance had come through it virtually unscathed. His Granddad had encouraged him to pity rather than fear or hate his tormentors – telling him that only sad souls with closed minds were unable to accept change, or anyone who looked, sounded or acted differently.

'Ignore them son,' he had said. 'They will soon tire of it when they see how unaffected you are by it. Let them see that it upsets you or worries you and it will only add fuel to their petty fire.'

He had been right in this, as in so many things, and Patrick's school life had slowly improved. As his Granddad had predicted the bullies had been made impotent by his disinterest in them, by the lack of effect their vile taunts and ready fists had on him - and he gradually earned the reputation as a strong, honourable boy.

Once the bullies had been thus dealt with Patrick had begun to attract a wide circle of friends, from all the social and ethnic backgrounds the school held, earning their respect as he had earned the grudging respect of those who had once tormented him during his earlier school years.

Many of his friends from school remained close allies to this day. Now, of course, his small group of loyal friends had expanded to include their wives girlfriends, partners and offspring and they regularly met up at each other's houses. As they were all very fond of one another and got along famously, it was like the comprised one extremely diverse extended family.

Patrick's marriage was rock solid and joyous, his social life was full and happy and his working life was also completely sustaining and rewarding. Outside his family and friends nothing was more important to him than his work. But still the hollowness gnawed away at him as it would a man who was starved of food, but Patrick's hunger was for knowledge - for answers.

* * * * *

When his Grandfather had first been diagnosed with Alzheimer's, Patrick had been only seventeen. He had already left school and had taken a job in a local record shop. Although he loved music and helping people find what they wanted – often advising them on gifts for loved ones, he had felt neither satisfied nor rewarded by the work he did there.

The next few years as his Granddad sank deeper and deeper into the grip of his illness had been difficult for both of them. Patrick's Granddad had remained cheerful and positive until almost the end, denying the illness one of its worst, most notorious victories – that of becoming aggressive and bad tempered.

Less than a year after the diagnosis, a year during which the boy Patrick had devised various strategies to make it easier for his Granddad to cope and remain independent – Patrick knew what he really wanted to do with his life.

He had become fascinated – if enraged, by the way this illness which so cruelly destroyed minds, abilities and families could take over and destroy both individuals and families. And became determined to find ways to help others going through the same thing he and his Granddad were experiencing.

The first thing he needed to do was obtain as many qualifications in geriatric nursing and specialist mental health and psychiatric nursing as possible. This he did, undertaking several courses concurrently, working day and night to qualify as quickly as he could. Then as each course was passed and his diploma signed, he opted for another. This final course was a psychiatric nursing certificate with a speciality in dementia, and passing this one became the gateway to his going on to train with Admiral nurses who were specialists in dementia care.

Having got all these qualifications, in record time, his aim was to set up a centre where sufferers could go on a daily basis or for a day or two - maybe even a week or two, giving them and their primary carers a rest from each other and the grinding horrors of the illness. As well as providing the sufferers with the opportunity to relax and hopefully have some fun into the bargain.

At first his plans had been stonewalled by the council, who considered that the dementia care they offered was more than adequate and who told him they had no funds for anything more.

'In these days of cut backs and recession the demands upon our resources are becoming more and more strained.' he had been told. 'We have none to spare for crackpot new schemes which are totally unnecessary. The service we already provide is more than adequate.'

'Have you ever had anyone in your family or among you circle of friends who have suffered from this cruel illness?' Patrick had asked.

'I don't know what business that is of yours young man,' the pompous council official had said while looking down his nose at the man he to whom he had not even offered a chair.

'It is obvious that the answer is 'No' by your very attitude and I hope that makes you feel blessed because if you had got first-hand knowledge of it you would not be so dismissive of my request,' Patrick as said as he turned and left the room.

Patrick had been taught well by his Grandfather though. His Granddad had never given up on anything he believed in and Patrick was not about to either. He would get funding and secure premises elsewhere.

The first stage in his dream was to scout around the town to find suitable premises. Many he looked at were too old, had too many stairs or were too expensive to rent, but then he discovered that the local health centre had a large suite of rooms which were standing idle. They had apparently been earmarked for a small emergency centre to ease the strain on the local hospital's A&E department and for specialist sport injury treatment. When their local Hospital trust had "rationalised" its provision however all these facilities had been switched to other centres miles away, leaving the suite of four rooms pristine and unused.

They would be ideal for what Patrick had in mind. There was one main room which was large enough to have many functions. It could be used for occupational therapy, entertainment, dancing and one corner of it could serve as a dining room, at meal times. In addition there was a fully equipped kitchen, toilets, including facilities for the disabled and two smaller rooms which could serve a variety of purposes. Just as importantly it was all on ground level with access straight off the car park. There was not a stair or a step in sight and it even had its own separate entrance and a small garden where sufferers might enjoy pottering around weeding or growing flowers or even just sitting to take advantage of warm sunny days.

Patrick wanted these premises and with the quiet determination he had inherited from his Granddad set out to ensure he got them.

He drew up a business plan detailing his proposals before taking it to various banks asking for a loan, which after much persuasion and even a little mild coercion he was granted by a local branch manager.

The manager, Mark Hughes, was struggling with his own case. His mother was living at home with him and his young family as neither he, nor his wife wanted to use the present facilities which they considered lacking at best and dire at worst. Mark's mother, much later in Patrick's struggle, after his centre was finally opened, was destined to be among his very first clients.

Patrick then approached the Health Authority asking for permission to use the rooms for a day centre. At first they refused outright, but when he explained that it was to be a private venture in which their only input would be to rent him the rooms they reluctantly agreed. He was granted a twelve month lease with a review at the end of that period to assess whether an extension should be granted.

Patrick's original idea had been to work in affiliation with the Health Authority but as this possibility was denied him, he had reluctantly decided to make his facility a private venture. This meant that carers and sufferers would have to pay to use it as it would have to be run along business lines to ensure enough money was raised to pay quality staff, buy equipment, food and everything else they needed.

Patrick had really wanted to be able to provide a free service as he wanted no one who needed help to be excluded, just because they couldn't afford the fees he would have to charge. At first he had been bitterly disappointed by this development, but Marie had convinced him that it was better to be able to provide this kind of quality care rather than none at all, even if some charge had to be made.

Patrick saw the sense in this and determined to make the charges as low as possible. Perhaps he would be able to interest Dementia charities to support him enabling him to reduce charges, or maybe they could hold regular fund raising events to offset costs. He would try – on this he was determined.

At least he now had his loan from the bank and premises to use, enabling him to bring his dream to life. His head was buzzing with ideas and plans now that it looked as if it might really happen.

The centre had become more than just a possibility and Patrick would never forget the day he took possession of the keys. Marie and Saskia had come with him to share in his excitement and success when he first opened the door on his fledgling centre.

There was so much still to be done before he would be able to open those doors to the people who most needed it though. It needed painting throughout, because, although never having been used, it had become musty and dingy through disuse, and Patrick wanted everything to be the very best for his clients. It also needed equipping with tables and chairs which could be used for both dining and activities, more comfortable chairs for listening to the radio or reading and a thousand and one other mundane things like pots and pans, books, games, towels, crockery and cutlery – the list seemed endless. Then there were the less vital, but still important things like cushions and pictures for the walls which would give the large spaces character and softness, taking away the rooms' clinical atmosphere.

In one respect Patrick had been very fortunate in the location of his new centre though for they would need nothing more than very basic first aid equipment. The fact that they were adjoined to the health centre made anything more sophisticated unnecessary because qualified doctors and nurses were on hand just next door, if ever there was a medical emergency.

Having taken possession of the keys and viewed the rooms more closely, Patrick had suffered a severe crisis of confidence wondering where he was to get enough money to buy all the specialist and every day items he would need. Here again Marie had come to the rescue suggesting that she compile a letter explaining their intentions and asking the businesses and firms in their local area to help if they could.

Marie's letter had borne more fruit than anyone could have imagined. Alzheimer's and Dementia were such well-known, dreaded illnesses and tragic stories of the effects these dreadful illnesses were to be found among many families of the employees and in the firms Marie contacted. This meant that many of people she contacted had been personally touched by their own tragedy and most were more than happy to help.

Some were only able to give small items like a couple of new books, packs of cards or a game of draughts, others had provided enough pots and pans to cook for an army or enough tables and chairs to furnish the dining area. And Patrick had gratefully accepted it all. When the centre finally opened its door each and every donation was honoured by a certificate of thanks proudly displayed on the walls of the entrance hall itemising both the giver and their gift. Patrick called the display his "Role of Honour Wall."

The next task had been to find quality, dedicated staff. This was harder than it might have initially seemed, for Patrick wanted staff who were not only well qualified, but who had the same ethos as himself. Patrick was determined that his centre would be a sanctuary where sufferers could enjoy themselves, as much as they were able, and be somewhere they looked forward to visiting - if their illness had not progressed to the stage where looking forward was no longer a viable possibility for them. Not only did the staff need the right qualifications though they needed the right attitude.

Some interviewees felt that a strict regime and discipline were essential when running any establishment for the elderly, and were not afraid to offer their opinions on the subject.

'They can be crafty old devils you know – they'll take advantage of any kindness seeing it as a sign of weakness,' one candidate had told Patrick.

'These crafty old devils you refer so callously to are someone's mother, father, grandparent or sibling. Each one should have the right to demand the best care and attention it is possible to give them.'

'Well maybe in an ideal world, but you must admit that given an inch then any of them will take a mile. You cannot allow them to get away with anything in my experience.'

This remark had met with a rare display of anger from Patrick who ceremonially tore up the application in front of this man, who would most certainly not be given a position, and marched him to the door in less time that it takes to tell.

So the struggle to find the right staff continued. Several of the interviewees he saw, although very well qualified, told him that in their experience it was best to distance themselves emotionally from the clients they worked with. 'It is no good getting too involved with them, it just depresses you and you end up taking their troubles home with you,' had been an observation he had heard regularly.

The names of those who spoke in this way had been swiftly removed from his list of possible candidates. But eventually he had gathered a group of like minded carers and was ready to open. Some of the carers were indeed well qualified, but others - the lay-carers - as he called them were often people who had watched or cared for a loved one going through the same things as his clients were. These were to prove to be some of the most valuable members of his staff, in fact, for they had witnessed first hand the ravages of the disease and could empathise with both clients and their families with warmth and true understanding.

There was still a lot to be done even after the centre had opened officially, more equipment to buy, policies and care packages to be drawn up, and local entertainers contacted with a view to coming on a weekly basis to sing, dance, play instruments, perform magic – anything which would give his clients some fun.

One of the most popular of these was a group of Morris dancers, who never failed to bring smiles to the faces of their audience whenever they performed.

None of the items on his to-do list worried Patrick overly now they were officially close to opening, as he wanted his centre to be a living growing thing adapting to individual needs and circumstances. In many ways it was the amorphous quality of the care he would offer which excited him most. In most of the centres he had worked in - gaining practical experience while training - the care offered had been rigid and the clients were made to fit the model of each centre, rather than the centre bending to the individual needs of each sufferer.

These experiences had made Patrick determined that at his centre every client would be treated as an individual and the care offered would be changed to fit their needs rather than the other way round. What he was aiming for was the kind of atmosphere in which everyone felt like highly valued members of a family – albeit an extremely dysfunctional one!

Almost before Patrick knew what was happening the frantic rush to prepare for opening was over and the day he had waited for, for so long finally arrived.

That had been five years ago. Five years during which the "Thomas Charles Centre" – named in honour of his Granddad had grown in popularity and had earned a reputation for the excellence of its care.

Cutting the ribbon to officially open the centre, on that day five years previously, had been one of the last things Patrick's Grandfather had done – he had died only weeks later, making the empty space which Patrick had always been aware of in his life deeper and wider.

It was an abiding sadness in Patrick's life too that the centre which had done, and continued to do, so much to help improve the lives of Alzheimer's sufferers and their primary carers, had come too late to help his own Grandfather.

Ever since his Granddad had died, the gaping hole he had always been aware of in his life seemed even bigger. He often felt guilty, when he had so much to be thankful for, that he felt this way. He had a wife who was not only beautiful outwardly, but had a beautiful spirit as well. She was kind, generous and understanding of the deep sadness he lived with and the ambitions which drove him.

She was however concerned that Patrick was becoming more and more affected each day by the need for answers to the questions he needed to ask, for explanations and didn't know how to help him. He seemed to be growing away from her, was becoming more distant, quieter and each day, she found it harder to reach him. Marie was becoming forced to see that nothing would improve until he found those answers to questions he had always wanted answered but had never been able to ask.

Chapter 2

The 'Thomas Charles Centre' had been up and running for only a comparatively short time when it was followed by Patrick's new centre catering for longer term residential care. This was designed to take in sufferers for up to two weeks at a time ensuring their primary carers had the opportunity for respite care and rest or even a much deserved holiday on a regular basis. With the success of both centres Patrick should have been happy – but he was at his lowest since his Granddad had died.

One morning when the newspapers, which were regularly delivered to the centre each day for the clients to look at, failed to arrive, Patrick walked to the newsagents to collect them.

On the way back to the centre he saw one of the cafés had put tables and chairs outside on the pavement for customers to be able to enjoy the glorious weather they were experiencing.

It was a real Indian Summer. September and now October had been sunnier and warmer than much of the actual Summer months had been and everywhere people were out enjoying this unexpected pre-winter bonus.

Patrick impetuously suddenly decided to join them. He felt he needed a little time to himself away from the demands of the centre and his impulsive decision was to prove life changing.

There was only one unoccupied table and so he sat there placing his order for a coffee and toasted tea cake. The waitress was a jolly lady a good few years older than himself, although just speaking to her for a few seconds had convinced him that she would be able to pass for a good few years younger that she probably was. She was one of those people who were perennially young at heart and her good humour and her broad smile warmed him.

He was surprised when she brought his order to see two cups on the tray she carried, and even more surprised when she asked if she might join him.

'It's my break and there's nowhere else to sit,' she explained, although, unbeknownst to him, the lost look on his face and his obvious sadness had been her primary motive. Here was someone who needed the opportunity to talk was her instinctive reaction to Patrick. She had recognised the need in him immediately, and knew there was no-one better to talk to than a stranger with no emotional ties to him.

Before long they were chatting as if they were old friends. Her name was Peggy and she told him that she knew who he was because an aunt of hers had been a client at the centre before she died.

'I remember her,' Patrick assured her. 'She was a lovely lady – she reminded me of my own Granddad who, like your aunt, managed to remain cheerful, most of the time, despite the ravages of the illness, almost to the end of his life.'

'My aunt wouldn't have been like that without the centre though – I'm sure of that,' replied Peggy. 'All the family were so grateful to you all at the centre. They often say, even to this day, that they would never have been able to cope with her illness without the breaks you gave them. Alzheimer's is such an awful thing for every member of a family affected by it. You seem to be able to work some kind of magic there though. '

'No magic – just care, respect and encouragement. We try to find something ... anything the sufferers are still able to do and build on that. It helps them keep positive and cheerful.'

'If you don't mind my saying so you look anything but positive or cheerful yourself this morning though. Do you want to talk about it? A trouble shared is a trouble halved, they say, and there's nothing like being able to talk things over with a complete stranger is there? You can tell someone you have never met before so much more than you can tell your nearest and dearest I always find.'

This was true Patrick realised. He had talked his problem over with his Granddad so many times but he had been reluctant to ask too many searching questions for fear of upsetting his Granddad or opening old wounds. He was always reluctant to talk to Marie about it too, because he knew how she worried so.

'You're right, but my problem is an old one and talking about it before has never helped.'

'Give it a try anyway – you never know.'

Admitting defeat in the face of her quiet determination and obvious kindness, Patrick just nodded before taking a deep breath, as if to gather himself for the task ahead, and beginning his story.

'I was brought up by my Gran and Granddad. Gran died when I was only ten – after that it was just

Granddad and me. I can't begin to tell you how great he was. He was my biggest fan, my encouragement, my inspiration – in short my best friend. He helped me in almost every aspect of my life, being both unfailingly supportive and encouraging. But there was one thing he could never help me with. He could never explain to me why my mother had left me at the age of just eighteen months.'

'Left you with your Grandparents you mean?'

'No – not really and that's the main problem. I might be able to understand it better had she done that, my Grandparents might have been able to explain it to me and each one of us may have been able to forgive her in our own ways. My Dad had left before I was even born according to my Granddad. Mum and I were living in two rooms of an old house in a run down area, according to what Granddad has told me since. She took in sewing to help pay the bills as she couldn't leave me to go out to work. Even then Gran and Granddad had been wonderful to us, babysitting me, helping out with bills and generally supporting her – even though she was not their blood relative. She was their daughter-in-law, you see, it was my Dad who was their son. But Granddad told me she was a super mum and loved me.'

'So what happened?'

'One day the other residents of the house heard me crying. That isn't unusual for an eighteen month old baby of course, but the crying went on for hours and hours, even days, until eventually someone called the police. They broke into our flat and found me in my cot starving hungry and very cold - wearing nothing but a nappy which had obviously been unchanged for days. It was freezing cold in the flat and so they took me to hospital. For a while it was touch and go that I would survive. I was emaciated, dehydrated and suffering from hypothermia.'

'And there was no sign of your mother?'

'No, it appeared as if she had just walked out and disappeared off the face of the earth. She had taken nothing with her, no clothes or personal items, her coat was still hanging on the back of the door – even her handbag was still on the table. It was just as if she'd popped out for a minute and was coming straight back.'

'And you have never seen or heard of her since?'

'No, nothing. It's haunted me all my life. Nobody, not even my Granddad could explain where she had gone and more importantly why she had abandoned me. I have wanted answers to those questions for as long as I can remember and it has been like a gaping hole in my life.'

'Have you ever tried to find her?'

'I wouldn't know where to start. I think Gran and Granddad tried at first and the police made initial enquiries of course, but gave up when it became obvious they were not going to succeed in finding her. They checked all the local hospitals, reports of road traffic accidents, local shelters for the homeless, doctor's surgeries everywhere they could think of, but found nothing. Sometimes I think it wouldn't have been so bad if I had been adopted – there is something almost shameful about being abandoned you see. You feel rejected and totally worthless. If I had been adopted it would be proof that at least she had cared enough to make sure I was safe and that I had the chance of a better life. There would at least have been records of it as well – but as it is the police nor anyone else had anything to go on. As it was all they were looking for was a missing person and everyone knows how effectively they can appear to vanish off the face of the earth.'

'That must have been terrible for you.'

'It was – to be truthful it still is. Never a day has gone past without me wondering why she left me. I have always thought it must have been my fault you see. I must have been a bad baby. Perhaps I cried all the time – although Granddad asked the other people who lived in the building and they hadn't heard me cry for long periods before those days. I have a daughter of my own now and there is nothing in this world which would make me abandon her. I cannot even imagine what circumstances would lead a loving parent to just walk out on their child. I would do anything to protect my own daughter – so why did my Mum leave me? All my grandparents and I were left with were questions. No reasons, no explanations, no apologies ...Nothing!'

'Did she have no other relatives living locally to whom she might have gone?'

'No, only me and my Grandparents. Granddad came from Jamaica with his family just before my Mum and Dad married. Once they were settled Dad arranged for Mum to come to England and they were married here.'

'You said that you have always thought it was your fault, that you were a bad baby.'

'What other explanation can there be?'

'Plenty believe me, but as to your being a bad baby – there is no such thing. By eighteen months babies haven't usually developed the reasoning power to cry just to annoy someone. If they cry it's because they are hungry, need changing, are tired, are in need of comfort or are in pain. So it certainly wasn't your fault. Perhaps your mother was suffering from post-natal depression.'

'Surely I would have been too old for that to be the case. That only affects mothers with very new babies surely.'

'No that's not the case at all. Recent studies have shown that it is possible for mothers to develop it up to five years after giving birth.'

'I didn't know that. But even if that's true, why didn't she take me to my Grandparents rather than just abandoning me.'

'I don't think any of us can begin to imagine how someone suffering from that would feel. In a severe case it could almost be as if the mother was having a complete nervous breakdown. The word depression doesn't do the illness justice really. Many people imagine the mother just feels a little bit low, due possibly to dramatic changes in their hormone levels as a result of giving birth. It's much worse than that. I have spoken to mothers who have told me that they lost all reason – they couldn't think rationally, make decisions or even function. Even the simplest tasks like feeding and changing a baby, making food for themselves, washing and dressing themselves each morning are beyond them.'

'And you think that may be what happened to my mother?'

'Well of course I don't know for sure. If she is never found you may never know. But from the little you have been able to tell me it certainly seems a very real possibility. After all, before that awful day, she appeared to care well for you. She did work at home to support you both you told me. Surely that means she wanted to give you the best she could without leaving you alone.'

'I would like to think that was the case. It would make it easier for me to understand and that's all I have ever really wanted.'

'So you wouldn't want to trace her even if it was possible?'

'Well yes, I would. Apart from the fact that I have a million and one questions I would like to ask her, I would love to see her, although sometimes I wonder if it would be a good thing. I often wonder, you see, if I resemble her at all, or am I more like my father? Or why when I can't sleep at night do I always find myself humming John Denver songs? Did she sing them to me as she settled me to sleep? And why am I terrified of cats? It's silly things like that - apart from the more obvious family history details, which I would love to find out.'

'But you have never tried to trace her you say.'

'As I said, I wouldn't know where to start – I don't even know if she's still alive and if she is, whether she is still in this country. She may well have gone back to Jamaica in which case it would be impossible.'

'Not necessarily. The Salvation Army have a missing persons' bureau and have been very successful in tracing relatives over the years and in most parts of the world. It is called' The Salvation Army Family Tracing Service'. They undertake searches for many people every year, but there are certain cases they won't become involved in.'

'Like what?'

'They do not normally undertake searches when adoption is involved, for fathers looking for illegitimate offspring, for minors under the age of sixteen and just for people looking for friends with whom they have lost contact.'

'How do you know all this - are you a member – do you work for them?'

'Not exactly. I first became aware of them when they found my sister for me.'

Chapter 3

Peggy offered to meet Patrick again the next day when they arranged that she would go with him to the offices of the Salvation Army Family Tracing Service. Patrick still could not believe Peggy had persuaded him into it, but in her gentle way she had done exactly that, and with apparent ease.

Because he had been reluctant to talk about the situation over the telephone, Peggy had said that it would be better to go to the London offices to speak to someone in person. But much as Patrick had been uneasy about discussing his problem over the phone, the thought of driving through London filled him with dread.

A whole day's absence meant that he would have to get cover at the centre as well, and he knew having a rare day off would cause speculation, but he was now committed. And although he was excited about what any investigation might bring to light, he was nervous about telling anyone other than Marie the reason for it in case the journey led to nothing, which was probably the more likely scenario.

As soon as he was back at the centre after unexpectedly meeting Peggy he rang Marie at home telling his wife about his conversation with his new friend, and the amazing coincidence of meeting her.

'That's good news – isn't it?' she asked warily knowing how depressed he became whenever he thought of his mother.

'I suppose so, although I'm not really expecting them to be able to do anything,' he replied with that certain flatness in his voice which always signified the onset of such a depression. 'What I can't get over is the amazing set of coincidences. I mean I have to go to fetch the papers for the first time in months, because the newsagent had failed to deliver them. I decide to stop at that particular café – the very one where Peggy works. There are no other free tables so she sits with me for her break. We get chatting and then it turns out that the Salvation Army have traced her sister for her, so she knows all about the tracing service they provide. The odds against all that combining at just the right time must be staggering.'

'Perhaps it was meant to be – your Granddad always said if something was meant to happen it would.'

'That's true – I wonder what he would have thought of it though, trying to trace my mother I mean. In one way it seems as if I'm being disloyal to him and Grandma.'

'I don't think he would ever have thought that. He told me once that he knew you would never have complete peace until you understood why she left as she did. I actually think he wanted to know and understand it too.'

'You're so good for me you know – do I tell you often enough how grateful I am for your love and support or how much I love you?'

'No you don't, but you don't need to you big idiot,' she replied laughing now and was relieved to hear his answering laugh before he rang off.

The rest of the day dragged. Late in the afternoon Marie rang him back to say she would cover for him at the centre. It was something she did occasionally when a member of his staff was taken ill suddenly or had a family emergency. She had no qualifications herself and was therefore limited as to what she could do there, but the old people loved to see her, especially if she took little Saskia with her.

Saskia's love of life and everything in it, her enthusiasm and her boundless energy were like a tonic to the old folk who remembered their own youth or that of their children when the little girl was with them . Every time Saskia visited the centre it was as if she brought the sunshine in with her, warming even the saddest heart with her sheer joy of life.

Marie too was always a hit, she would spend hours listening to their stories – often over and over again – without any sign of impatience or irritation at having become embroiled in their conversational loops.

Sometimes she would play cards with them or, being an accomplished pianist, would organise an impromptu sing-a-long of all their old favourites.

* * * * *

Another surprise awaited Patrick when he returned home on this most surprising of days. Marie had spent the time, when Saskia was having her afternoon nap, going through his Granddad's personal papers. It was a job Patrick himself had been meaning to do ever since his Granddad's death, but had put off more than once, not wanting to experience the rush of sadness he knew would overwhelm him if he were to attempt it.

Among all the other document Marie had found, there was not only the certificate of Patrick's birth, but the certificate of Patrick's parents' marriage. This contained not only the names of Patrick's own parents themselves but the names of their fathers.

'I wondered if these might help to find her,' was all she said as she handed him the old crumpled documents.

'Thank you Marie,' was all he could say hugging her tightly as if drawing strength from her. 'I'm still not sure that I would want to actually meet her though. One minute I long to, then the next I am adamant I wouldn't agree to it. What I really want, I suppose are answers to the questions that have plagued me. I just want to understand why she left me.'

'I know, but the only way to get the answers you need to understand her motives, would be to meet her face to face surely. After all she is the only one who knows the whole story and her reasons. All anyone else could do is just guess or surmise.'

'You're probably right, but just at the moment I don't think I could either meet her or look her in the eye.'

'You'll make the right decision for you, if and when the time comes I'm sure of that. And if you want me to be there at any stage of this journey I will come with you.' So saying she enveloped him in her arms and there he stayed for many contented minutes drawing warmth and comfort from the strength of her love for him.

Patrick hardly slept that night, wondering what the following day would bring. He tossed and turned until the early hours then, giving up all hope of sleep got up to make himself a drink. He should not have been surprised when, a few minutes after the kettle had boiled, Marie appeared tousle haired and bleary eyed in the kitchen.

'Is there enough in the pot for me?' she asked smiling.

They spent the rest of the night talking about the possible outcomes of his meeting with the Salvation Army's representative, and how each scenario might make him feel.

By the time daylight poured in through the kitchen windows, casting shadows from the watery sunlight over everything, Patrick felt he was as prepared as he could ever be.

Because of Patrick's horror of driving in and around London Peggy had suggested they opt to travel by train and then take the tube or taxis, which hopefully would relieve some of their anxiety about the journey.

As the train slowed on its approach into London, Patrick and Peggy looked on out a scene of horror. The main road alongside which they were travelling was full of cars at a complete standstill and an eerie quiet replaced the sound of roaring engines impatient, angry horns and squealing brakes. The tailback stretched for miles and they were almost at their destination before they heard the wail of many sirens approaching the source of the traffic jam.

Several cars had collided leaving only the crumpled and smoking remains of them piled in a multi-coloured heap, resembling the kind of modernistic sculpture favoured by galleries like the Tate Modern.

There were several dazed and shaking people gathered around as if in shock – some already shrouded in blankets which looked as if they were made from aluminium foil. Peggy and Patrick could only hope that everyone had escaped the carnage and that there were no others in the mangled remains - that was too horrific to even contemplate.

'I'm glad we decided to come by train,' Patrick observed when he found himself able to speak.

'Yes, it was a good decision,' Peggy replied simply.

At last they were at their destination – a huge cathedral like building filled with the hum of countless conversations and the tattoo of a thousand footsteps. Here they were to connect with the underground train which would carry them further into the throbbing heart of the city.

Several tube stations and a short walk later they were standing outside the building which had held so many hopes for so many people over the years.

'Shall we go in – your appointment is in ten minutes?' Peggy enquired as Patrick remained rooted to the building's lowest step. She was a little nervous herself now, she had often talked to other seekers who had given up taking this vital first step or had failed to even cross the threshold, their nerves getting the better of them and weakening their resolve.

'Give me a minute,' Patrick said with an tremble in his voice.

Peggy was seriously concerned now, but she need not have been. Patrick was made of strong stuff so she breathed a sigh of relief, not even realising she had been holding her breath, when a few minutes later, he squared his shoulders and headed for the door.

Patrick's interview was with a kindly gentleman whose upright, military bearing ensured that he still had a commanding reassuring presence about him. Before even they had even begun to discuss the reasons for Patrick's visit, tea and biscuits were served in a cosy anteroom adjacent to Charles' more formal office. And, it was only after their refreshments had been consumed and pleasantries exchanged that Charles escorted Patrick into his inner sanctum and the interview began. It lasted no more than an hour, but to Patrick it felt much longer.

During that time Patrick was asked far more questions about his family than he had answers to, nevertheless he was surprised that he knew more than he thought he did. Things his Granddad had told him about the family home in Jamaica, about how his parents had met, even about his mother herself came back to him under Charles Austin's gentle but deceptively insistent probing.

Patrick gave him the documents Marie had discovered and they were promptly whisked away to be photocopied by a hitherto unseen secretary who had been summoned by the sound of a buzzer placed by "call me Charles'" right elbow.

'Now the most important question of all,' Charles Austin said as he resumed his seat in the interview room after receiving the documents back with old worldly manners which Patrick already recognised as typical of him.

'What are your motives for wanting to find your mother?'

'I want to know, to try and understand why she left me. Why she just walked out on me, leaving me alone and neglected to God knows what fate when I was just eighteen months old.'

'Very understandable my dear boy, but I hear a lot of anger and resentment in your voice. You must understand that we would not be prepared to put your mother, should we find her, in any situation which might be potentially harmful to her – emotionally or physically. Therefore I must ask you if you would be willing, if our search is successful, and that you decide you wish to meet her, you do so in the company of one of our officers.'

'I wouldn't try to hurt her, if that's what you mean – in fact I'm not sure I even want to actually meet her. Sometimes I long to and at other times I really don't think I could. But mainly I just want answers to a lot of questions.'

'Fair enough, but cases of abandonment like your own naturally can leave behind a deep residue of hurt, anger and resentment, so I think mediation would be the best way forward should you meet her and if I might suggest some counselling for yourself to help you come to terms with all those negative emotions in the meantime.'

'I can't afford the time to keep popping up to London for counselling and I'm pretty sure I don't need it in any case. The thought of pouring my heart out to a complete stranger fills me with horror,' Patrick replied testily.

'You wouldn't need to come to London or talk to a stranger. Peggy is one of our trained counsellors and as I understand it you have already opened up to her somewhat. I am not suggesting you need therapy, dear boy, or anything like, that but it does us all good to talk about things which have affected us badly. I wouldn't be here today if I hadn't met a wonderful man in this very building who encouraged me to pour out what I had witnessed. I was unfortunate enough to see far too many young men killed or injured on far too many battlefields you see. But talking it through with my own counsellor help me come to terms with it all. We tell ourselves that can't burden our nearest and dearest so say nothing until the burden we are carrying becomes far too heavy and we break under the strain.'

Patrick could see the wisdom and the truth in these words. For years he had avoided saying anything to Marie which might upset her too much. She knew, of course, that he had feelings of unresolved anger towards his mother and that he wanted, possibly more than he wanted anything else in his life, to know why she had abandoned him. But he had never been able to share with her the depth of those feelings, or the despair which washed over him, more often than he cared to admit, when he thought how unlovable, how worthless he must have been for her to leave him like that. It was as if he had been discarded like he had been a piece of rubbish.

These were the feelings which had driven him to make a success of his life and one of the reasons he had chosen to try to improve the lot of others who were often abandoned by society and even by their own minds. But if he were truthful with himself he would admit that he was proud and confident about the worth of his work. As far as personal confidence was concerned, however, he was forced to admit he had little or none. In many ways he still considered himself worthless and unlovable and, no matter how many times his family had assured him otherwise, these feelings never left him and were the legacy of his mother's actions all those years ago.

'I didn't know Peggy was one of your counsellors,' he said quietly.

'Well it is not something she would advertise, but she is good. She has a way of recognising souls in torment and instinctively reaches out to them – just as I'm sure she must have reached out to you. My advice to you would be to take advantage of her wisdom and her kindness. The kindness of strangers is a wonderful thing you know,' Charles said with a smile.

The interview ended shortly after these words with the promise that Charles would be in touch as soon as he had any news to impart, even if the search proved fruitless meaning that, in effect, there was no news to give him.

All this time Peggy had been patiently waiting in Charles' outer office having vehemently refused to accompany him for his interview.

'You don't want me there,' she had told him. 'You need to be able to talk to Charles in complete confidence so that nothing or no one will cramp your style. Go on in now, you will be fine with Charles.'

Almost before they knew it Patrick and Peggy were back on the train, but their homeward journey was very different from the one they had taken to the capital that morning. For one thing they were in a carriage which was completely empty except for themselves. There were no crowds of commuters frenetically tapping away at laptop keyboards, no intrusive ringing of mobile phones or the chatter of ensuing conversations. This time the air was still, calm and quiet.

'How do you think it went?' asked Peggy taking advantage of the opportunity for private conversation.

'Alright I think, I saw a man called Charles, as you know,' replied Patrick noting that Peggy nodded her head approvingly at the name. 'He seemed quite hopeful that they would be able to discover something, even if it was only that she had died.'

'How would you feel if that were to be the case?'

'Cheated, I think best sums it up. I have waited so long for answers. So long to be told that it wasn't my fault that she left. My Granddad always told me I could do anything - become anything I wanted to be. He strove to give me enormous confidence and a real feeling of self-worth despite my inclinations to think otherwise, but deep inside I have never believed it. Without his support I don't know what would have become of me, because even though he tried to help me work through my feelings of inadequacy - in many ways he failed. You see her rejection was so entrenched in me, deep down, that I have always felt totally worthless, unimportant, insignificant.'

'Because your mother left you.'

'Well yes, I mean if I had meant anything to her, if she had valued me, at all she would have stayed, she would never have been able to leave me behind like last year's unwanted Christmas present, would she?'

'Do you feel anger as well?'

'You bet I do!' Patrick spoke the words explosively, openly admitting his feelings for the first time. 'I mean I could have died if the neighbours hadn't alerted the police. That alone would be enough to make anyone angry surely.'

'Of course it would – it's perfectly normal that you should feel as you do, but it is important that you should work through these feelings,' insisted Peggy firmly. 'Harbouring such resentment and anger is very self destructive - you must realise that.'

'I suppose, but how do I stop myself feeling that way. I'm thirty five now and in all the years since she left she has never once tried to get in touch to find out if I'm still alive, and if so how I was doing.'

'You've had no word from her at all?'

'No, not even a birthday or Christmas card and I am sure she never contacted my Granddad – he would have told me if she had. As far as she is concerned I don't seem to exist. I certainly don't matter to her at all – that's for sure.'

'What I am going to say now may sound crazy to you, but I'd like you to try what I suggest,' said Peggy tentatively. 'It has worked for many of the others I have counselled, so just promise you will hear me out before you dismiss it. What I would suggest is that you imagine yourself standing in a place where you have always felt happy and at peace. Maybe it's a shoreline or a wood, a bench in the park even. The place doesn't actually matter it is how it makes you feel that is important. Once you are fully in that place and feel the peace wash over you, imagine yourself sealing all your anger and resentment in a bottle or a box – something like that. Something you can completely seal without fear that it will ever be opened again, and then imagine yourself disposing of it so it can't hurt you anymore. Imagine a door opening up from your peaceful place, you go through the door, putting the box or the bottle - whatever you have put your negative feelings in - on the other side of the door and then coming back to your serene happy place once again and locking the door. Once you have done that settle back into your happy place, letting the calm wash over you, recapturing the peaceful feelings and thinking of something which gives you happiness to replace the negative emotions.'

'It does sound crazy!' was all Patrick could say.

'I know but it has been proven to work – psychologists use this technique with great success. It is as if you have control of the negative emotions for the first time and can decided to put them away, so that they can no longer harm you. Try it - you have nothing to lose after all. It probably won't work the very first time you try it but keep doing it until you feel it helping. Even if it doesn't work for you - and I'm sure it will if you keep going with it – you can't feel worse than you do now can you?'

'Alright I'll give it a go, but I'm far from convinced.'

'You and most other people who have been asked to try it,' Peggy giggled. 'You may not think it's working and it may not be at first, but if you keep trying you should eventually be able to look at your situation more positively and find that thoughts of, in your case anger towards your mother, are no longer causing you as much distress or anger. I'll come and see you at the centre now and again to see how you are getting on, I'll even help you with the process if you want me to.'

'Thank you, I may not be too hopeful but trying anything is better than doing nothing. Surely it will be better than feeling as I do now.'

The time had flown by and their journey together was almost over – in one way. Their other journey together was just beginning.

Neither of them could know what the outcome would be – whether Patrick would ever be re-united with his mother. Whether he would ever get the answers to those questions which had plagued him all his life; or whether his mother would even still be alive and able to answer them. But whatever happened Patrick somehow felt better for merely trying to find those answers. It was as if by being more proactive and taking positive steps he was feeling more positive in himself. He also knew that Peggy was right about him confronting all the anger and bitterness which he had stored up and revisited over the years. How many times, he asked himself with new honesty, had he advised relatives and primary carers of his clients to seek counselling as a method of dealing with all the resentment and hostility brought about by losing a loved one to such a cruel illness.

When it came to himself though he had convinced himself, like hundreds of others before him, that he could cope without baring his soul to a stranger. Just the thought of it made him feel vulnerable and weak – and he had always tried to think of himself as strong enough to deal with anything.

Now however Peggy had helped him to see that it needed more strength to confront the problem than to ignore it and so in a way he had two journeys to travel – but with the help of Peggy and his loving and supportive family he saw now that he would reach its end and that he would be the happier for it.

What would have become of him had he not met Peggy as he stopped for an unscheduled cup of coffee, he would never know. That chance meeting and subsequent interest in his woes and kindness towards him had the potential to change his life – improving it beyond all recognition.

Peggy's Story

Chapter 1

Although she had always considered herself to have been unfairly saddled with what she thought of as an out-dated, old fashioned name – or perhaps because of it, Peggy was almost fanatically modern.

At almost fifty, she was often mistaken for someone much younger. She wore her hair styled and coloured in a modern way, her clothes were on trend – if budget priced, and her attitude fiercely up to date. She kept in touch with modern trends in music, was well read and kept up to date with the news and public opinion, with an almost compulsive regularity, and was therefore well informed on many subjects.

But her Achilles' heel was technology. Despite her almost obsessive modernity – computers, the internet and interactive anythings and everythings were beyond her. And the language of computing with its megabytes, zips and rams was as incomprehensible as fourth year Latin had once been. And as for mother boards, well to Peggy that just implied a housewife with too little to do now her children were old enough to be reasonably independent.

She did have a mobile phone, but it was one of the very basic ones - it didn't connect to the internet, take photos or movie clips, let you watch matches, tell you the latest news, give you the football scores, or sing you songs. It just made telephone calls which in any case was all Peggy thought you should ask of a phone and certainly all she asked of it. What else would you want a phone to do anyway she wondered. Surely if you wanted to take photos or movies you would use a camera and what was the matter with using the television or newspapers to keep up with events.

Peggy was also very optimistic in her outlook, always a bottle half full person and throughout the troubles of her life she had always tried to remain positive and optimistic. An attitude which, she was convinced, had helped her through her worst days – of which she had had more than her fair share.

Peggy liked people and could usually find the good in everyone. She also had a raging desire to help those in distress, and was well known for her ability to tackle any and all problems. But technology defeated her and she found little to be positive about anything remotely connected with it.

Never one to admit defeat, Peggy had tried to learn how to use a computer - once taking a short course of lessons. It had been beyond her however. This may have been because the tutor, who obviously knew his way around computers backwards, and would have possibly married one had it been legal, talked way over her head. He had a high and mighty attitude and had assumed his students already had a certain degree of knowledge; which she did not. During one class things between them came to a head though and forced Peggy to rethink her attendance.

'I really think this course is beyond you my dear,' he had told her in his infuriatingly patronising way one evening after she had struggled and failed to load something or other.

'I really do need to learn though,' she had pleaded.

'I think not. I am not prepared to waste all my time on someone so obviously totally inept. In my opinion it would be better for you to go to a flower arranging or baking class.'

Peggy, although incensed by his attitude, had to admit that as far as computers were concerned she was woefully ignorant and in many ways wished she could remain so.

Because of her desire to help others she had trained as a counsellor, and did voluntary work for many agencies. She was, what she liked to refer to as a freelance counsellor. She was not tied to any one agency but her name was on many of their records and she was often called upon if her own experiences or circumstances could be deemed helpful to those who needed help.

Her desire to help may have been innate, but it may also have sprung from her own experiences, as her own life had not always been steady and secure – far from it. At times, when she was in her darkest most despairing places, she had often longed for someone to share her burdens and troubles with. Someone who was not known to her - who would not be hurt by her disclosures or be adversely affected by them. Someone who would not take her burdens upon themselves, worry about them constantly and make them their own.

It was this desire which had led her to train as a counsellor. She knew how much they could help.

Peggy had been widowed early, lost a child to cot death and discovered a sister she never knew existed, making it possible for her to be empathetic with others going through their own tragedies in many areas of life. Although no two people could ever feel the same in any given set of circumstances Peggy was at least able to identify with their sorrow, anger and grief. To tell them honestly that although circumstance differed, she had been affected by something similar and could relate to their feelings and pain.

Bill, her husband had been the light of her life and a more optimistic, cheerful man it would be hard to imagine. Two of his favourite sayings had been "make the most of every day because life is too short" and "it's not worth worrying I may be hit by a bus tomorrow."

He had been twenty six when his prophecy had been ironically fulfilled and that very thing had happened on a dark winter morning on his way to work. It had snowed heavily in the days before the accident; heavy traffic had melted the snow to slush on the main roads of their town only for it to freeze hard again over night. Bill had been walking along the pavement when a bus filled with early morning commuters had hit a patch of black ice, veered uncontrollably off course and slammed into the wall of a shop pinning Bill between it and the wall, literally squeezing the life out of him.

Afterwards Peggy wondered if the Gods had warped senses of humour or were twisted mischievous control freaks for why else should they choose to despatch Bill in the very way he had joked about so often. It was almost as if they were saying "all right Bill — you asked for it so you'll get it."

At the inquiry, the bus driver had been absolved of any blame, and Peggy was glad of that. Although one look at the poor man told her that he was still suffering from the after effects of the crash and that, although others might, he would never be able to absolve himself of blame. It had been a dreadful accident which nobody could have either foreseen or prevented and she didn't want the driver to suffer more than he had. She had felt so sorry when he had told the committee that he was still haunted by the accident — especially the look of surprise on Bill's face as he had looked with already dead, unseeing eyes through the shattered windscreen of his bus.

Peggy had known that Bill would not have blamed anyone for such a freak occurrence and although low and miserable at times, her natural optimism and positivity had made her able to continue with her life and the task of bringing up their two young children alone.

It hadn't been easy and even her resolve and determination had been sorely tested on many occasions, but Bill's example and his constant presence in her life saw her through the difficult times. It was as if he was sitting on her shoulder always ready to offer advice and give her hope. Sometimes she would swear she could hear him chuckling in her ear, or tell her to smile the smile he had always loved.

Bill's parents had been wonderful too. 'We will be here for you as much or as little as you need us sweetheart,' Bill's dad had said.

'We will of course, we will Peggy,' her mother in law said. 'But we will wait for you to call us. There is nothing worse than interfering in laws is there?'

In this kind unobtrusive way they had made it clear to her that they would support her in any way they could. They offered offering babysitting on a regular basis even if ever she should need to find a job. They also helped with the jobs which Bill had once joyously, if not competently, done around the house or by cooking the some meals for her freezer. But they told her they would never interfere. Help was there if she needed it, and it would be happily and freely given, but only if she wanted it.

In this way they had been her safety net and there had been many times when Bill's dad, Peter, had been called to mend leaking taps, sort out the cantankerous washing machine or mend a multitude of other household gadgets. While he was whistling tunelessly in the background Bill's mum, Janet, would be stocking the freezer with casseroles, pies, sauces for bolognaise or carbonara and all manner of cakes "just to keep you going." Then they would, with understanding and generosity, leave her alone until she called on them for help again, or invited them to visit and spend time with their beloved grandchildren.

This life line became even more important only six months after Bill's death when their baby son, who had been just four months old when his father had died, fell victim to cot death, or "sudden infant death syndrome" as it is now called. Peggy sometimes wondered whether the boffins, who had renamed it, thought that by giving it a fancier title it was made magically more bearable for the bereaved. But whatever it was called Josh was dead and had died in his cot; and there was simply nothing which could make that easier to bear.

Despite her public face and the smile she always wore outside the house, there were times when the effort of remaining cheerful and positive was just too much for Peggy. She just about managed to bravely pin on a public smile and laugh with the world when she was out and about, but it was often a different matter when she was at home at night, alone after she had put little Karen to bed. There is only so much anyone can bear and she had lost two of the people she loved most in the world, suddenly – in the most tragic of circumstances – and in very quick succession. But her down times, as she called them nevertheless made her feel guilty, as if she was pandering to her grief and allowing it to overwhelm her instead of confronting it head on or coming to terms with it.

In time, a very long time it had to be said, the down times became fewer though; less serious and shorter too. The effort became less and the cheerfulness greater as well as more genuine, and Peggy felt she was just beginning to come out of the long dark tunnel she had felt herself enclosed in since Bill's untimely death. Since the dreadful time too, when she had gone in to the nursery to rouse Josh with a tickle and a kiss just as she had every other morning of his all too short life..

That morning was to become the start of the second most horrendous day of her life. Any optimism or positivity she had achieved during the months since Bill's death evaporated in the few seconds it took for this new nightmare to become a reality. It felt as if her double tragedy was too much for her to bear, her hard won optimism vanishing as quickly as morning mist.

Even though he was such a young baby, Josh had always been a good sleeper and Peggy had been grateful for that during the weeks and months after Bill's death when she had spent most of her nights sobbing into her pillow and had needed all her strength just to put her feet to the floor some mornings in order to carry on with the day.

Now though her little Josh's sleep was permanent and the shock of finding him cold and blue, but otherwise looking as perfect as normal would stay with her for ever. As would the sound of her keening as she tried, hopelessly to wake him. She had heard other mothers who had suffered the same loss say that at first they had not realised that their baby was dead and not just sleeping – but Peggy had known in an instant. There had been no respite of doubt for her, no tiny hope.

At the sound of her mother's anguish, little Karen had woken and with understanding beyond her tender four years, had known something dreadful had happened and had somehow managed to telephone Nana and Gramps.

This devastating blow, coming so closely on the heels of the first had sorely tested Peggy's naturally sunny nature – as it surely would that of any wife and mother. And there had been dark days, many of them, when only Karen's need of her had forced Peggy to deny her natural inclination to shut herself away from the world and derive what little warmth and comfort she could from staying in bed.

But gradually over the days, weeks, months and years which followed her second tragedy Peggy's innate optimism and positivity re-established itself, just as it had after the first one. This was helped by the fact that Karen had inherited her father's joy of life. It was hard to be depressed when Karen was around and that was one of the many reasons Peggy missed her so now.

Ten years ago at the age of just twenty Karen had met a young man who was travelling around Europe before taking up his first teaching post in his native New Zealand. They had fallen instantly, hopelessly in love and, all plans of future travel suspended, Karen and Toby had spent the remainder of his holiday together, making plans for the life they knew they were to have together.

When Karen had announced that she would be following Toby to New Zealand as soon as everything could be arranged and would live there, Peggy had been shell shocked. Her grief had been almost as raw as it was sixteen years before, after the deaths of Bill and Josh.

Chastising herself for her selfishness she had thrown herself into preparing for the first of their two weddings. They were to have a small ceremony in their home town to which only Nana, Gramps and a few of

Karen's closest friends were to be invited. This would then be followed by a much bigger celebration in New Zealand for Toby's family which, by all accounts, was the size of a small army.

It had been losing Karen's cheerful presence in her life which had prompted Peggy to look for the sister, she had heard whispers about, but who had never been even been mentioned when Peggy was growing up. The only times Peggy even heard the name "Angela" were after her aunt had developed the Alzheimer's disease which had loosened both her tongue and her inhibitions. Nevertheless her curiosity had been aroused.

At the local library one day she had spotted a flyer for the "Salvation Army's Family Tracing Service" and had decided to ring them to make tentative enquiries.

It had been Peggy's aunt on her mother's side who, several years before, had talked of this mysterious sister about whom no-one else had ever spoken. But as Aunt Jennifer had been suffering from Alzheimer's at the time of her disclosures Peggy was never sure whether the sister, named apparently Angela, was real or a figment of poor Aunt Jennifer's deteriorating memory.

Peggy finally came to the conclusion that Angela did exist. It had been the way the rest of her family had tried to silence Aunt Jennifer, when she started to talk about Angela, in her rambling way, which had convinced Peggy of her existence.

'Hush now Jennifer,' Peggy's mother had said repeatedly, before trying to steer the conversation in a different direction.

'Stop all that nonsense Jenny my girl,' chastised her grandmother - who unlike her daughter was still as sharp as a pin mentally. 'You and your stories – I swear you should have been a writer. You could have made a fortune writing for Mills and Boon.'

'She's going back to her childhood again. You had an imaginary friend called Angela didn't you Jenny. That's who you are thinking of,' said Peggy's mother on another occasion looking flustered while reaching for a plate of newly made scones. 'Have a scone now Jen and let's hear no more of your nonsense.'

These were the kinds of disclaimers Peggy had heard so often, but now she knew the truth behind them.

Angela had indeed been real, and after an extensive search featuring many false leads, hopeful ups and despondent downs they had been united and were now the best of friends. It had not been an easy search, as many of them are not, especially as, like with many adopted children, Angela's Christian name had been changed by her adoptive parents and she was now called Ellen.

The search had given Peggy more than a long lost sister though; it had given her another direction; a purpose in her life to help fill the void left by Karen's emigration. It was also how she had first become involved in counselling.

More often than not, people involved in searching for lost relatives became aware of some kind of trauma or breakdown within the family unit. Whether the cause or the effect of the separation - a family rift, argument or scandal was invariably something the searcher for a relative had to face. The negative feelings these discoveries unleashed often needed the sympathetic understanding of a counsellor in order for acceptance and recovery, even forgiveness to take place.

Several courses and qualifications later Peggy had been much in demand, and was now busier than ever before. She had discovered that her work had created in her the ability to recognise a tortured soul and sometimes she even tentatively approached them, encouraging them into a conversation – just as she had with Patrick.

He had looked so lost, so sad when she first saw him. He had the look of someone who had no idea what to do or who to turn to. All Peggy had done was make him aware that she was there for him if she needed him – just as Bill's dear parents had done for her all those years ago.

Helping folk through the worst of their troubles gave Peggy an enormous amount of satisfaction and great joy and helped ease the loneliness of her solitary life; at least during the day - the evenings and nights were a different matter.

For months now Karen, Toby and their two boys, whom Peggy had never seen except in photographs, had been nagging her to get a computer so they could e-mail, or video-link each other.

'It's so much quicker than writing letters Mum,' Karen had told her. 'It's more like having a real conversation, but not nearly as expensive as overseas telephone charges. It's really easy to e-mail once you get the hang of it. Why don't you buy a computer and learn, the boys would love to be able to talk to their Nan more often.'

'I'll think about it I really will.'

'You always say that Mum but you never do anything about it do you.'

'I know ... I will though I promise ... soon.'

'Please do, the boys are growing up so fast and you are missing out on it all by not being able to talk to them more often or more freely.'

It was true, telephone calls had to be rationed because of the expense, but buy a computer – worse still - have to admit she would never be able to use it! To have her daughter and grandsons mock her for her incompetence, even if in a fond way; Peggy could not bear the thought.

Chapter 2

The subject of computers and e-mails had become a constant topic in Peggy's letters and telephone conversations with her far away family and it was obvious that none of them understood her reluctance to buy the computer which, to them seems the answer to their communications problems.

The short answer was that Peggy was terrified of them. She could type, that wasn't the issue, and had used her beloved straight-out-of-the-ark manual word processing machine for years for all her business correspondence. But her trusty old machine had never let her down, alright so it had needed the odd drop of oil or new ribbon to keep going but it had never crashed as she had seen the computer system at the doctor's surgery do.

She had only gone to pick up a repeat prescription but had soon become embroiled in a scene of utter chaos, there had been complete panic that morning. None of the doctors had been able to access patients' records. All evidence of orders due, test results forwarded from the hospital - along with the vital ability to print prescriptions had disappeared in a flash. The result was the nearest to pandemonium that Peggy ever wished to witness.

The practice manager and the receptionist were dashing around giving very passable imitations of the proverbial headless chickens, ringing help lines, constantly apologising to patients for the delay to their appointments, trying to find old paper copies of records and generally showing signs of being exceedingly stressed; their faces as red as beetroots as their blood pressure soared.

Peggy didn't want that. How would she be able to cope with such a crash, she had thought to herself as she had witnessed the scene of chaos unfolding before her. If these people, so skilled in the use of computers, so professional and well trained, couldn't handle such a breakdown, how could she be expected to? She trusted her old faithful and was determined to see off any and all attempts to breach her defence of it – until Karen mentioned the web-cam.

Suddenly the thought of being able to see her family as she talked to them, the possibility of chatting about their lives with all the every- day minutiae of which their lives were made up. To hear their laughter, even learn to recognise their voices with their strange New Zealand accents was all too tempting. This was the kind of chat which phone calls were too expensive to allow, and the thought was too far tempting to resist. The idea of seeing them as if in a film as they chatted was too seducing for words, and would be almost as good as seeing them in the flesh ... almost.

But how was she to even look at the monsters her mind had made computers into, let alone tame one to her use? The first step, she supposed, would be to visit one of the large chain stores specialising in computers and the accessories which, it seemed, they all needed.

Seven or eight times Peggy approached the store determined, each time, to cross the threshold. But every time just the vision of banks and banks of products and row upon row of computers of all shapes and sizes, seen through the large glass windows, was enough to kill her determination stone dead.

On what seemed like her hundredth attempt Peggy did manage to walk into the store, only too be immediately accosted by a pimply youth who didn't look old enough to be at senior school never mind working. Scenting both a victim and a nice fat commission, the youth went in for the kill, dragging her up and down aisles of merchandise telling her she needed one of virtually everything on display in the huge store.

'Good morning Madam and welcome to "Computer Heaven" Are you looking for anything in particular today?'

'I er … I need to er… buy a computer.'

'Have you already got one and this is to be an upgrade, or will it be your first machine?'

'My first.'

'Ah right, excellent - it will be my great pleasure to assist you,' the pimply youth said rubbing his hands together mentally at the thought of such a gullible victim.

After half an hour of his aggressive sales technique Peggy felt as if the walls were closing in around her and she felt as if she was about to faint. Squeaking 'I'll think about it,' she fled for the door and calming fresh air, as fast as her wobbly legs would carry her. It was no good, she thought as she ran across the car park to the safety of her dear little Clio, she could never go back in that store – or any other like it again. Not until hell froze over anyway!

After such a fright and the shame of being unable to stand up to a mere lad, there was only one place to soothe Peggy's nerves – the park. For as long as she could remember, even before Bill had been killed, she had sought solace among the trees of her local park. Something about being surrounded by nature was both soothing and reinvigorating at one and the same time. Nature in any form was capable of bringing solace to the soul, but for Peggy it was mainly trees which brought about a peace and calm in her. There was something so reassuring about being among living entities which had witnessed all manner of tragedy and conflict during their lives of several hundred years. The green canopy and the softly whispering leaves always soothed her, no matter what her anxiety was. To physically embrace such a giant gave her the ultimate high – but worrying that she would be thought mad she wisely restricted her tree hugging sessions to times when she was alone in the park – preferably after dark.

This was the first place she had wanted to flee to after Bill's death, but well meaning friends and relatives who could not understand her need, had feared that she was suffering some kind of breakdown and had stopped her. As soon as the funeral had been over and the tide of well meaning relatives, friends and neighbours had slowed to a trickle she had bundled Karen into her coat, Josh into his pushchair and made for the sanctuary of the park's trees.

They never failed to relax or restore her and she needed their abiding strength and majesty today. Slipping deep into the small wood which bordered the park, Peggy found her favourite tree, a towering majestic oak which must have been an acorn over three hundred years ago. Leaning her back against it she breathed in deeply, feeling its strength through her coat and listening to the canopy softly whispering to her.

'Are you alright?'

At first she though she had finally lost her mind and that the tree was really speaking to her – but, no the voice was definitely both male and human. The voice broke into her thoughts once more asking the same question and shocking her back to the present, covering her with embarrassment that she should be caught tree hugging in such a conspicuous manner. This man would think her a complete lunatic she thought to herself, before wondering why on earth she should care what he, a stranger, thought of her.

'That's my favourite too,' he said surprising her again. 'I love the texture of the trunk and the rigid solid feel of it don't you?'

'I didn't think anyone else would enjoy tree hugging!'

'Why not? I'm sure there are those who would think it foolish and a bit weird, but what do we care about narrow minded folk like them. I bet they've never tried it so how can they judge. I always come here when I'm a bit low or when I've got a problem to sort out ... are you the same?'

'Yes, for as long as I can remember this has been my special place and my special tree.'

'Well I hope you won't mind sharing it with me – do you fancy a coffee at the café - it's gone really cold all of a sudden. I promise you my intentions are totally honourable, well if you discount the jam doughnut I was hoping to have.'

Peggy laughed at his words - liking this man for his warmth, understanding and humour. 'I'd love to', she heard herself say although, at first, she had been determined to pleasantly refuse his offer.

Peggy was not known for impetuosity or capriciousness but here she was accepting a drink from a complete stranger who, despite his assurances to the contrary might be a serial rapist or an axe murderer for all she knew. But it was only a cup of coffee in a crowded, public place in broad daylight, so she relaxed and followed as he led the way out of the wood.

They had to wait a few minutes, while an overworked and undoubtedly underpaid waitress cleared the dirty dishes from a table for two for them. As a part-time waitress herself Peggy was always acutely aware of others who did the same work, and was often embarrassed if she felt she was adding to their workload. This waitress smiled at them sweetly though and showed no sign of being overly harassed. So Peggy relaxed once more and took her seat.

'Tea or coffee?' asked her host.

'Tea please, but I don't want you to pay, let's pay for our own – after all I don't know you, so I don't think it would be right to let you buy it for me.'

'Well it's only tea and a cake – hardly a twelve course banquet, but if it would make you uncomfortable to accept then we'll go Dutch by all means. If it helps put you at your ease at all, my name is Barry. There you tell me yours and we won't be strangers anymore.'

'I'm Peggy,' she replied with a smile. 'so how come you are foot loose and fancy free at this time of day and not at work? If that's not too personal a question.'

'Not at all. I've got my own little business which means that when work is slow I can treat myself to the odd afternoon away from the shop and a bit of furtive tree hugging. So what's the guilty secret to your being here?'

'Oh nothing guilty or underhand, just that I'm a waitress and I'm not on the rota until tonight. I usually work days in a café but there's a special function tonight at the restaurant the boss owns, so he's called in as many staff as he can to cover that.'

'So you're having a rare afternoon to yourself too, and what did you choose to do with it before I found you hugging a tree?'

'I went to the computer super store in the retail park across town.'

'Oh that place,' Barry said his voice suddenly filled with, if not anger, then at least irritation and derision.'

'Have I said the wrong thing or offended you in some way?' Peggy asked confused as to how such a thing could have happened.

'No – sorry, it's nothing to do with you, it's just that I have my own computer business, that's what I do. These big shops really annoy me, they buy in bulk so can offer goods cheaper than I can, and that's fair enough I suppose. But it makes it very hard for small stores like mine to keep up with all the latest models and innovations. What really annoys me though is that when they have taken your money they lose all interest. They don't offer any decent after sales service or even advice. They only want to make sales so any advice they give would be tailored around making that sale and if there's a problem after you've bought a machine they don't want to know. Sorry, sorry - hark at me going on about my troubles and my grievances to a complete stranger.'

'Please don't apologise – as it happens I tend to agree with you. I went in for advice and help, and all I got was a demonstration of ever more expensive computers, followed by a hard selling approach telling me that I would need a wide range of other gadgets. I came out more confused and terrified of the darn things than when I went in!'

'That's exactly what I mean. Don't get me wrong there is a definite place for that type of store in today's market – but you need to know what you really want and need before you even cross their threshold in order to get the best out of stores like those. For someone who isn't familiar or comfortable with computers those places are hopeless. In fact they are worse than hopeless – they are minefields for the inexperienced computer user.'

As the time passed and, while they were waiting for their order to arrive, Barry and Peggy talked about a huge range of things. They discovered that they had similar tastes in many of them, quite apart from their affection for trees and their habit of illicitly hugging them! They both loved detective fiction, in books and on the television, they both had large collections of the country music they both liked, and had both loved ballroom dancing when they were younger.

Peggy told Barry about Bill's accident and how she hadn't danced since, as she was too shy to go on her own. Barry told her that he and his wife had danced right up until a few months before her death five years ago. He confided that he missed dancing, but wasn't sure whether it was the dancing itself or dancing with his wife Meg that he missed most, but was pretty sure it was the latter.

'Probably a little of both I should think,' Peggy told him. 'The two things are so fused in your memory that they are inseparable.'

'You sound as if you know what you're talking about, you're not a psychiatrist in your spare time are you? You know - if business is a bit slow in the café - you nip off to sort out a few mental health issues in between serving customers.'

Peggy laughed hard at such a ridiculous idea, but then she had laughed a lot since they met – probably more than she had laughed for several months.

'Not quite,' she told him when their laughter had finally stopped. 'But I am a trained counsellor. Although I am nowhere near as qualified as a psychologist for example. I find that people often just want someone to talk things over with . Someone to listen, to offer help and advice or to put them in touch with others more qualified who would be able to help them.'

'So we're both in the business of offering help and advice, but in very different areas of life. You sound as if you deal with real life, you know the important stuff -

helping people improve their lives and shaping situations - whereas I only deal with machines.'

'How easy would it be for someone who has never handled a computer before to learn?'

'You?'

'Yes, that's why I went into the superstore, you see, to buy one but as you said I didn't receive much individual help. I just felt as if I was being pushed into buying the most expensive one the salesman could push onto me.'

'Can you drive?' asked Barry

'Well yes, I can, but what on earth has that to do with learning about computers,' came Peggy's bewildered reply.

'I always tell folk who come to me for training that if they can learn to operate a car they can learn to operate a computer – after all, unlike a car, a computer hasn't got the potential to kill you has it?' Barry laughed.

'You train people in the use of computers too!'

'Well yes, it's not much point selling them one if they aren't able to use it. If I did that I would be as bad as the super stores I've been complaining about wouldn't I? But yes, I run training courses for everyone, not just those who have bought from me.'

'Do you think you could teach me?'

'Well, I'm sure you could learn, it all depends on what you need to know and why you want to learn. I always find that if someone has a specific reason for learning it tends to come easier to them. It gives them drive and focus, because they already have a goal in mind.'

'My daughter now lives in New Zealand with her husband and children. They have been nagging me for ages to get a computer so we could e-mail each other. They say it is much cheaper than telephoning, and now they have a web cam and if I got one too I would be able to see them while we chat. It would be the next best thing to having them in the same room with me.'

'Can't think of a better reason than that. Look take my card, my shop's address and telephone number are on it. Think about it and give me a ring if you're interested – no pressure. Take your time, it's important that you feel the time is right for you. If it is you'll learn all the faster.'

Peggy thanked him as she pocketed the card and left the café. Barry had made a big impression on her, not only because he seemed kind and was amusing, but also because of the appreciation and courtesy with which he had spoken to the waitress. In Peggy's line of work that attitude was not only rare, but extremely welcome as it helped to lift the spirits of anyone who spent most of the day on their feet!

She suddenly felt more buoyant, her footsteps seeming lighter as she acknowledged, for the first time, that mastering a computer might, just might be possible. She had confidence in Barry. They had seemed to gel from the first moment she became aware of his presence as she stood drawing strength from 'her' tree, and she knew they could become good friends given time.

The fact that he was in computers, and had offered her help with them too, when this was her particular bête noir, was such an amazing co-incidence that she found it hard to believe even though she had just experienced it. She found herself thinking back to Patrick, who had said the same kind of thing when they first met. A set of random events had brought them together when Patrick needed it and now something similar had happened to her. Perhaps life was like that and there was always help available if you only looked for it, or at least acknowledged it when it presented itself to you.

Peggy had always believed in helping others, that was why she had trained in counselling, but she had never expected to receive help from anyone herself, at least not a complete stranger anyway. Perhaps there was something in the kindness of strangers thing one of her lecturers had talked about so often.

Chapter 3

In truth Peggy didn't have to think too long or too hard about contacting Barry again. She had mentioned meeting him to Patrick, when she had visited him at the centre the other day for one of their now regular sessions. By this stage in their relationship their sessions were not so much counselling sessions as chats between old friends, but that was exactly the kind of atmosphere Peggy aimed to generate.

The intimacy produced in this way was not only helpful by creating a relaxing atmosphere but led to much more frank and open revelations. Even without realising it Patrick had opened up to her more that he had to any other living soul, laying bare his fears and regrets as well as his and anger and bitterness.

'Isn't that just how things happen sometimes though – look at the way we met,' Patrick said when she had told him about meeting Barry, his words echoing her own thoughts precisely. 'There were a whole lot of coincidences there, starting with the newspapers not being delivered right up to me deciding for the first time to stop at the very café where you worked. My Granddad used to say people are fundamentally good and are usually willing to help you if you are willing to let them. More folk would still stop to help someone who had fallen over for example, than walk past them, even in this day and age.'

'I know what you mean – it restores your faith in human nature doesn't it when the news is usually full of stories of people taking advantage of others for their own gain. I think I'm going to go for the lessons, you know. Barry seems such a nice man and I'm sure he will not 'rip me off' as the youngsters say today.

'I'm sure he won't, give it a try, after all you don't have to go back for a second time if you don't think it's for you. Just think of the benefits if you do master it though. You will be able to talk to your family face to face as it were – or almost as good as anyway.'

So Peggy rang Barry that same day asking if she could book lessons with him and was surprised when he said she could start the following evening.

When her eight o'clock appointment was fast approaching she left her house and drove the short distance to Barry's shop. Normally Peggy would never have dreamt of taking her car out for such a short journey, but the wind and the rain were particularly vicious that evening and she would have been soaked through before she even reached her front gate if she had attempted walking there. And 'drowned rat' was not the impression she hoped to create for her first lesson.

The gale was buffeting her tiny car all the way there and the butterflies in her stomach were doing as good a job by buffeting her from the inside. By the time she reached Barry's small shop she felt as if she had taken part in - and lost - a wrestling bout.

Taking her courage in both hands she approached the shop doorway and went through noticing the old fashioned bell, which seemed to tinkle reassuringly as she entered. The bell gave out such a comforting welcoming sound, that somehow she was reassured just by hearing it. There was no-one in the shop, so Peggy took time to slow her breathing to a more normal level while looking around her.

For a business selling such high tech modern equipment the shop itself was quaintly old fashioned. From its tinkling bell to the deep well-used leather chairs arranged in front of a long bench which ran along the back wall, to the muted décor it looked thirty years behind the present day; harking back to a time when computers were not a necessary tool in almost every household.

Fixed to the wall behind the bench were the only things which gave any impression of the modern day purpose of the shop. It was a row of electrical sockets which made Peggy rightly surmise that this was where her lesson was to take place.

There were no intimidating computers on the bench however – no screens almost as big as her television at home, no printers, speakers, or great silver boxes which seemed to tower over everything else. In fact there was no sign of a keyboard, or any of the hundred and one other things she had been told it would be necessary for her to buy. There wasn't even one of those funny things the man at the superstore had called a mouse. Peggy had wondered then why such a name should have been given to the gadget, for anything looking less like a mouse was hard to imagine.

In fact there seemed to be nothing remotely scary waiting for her on the bench, just a slim black box about the size of a large book. There weren't even banks of display shelves housing all the smaller gadgetry she had seen in the superstore. In fact it looked more like a somewhat old fashioned living room than a shrine to technology. Alarmed, Peggy wondered if she had mistaken the date or time of her first lesson. She was just about to ring the old fashioned brass bell on the counter which bore the missive "ring me for help" when she heard movement.

'Hi,' said Barry grinning broadly as he stepped from behind a curtain in the very back corner of the shop with the air of a magician appearing from one of his magic cabinets. 'Glad you could come, I always worry that first timers are going to back out on me. They are usually so terrified you see.'

'I am – and I very nearly did, but it's reassuring to know I'm not the only one to be terrified and intimidated by computers.'

'You must be joking! There are hundreds of folk of our generation who can't face the mere thought of using them - let alone the reality. Our kids and grandkids won't feel like that because they've grown up with them. They embrace technology because for them it's always been there, but it's another matter for the likes of you and me.'

'Yes, it's hard to imagine now, but when I was growing up we didn't even have a telephone in the house or a television until I was much older – and I'm hardly ancient. My parents weren't very well off, so I suppose we came to things like that later than some people.'

'Well you've cleared the first hurdle – the first and worst, as I like to tell my newbies,' he said with a chuckle. 'You didn't back out - you are here and ready to give it a go, it's all down hill from here,' he said smiling at her most reassuringly.

'Where are we to have the lesson?' she asked looking around her in confusion once more.

'Right here,' he said going towards the slim black book like box, pressing a button and lifting the lid to reveal a screen and keyboard all built into it – again reminding her of a magician.

'That's a computer!' she almost shrieked. 'But where's the tower thing and the thing called a mouse and everything else the man at the superstore said I would need to buy.'

'Right here,' he said again. 'This is called a laptop and it has everything you need, for basic computing, with the possible exception of a printer. I find it is better to introduce my beginners to this type of machine – it's much less intimidating that the desk top type.'

Peggy couldn't agree more, as there seemed nothing scary about this computer. In fact it was hard to imagine a more innocuous, benign looking machine and suddenly Peggy wondered, for the first time ever, if it might be possible for her to learn enough to enable her to be in better contact with her family.

'I thought I'd teach you how to write a letter during this first lesson. Once you can do that you will find it useful for business letters because the computer stores a record of everything you write and you just print off a copy to send. Don't worry,' he reassured her. 'It's easier than it sounds.'

And it was. Before the end of the lesson Peggy could switch on the machine, find the Word file she needed, start a new document, type a letter and save it. Barry suggested they leave printing it out until the following week, because in that way he would be able to assess how much of the first lesson she had absorbed and remembered, before being faced with learning a new skill or being faced with the prospect of mastering another machine.

Peggy was thrilled – even taking into account that she had an advantage through already being able to type, she had done really well and had learned a lot of new things.

She had also become almost fond of the friendly little laptop computer after just one lesson. It had behaved itself beautifully, had done everything she had asked of it and had been a lot easier to use than she had feared. The keyboard held no surprises of course, but the absence of the mouse thing was also a bonus as she found it really easy to operate the built in pad which replaced it.

Six weeks on and Peggy often wondered what she had been so terrified of. With Barry's expert tuition and patience she had already mastered most of the things she would need. She could both send and open any e-mails she had received. She could attach things to the e-mails she sent, meaning she could send photos and could open attachments anyone sent to her. She could create new documents and access any old ones stored on the computer's hard drive and could print off anything which needed to be produced as a paper copy.

Barry was really pleased with the way she had picked up these new skills so quickly, and often referred to her as his star pupil. After each lesson was over it became a regular thing for them to sit in the back room, with a cup of tea and a piece of the cake, or one of the scones Peggy had got into the habit of bringing with her.

Her offerings seemed little enough thanks for all his attention and kindness and she was pleased to do it. Cooking for one was never as satisfying or rewarding as cooking for someone else, especially someone who really appreciated the results, as Barry so obviously did. He had once confided that he had missed his wife's excellent home baking, since he had been left on his own. So baking seemed to benefit them both. Barry in the eating of her offerings, and her in the making of them, as Peggy had always enjoyed cooking and had always found it soothing. It seemed as if they had discovered another pleasure they could enjoy.

The course was ten weeks long and by the end of it Peggy had almost as many mixed feelings as she had when she had first walked through the door, hearing the cheerful tinkling of the bell for the first time. She had certainly learned all she needed to, even mastering the complexities of the web-cam and skype although in actual fact it was hardly complex at all. As with most things Peggy found that the anticipation and dread were far worse than the reality.

Barry had shown her how to install the program which set the web-cam up, which was the most complicated part of the processes, and had then talked her through the procedures she would need to activate it. He had promised to do the same for her, if and when she decided she was ready to buy her own computer, a prospect she was finding more and more tempting each day.

She had long ago changed her mind about computers, now viewing them as a friendly helpful tool, if used wisely and with due caution, rather than as a dangerous sinister foe.

Peggy had certainly mastered the computer and was understandably proud of her achievements, but the mixed feelings she was experiencing now were altogether different from those of ten weeks ago.

Now she was regretting, mourning even, the end of the course primarily because she would miss the evenings she spent with Barry; grieving for his interesting, amusing company, as she resumed her lonely, almost solitary, existence.

Life was a funny old thing, Peggy thought as she washed the single cup, saucer and plate which were the usual result of her solitary breakfast. Just as you got used to something, not necessarily liking or enjoying it, but at least used to it - like being alone, along came something else, some alternative, to cruelly show you what you had been missing.

Peggy had thought that in her solitary life she was now, if not happy or content with her isolation - at least used to it – accepting of it. But the evenings she had spent with Barry had demonstrated to her just how much she missed the company of other human beings and how stark and cold her life had been without it, in the past and would be again in the future.

As she went to put away her pitiful washing up, the very crockery she held seemed to mock her as if reminding her of happier times when every meal in this house had resulted in a sink full of dishes to be washed and dried amid laughter and cheerful conversation. The sudden memory left Peggy feeling as bereft and isolated as she had when she had first been widowed, lost her baby Josh, and years later when her only daughter had emigrated to the other side of the world. She had felt deserted then and, although this seemed a trifle strong and certainly a self-pitying description, it was how Peggy had felt at the time. And if she was honest, there were times, even after all these years, when she still felt the same. Times when she was lonely and depressed; then her aloneness threatened to choke her.

    She knew of course that Karen had the right to live her own life as she wanted to, and Peggy had always wanted her to have the opportunity to live it as she wished. Indeed Peggy had brought her up to be strong and decisive, to make her own choices and be independent ... but ...

    But what exactly? Would she really have wanted Karen to have forgone her chance of happiness, just to stay in England and keep her mother company? And if so - what kind of mother did that make her – what did it say about her own character? Of course that was not what she wanted for her only child. Peggy was pleased her daughter had realised that she must put herself first and lead the life she felt she must. It was just that Peggy was so lonely and nothing she had tried to fill her life with since Karen's emigration had gone anywhere near filling the great black hole her daughter's leaving had created. Moreover it was only since Peggy had been enjoying Barry's company that she had realised how truly empty and cold her life had become.

She squared her shoulders and made a decision, she would buy one of the cute little lap tops Barry had shown her how to use. He had shown her a little one with a pink cover which looked so pretty that it made it seem both cheerful and positive. She would also enable a web-cam on her new laptop to make to possible for her to talk to her family directly. Then taking all her courage in both hands, she would approach Barry with a view to meeting once or twice a week as friends. She would offer to cook him a meal once a week and maybe they might even go to the cinema or for a drink. They might even, in time, again take up the ballroom dancing they had both once loved.

One thing at a time though, first she would ask him for a meal and they would take it from there. After all Peggy really enjoyed his company, as he had said he did hers, so what harm would there be in two friends easing each others loneliness by spending some time together.

Suddenly her world was a more promising place to be, the colours around her were brighter, the sounds sweeter and the air warmer and more fragrant. She would ask him tonight at her final class and she intuitively knew he would agree because he enjoyed her company, as much as she enjoyed his and together they wouldn't be so lonely. Just one or two evenings a week would give them a focal point to each previously empty week – something for both of them to look forward to and that, when all was said and done, could be no bad thing.

Barry's story

Chapter 1

Barry felt as if he was emerging from a long dark tunnel. Ever since his wife had died he had been sunk in a depression so deep that until now he hadn't even realise he was depressed. But that had all changed once he had met Peggy. Now the sun seemed to shine brighter than it had since he became a widower and the bird's dawn chorus seemed more cheerful to his ears.

Barry had never thought he would be able to love again or indeed to become so fond of another woman that he might even entertain the possibility of another love in his life. Now, however, he recognised that it might happen, even that it might have started happening already.

He wanted to take the next step with Peggy and invite her to his home. She had already cooked several cakes for him as well as the offerings they had shared together after each lesson, and he acknowledged to himself that he ought to reciprocate her kindness by offering a meal at his home. And that was where he had a problem, a problem of epic proportions, forcing him to accept that the idea became a non-starter.

Since his wife, Meg, had died Barry had not had the heart to do anything to his house. It was still decorated as it had been and even more depressing, it still contained all his wife's personal possessions. Her clothing remained hanging in the wardrobes, her hair brushes, jewellery, perfume and the little make-up she had used, only occasionally, continued to stand on her dressing table gathering dust; hers the very last hands to have touched them.

Barry had, at long last, looked at his home with eyes from which the cataracts of depression and disinterest seemed to have been removed when he reached home after the final lesson with Peggy. His new awareness forced him to recognise that not only was it out dated and cluttered with things he should have disposed of long ago, but it was also filthy. And he felt ashamed.

He remembered, with sadness and regret, the pride Meg had taken in her home, modest though it was, and reflected on how horrified she would be, to see her much loved home in its present state. Meg had been the kindest, most generous of women, only roused to anger if the hard work she put into the house went unappreciated or was abused. Then her tongue would become really sharp and her mood would blacken.

Remembering this, Barry was almost consumed by guilt as he looked around each chaotic room. The carpets and the surfaces of the furniture were so thick with dust that they felt sticky to his touch. The kitchen cupboards overflowed with tins and packets long beyond their use by dates. The sink was stacked high with unwashed crockery and the worktops and floor were so badly stained that he could hardly see their original colour. The one bedroom he used was in just as dreadful a state, with the once delicate colours of the bedding yellowed and dulled by all too infrequent laundering, and as for the state of the bathroom …

Once Barry's eyes had been opened to the squalor in which he had been living, totally unaware, he was immediately galvanised into action. He went to the kitchen for a roll of black dustbin bags, took them back to the bedroom and began to sort out Meg's clothes. Many times he almost faltered in his task as a faint whiff of her favourite perfume, or even worse, her own unique fragrance assailed his nostrils, but this time he kept going until everything was sorted into three piles. The largest was to go to a charity shop although he acknowledged to himself that he would need to take them to one in another town, some distance away from his own. This he would have to do, if he wanted to prevent seeing some other woman wearing an article of Meg's clothing, which she had bought from one of the own charity shops in their own town.

The second pile was to be thrown away or given to a clothing bank for recycling, and the third contained one or two items which, even now, he could not bear to part with - such were the memories they embodied. These included a few pieces of Meg's jewellery. They were mainly inexpensive items he had bought her for anniversary presents or at Christmas or for her birthday. They had, nevertheless, been precious to her as they had symbolised the love they had shared.

Next Barry went in search of the vacuum cleaner he had never once used in all the years since her death; favouring instead a hand driven carpet sweeper, and then using it only when he had deemed it absolutely necessary. He spent more minutes than he would have thought he needed, working out how it worked before attacking the bedroom carpet. He was amazed that the machine had required emptying several times before the task was finished, such had been the thickness of the dust on the carpet. Soon though he could see a difference and watched with something approaching pride as the colours of the carpet were brought back to life. His next challenge was to strip the bed and throw the whole lot in the washing machine. It took him considerably longer to coax this equally unfamiliar machine into life, as he had got into the habit of taking his washing to the laundrette. There he had deposited his soiled laundry with an obliging and ever cheerful lady who, as if by magic, returned it to him a few days later freshly washed and ironed. He had thought this decision had been taken out of necessity, as he was too busy to do domestic chores, or at least had told himself that this was the reason. Now however he realised he had to accept it had been the result of his laziness. Facing this truth about himself was not easy, nor was the shame he felt in admitting he had never used their domestic washing machine. At last, after what seemed a mammoth struggle, the machine was whirring away though, in what he hoped was an appropriate and contented manner. At least he had remembered Doreen's words of advice when he had first used the launderette.

'It will be far easier for you and incidentally for us here, if you remember to separate the colours before you bring it in,' she had told him kindly. 'Some of the darker colours will bleed into the paler ones you see. So if you try to wash something red for example with white or pale clothes everything would come out pink.'

By now Barry was almost exhausted, but he was determined to polish the bedroom furniture and attack the bathroom before he called it a day. So armed with duster and spray polish and a whole array of other cleaning products, discovered in the depths of the kitchen's under sink cupboard, he made his way up the stairs again. Noting again with shame, that even the bottles containing these products were, in themselves, covered with the dust and grease of long disuse.

Forty exhausting minutes in the bathroom was enough to convince Barry that the old fitments were way beyond the help of bleach and the other assorted so-called miracle cleaners he had at his disposal. The bathroom would need much more drastic action to revive it. In all honesty, he admitted to himself, it all needed to be completely replaced.

At least the bedroom furniture was now glowing with a long forgotten lustre while exuding a fresh lemony smell. Somehow, he thought fancifully, the room seemed lighter, brighter, as if relieved of its burden of grief – its memories of Meg. Or perhaps that was just him. Nevertheless Barry had to admit that he felt a sense of relief that the jobs he had put off for so long, had at last been completed. He would never forget his beloved Meg of course, but the removal of all the minutiae of her life had somehow begun to release him.

Exhausted now Barry made his way to the kitchen to brew himself a pot of tea, only to find the scales, which had fallen from his uncaring, blinkered eyes over the last lonely years, made him take a really good look at the kitchen for the first time for ages. It was not just dirty. He was now forced to look beyond the dirt and the clutter, and he didn't like what he saw. He noticed, for the first time, how some of the cupboard doors were hanging drunkenly on hinges which had parted company with the carcases. Several drawer fronts too had long since fallen off exposing the untidy contents within; and the stains on both worktops and the floor alike were too horrendous to contemplate.

Suddenly making up his mind Barry searched through the yellow pages telephone directory for a kitchen and bathroom company in the immediate vicinity of his home. Such was his aversion to huge one-size-fits-all computer stores, that he was determined to avoid using one of the enormous DIY stores which were of a similar type.

Four information packed pages and almost an hour of meticulous study later, Barry found what he had been looking for, a family firm established over fifty years ago. He then looked the firm up on the internet and was pleased to find several reports from previous customers stating the firm's efficiency and reliability. He made the phone call immediately and an appointment was made for a representative to visit his home for an initial planning session and estimate of cost.

Having taken such drastic steps, Barry now found there was no stopping his drive to modernise. Meg had loved the 'Country Diary' range of wallpapers and soft furnishings and although the curtains still looked fresh: or at least they would once they had undergone the ministrations of a reputable dry cleaners, the overall effect of floral curtains and paper was now, to Barry's eyes, fussy and created a cluttered look.

Deciding that plain painted walls would look more up to date and more to his masculine taste he decided to ask his friend, who was a professional decorator, to strip the old wallpaper and paint the walls in muted co-ordinating colours. Doug was a long standing friend from their school days who, along with hundreds of others, had been struggling to find work in the current climate of recession and cut backs. Barry knew he would not only do a good job, but also value the income it would bring him. So Barry welcomed the opportunity to give his old friend a helping hand and at the same time improve his domestic conditions for himself.

Having been running on adrenalin for the last few hours Barry was suddenly exhausted and fell onto the settee feeling consumed by both tiredness and guilt. How, he wondered, as he rubbed his hand over his sore aching eyes, could he have betrayed Meg as he had.

The house had always been a shrine to her home making skills and physical evidence of her love for him and now with two phone calls he was preparing to eradicate all that in one series of rash actions.

There was no going back now however, he was committed to following through what he had started. Barry knew that the bereaved often claimed their lost loved one would approve of their actions – often merely in order to justify what they had done. But in this case he genuinely thought that Meg would approve. Better to have the house looking cared for and pristine again than leave it as the shrine to loss and disrepair which it had become.

As he sat nursing a can of beer he didn't really want, guilt swept over to engulf him again until he felt as if he was in the middle of a dense black hole. Perhaps Meg would understand and approve of his actions, but it still felt as if he was eradicating all evidence of her from their home. Putting his hardly touched drink down, Barry decided that further action was the only way to claw his way out of the depression, which had hit him as violently and suddenly as an unexpected blow. Dragging himself to his feet once more, he decided he would take the first consignment of the black sacks to the charity shop in the nearby town.

The town was only a few miles away from the one in which he and Meg had lived all their married life. Local women, from their town might still shop there, but Barry felt that at least he would have tried to avoid the agony of seeing someone else in Meg's clothes if he delivered them this far away from their own town.

The roads were quiet and dark as Barry drove the almost ten miles to the neighbouring town. At first he wondered why he had only seen three other cars on his journey, until he remembered talk that some high profile football match was being screened on the television that evening. It was this which was no doubt responsible for keeping many people either at home, or at the pub, glued to their televisions.

Barry knew that there was only one charity shop and this was on the main street of the small market town, so he found it easily. At this time of night the shop was in total darkness - the charity naturally wishing to avoid huge electricity bills But the chaotic, eclectic window display and chipped paintwork on the window frame, told their own story and were enough to advertise its presence.

It was obviously standard procedure for donors to leave bagged contributions in the small recessed doorway, as several bags had already been placed there before he had arrived. So he added his own to the pile and was just about to leave when a small sound reached his tired ears. At first Barry thought it was the high pitched cry of a small child and he looked around him peering into the darkness half expecting to see a mother and baby making their way along the street, but there was no-one in sight.

It took a few minutes for Barry to realise the sound was coming from the charity shop's own doorway – so he began to hunt for its source among the rain splattered bags. Before long he noticed movement in one of the bags closest to the shop's doorway. The bag was tightly tied but seemed to contain nothing which could have been classed as donations. Realising what he had discovered even before tentatively opening the bag and peering inside Barry was filled with a rage which seemed to grip his chest in a vice and fill his eyes with red hot anger.

'What the hell...' he almost shouted as he looked with horror into the black bag. 'What sick apology for a human being would be capable of this?'

The stench as he had opened the bag was enough to bring him to his senses for, sure enough, cowering together at the bottom of it were three tiny puppies. They had obviously been there for some time as they were covered in their own excrement and were gasping for the reviving air which they desperately sucked into their tiny lungs as soon as it met their nostrils and gaping mouths.

Although he had owned several dogs during his lifetime Barry was no expert on puppies. The dogs he had been privileged to share his life with had all be older and had all been adopted from rescue centres – the youngest having been seven months old when he had adopted him. These poor scraps were much, much younger, even to Barry's untutored eye, and they certainly didn't look old enough to have been separated from their mother. By way of experiment Barry offered his little finger to the mouth of the most alert puppy – although, truth be told, they all looked more than half dead. As he had expected the pup eagerly started to suck his finger in the hope of receiving some long overdue nourishment and, with this small pathetic sign that although weak and starving the pup was not yet ready to give up its struggle for survival, Barry's mind was made up. There had of course been no doubt what Barry would do – his mind had, in fact, been made up as soon as he had opened the puppies' plastic prison. There would have been no way he could have walked off and left them to their fate as their previous callous and cruel owners had done.

Cursing the heartlessness and cowardice of the miserable excuse for a human being who had dumped the pups, he took off his jacket, wrapped the pups in it as closely as he could and took them to his waiting car. His jacket would not survive after enveloping the three stinking pathetic little bundles, but Barry did not care one jot. Placing the bundle carefully on the passenger seat he drove off – carefully as he was still consumed by red hot anger and didn't want to risk an accident.

Having got the puppies safely home he quickly found out an old cardboard box, lined it with old towels and two of his ancient jumpers, put a hot water bottle under them and put the puppy filled box as close to the fire as he dare. So far so good, they were now safe and warm – but what they needed most was a decent feed – and quickly by the look of them, as one of them seemed to be fading fast.

Barry warmed some milk, put it in a saucer and tried, one at a time, to encourage the puppies to lap – but each one refused even though he pushed their noses into the milk harder than he would have liked to do. They did lick some of the milk from around their mouths, and finally a drop or two from his fingers, but in his heart Barry knew this would not be enough to keep them alive. Next he tried to spoon a little of the milk into each tiny unresponsive mouth, but it just trickled out uselessly, probably because his hand was shaking too badly to hold the spoon steady. He needed to get a decent amount inside them if they stood any chance of survival, but what could he do?

Chapter 2

Barry searched the house frantically looking for anything with which he could get milk into the puppies, but there was nothing. Before her death Meg had sometimes needed medication given by syringe and he looked everywhere he could think of to find an unused syringe cartridge. He even went into the loft looking for the old dolls Samantha, their daughter, had played with constantly. He remembered that she had spent hours feeding her dolls with pretend milk from a minute version of a baby's bottle, but his ever efficient wife must have given the dolls and all their paraphernalia away long ago.

Desperate now, he raked his fingers through his hair as he gazed around him for any sort of inspiration, knowing the puppies' lives were now in his hands and that he had only a very short time to get nourishment into them.

It was now well past midnight and he knew any shop which might have been able to sell him what he needed would be long since closed, but he put on his warmest jacket anyway and headed out into the bitter night's chill anyway. His worst fears were soon realised as he drove through his small town desperately searching for a shop, any shop which showed signs of life. Each and every one was shut up tight though, their normally welcoming windows dark and blank like closed unwelcoming eyes. Having no other choice he began to drive back to the town where he had found the puppies, knowing he was driving far too fast in his desperation.

Normally a careful, safe driver he was now careering through the narrow roads and around tight bends, like a maniac and should not have been surprised that he attracted unwelcome attention as he began to enter the town. The siren splitting the air, like an air raid siren of long ago, startled him however, and it was a few moments before he realised that it was anything to do with him. Finally he glanced in his rear view mirror and seeing the pursuing police car with both lights and siren blaring he pulled over into the car park of a long closed public house shuttered and dark after a long day feeding and quenching the thirst of the public - a deep profound dread in his heart.

'In a hurry are we Sir?' asked the officer who, true to the old adage, looked barely old enough to have left school to Barry's much older eyes. 'May I see your driving licence and car registration documents please?'

Having scanned the documents and thankfully finding nothing amiss, the officer then asked the reason for Barry's journey, where he had come from and where he was headed at such a time and speed. As quickly and precisely as he could Barry explained what had happened and how he was desperate to feed the pups before it was too late, apologising with nearly every breath for his unusual disregard for the rules of the road.

'Leave your car here Sir and come with me,' commanded the officer – his words filling Barry with a new kind of dread.

Was he to be taken to the police station, breathalysed and even locked in a cell over night? Barry was not concerned about the consequences to himself and his established reputation as an upstanding member of the community; rather it was the plight of the puppies which tore at his heart.

'Can't you leave charging me until the morning? Please officer if you lock me up tonight the puppies will be dead by the time I get back to them.'

Barry had said this as he reluctantly obeyed the command and climbed into the patrol car and only when he had settled into his seat belt and heard a soft laugh did he turn to face the young man.

'We're not going to the station Sir,' he said with another chuckle. 'You're in luck, I'm just going off duty and I'm taking you to my home. My Mum breeds bearded collies, she has done for years. She's never done it on a large scale, just having two or three litters from each bitch we've ever kept as a pet, but she's got everything you're going to need to raise those pups, if they are not too far gone.'

Barry was too amazed to respond with anything other than a grateful smile and a 'thank you'. He was still tense however after his near brush with the law and expected their journey to slowly drag but it seemed only minutes before they drew up outside a very ordinary semi-detached house in a quiet residential area of the town.

Unfamiliar with this part of town Barry could only follow the young policeman who had introduced himself as Tim Walker into, what seemed to be, one of the neatest and prettiest houses on the street. Even as he walked past the well tended lawn and flower beds still riotously blooming with flowers, even in these late months of the year, he felt the house welcoming him, just as his had done when Meg had been alive. And entering the house did nothing to reduce that impression as a voice called out 'Is that you Tim? Just give me a moment and your supper will be on the table.'

Once again Barry heard a chuckle from Tim as he turned in the hallway before leading him into the kitchen. 'Mum always says that, although I don't know who else she could be expecting. Dad left us when I was six and it's just been the two of us ever since, that is unless you've got a fancy man now that I know nothing about - eh Mum!'

'Give over our Tim,' said a jolly looking woman who smiled at Barry as she turned away from the cooker, wiping her hands on a flowery apron. 'What would I be wanting with a fancy man? You make enough work and worry for three mothers as it is – I wouldn't have either time or energy for anyone else!'

'Mum this is Barry – Barry my mum Sue, I met him earlier tonight and he tells me he found three abandoned puppies in a bin bag outside that charity shop in town. Just dumped there they were with the bag all sealed and no air to breathe.'

'I don't know how any human being worthy of the title could do such a thing. Some folks don't deserve to draw breath themselves, treating those poor pups so callously and cruelly. Anyway how can we help you?'

Barry went on to describe the conditions of the puppies and how he knew that he needed to get milk into then fast if they stood any chance of surviving the night.

'Right I'll sort you out some things you'll need. It's a pity our Sasha hasn't had her litter or she would take them on as well, but she's not due for another fortnight yet. Still I've got just the thing,' Sue said chattering away as she led him to a kind of utility room behind the kitchen where an obviously placid bitch lay contentedly dosing in a luxuriously padded bed. She lifted her head, opened one eye and obviously decided Barry was not interesting enough for her to make the effort to rise and welcome him. So she just sighed, as if irritated by the disturbance, then closed her eyes again, lowered her head to her paws once and going back to sleep.

'You'll have to forgive Sasha's bad manners, but she's always like this when she is expecting pups. For the last two weeks she becomes the laziest dog in the world, don't you girl? It's almost as if she realises she will have little or no peace once her babies arrive,' said Sue hunting through boxes and along shelves as she chattered away, selecting items and putting each into a capacious cardboard box. 'This will be her last litter; she's given us two other litters both with eight healthy pups apiece in them so she's due a well deserved retirement after this lot. I don't believe in putting them to a dog too often, it's not fair. I hate the idea of puppy farms and people who breed just for money. Although we needed the money when I first started breeding, and it was certainly very welcome. I do it now though because there's something so special about having pups in the house. Watching them grow in a loving family environment before sending them off to have wonderful lives to good homes, is a real joy for me. All the homes our pups have gone to are vetted carefully by Tim and me. No-one shows or breeds with them they're simply well loved family pets – and Beardies make the most loving, faithful companions you could wish for. What breed are the ones you found, do you know?' she asked all the while continuing to lift things from shelves and cupboards before placing everything into the rapidly filling box.

'I've no idea, probably cross breeds, but then I'm no expert.'

'Well never mind, it doesn't really matter when all is said and done. They all need love and care whatever their breed, that's for sure. I'm usually a very placid peace loving soul but if I ever caught hold of anyone who could be so cruel to a defenceless animal – well I swear I could wring their neck.'

'Best not though eh Mum,' remarked Tim with a smile as he joined them. 'I wouldn't like to have to lock you up – here let me take that from you. I'll carry it through to the kitchen for you.'

Once back in the warmth of the kitchen with its cosy newly cooked supper smells Tim placed the box on the now cleared table and went to switch the kettle on before making them all tea and making a start on the dishes. 'He's pretending his well trained,' laughed Sue. 'You must be having a good influence on him!'

Tim just laughed and raised his eye brows as if to say "don't take any notice of her - she's always like this."

'Now then Barry, I'll just talk you through this lot and then you'd better get back to those puppies. I'm afraid I can't come and help you tonight, but if you leave me your address I'll pop over and see them tomorrow. Now one question, are the puppies' eyes open?'

'Well I didn't really pay much attention, I was so shocked to find them, but from what I can remember I think they were closed,' Barry replied.

'Oh dear that means they're only about two weeks old or so, not able to lap yet so they'll need bottle feeding.'

'No they certainly can't lap. I tried to put some milk into a saucer and gently press their noses into it but they just had no idea what to do.'

'Well that is just what I thought, so we must concentrate on bottle feeding. This is puppy formula milk - not as good as mother's milk of course, but it's the best substitute I've ever found. I've put in some feeding bottles as well. It would be a good idea if you can use a different bottle for each pup, just in case they have any infections which might be transmitted by sharing the same one. The milk needs to be heated to blood temperature and you can test it by dropping a little on your skin, just as you would for a human baby. If it feels warm, and not too hot or cold to you, then it should be fine for them. After you have fed each one it's very important to wipe their bottoms with a large wad of damp cotton wool. This will stimulate them to open their bowels and bladders – normally the bitch licks them after each feed to make that happen. Without the bitch to do it, the simulation of wiping is essential otherwise they may become ill. There's a whole pack of cotton wool there which should see you through for quite a few days. As well as the milk you must try to get some of this re-hydration fluid into each one of them. They must be severely dehydrated at this stage and that can kill them quicker than lack of food. It might also be an idea to bathe their eyes once a day, preferably in the morning to stimulate them to open. This is a heat pad, you said that you'd put in a hot water bottle which was just the right thing to do, but this pad will maintain a constant warmth so you won't need to get up in the night to refill any hot water bottles. Just plug it in and away you go. Put an old towel or something on top of it and they should be very cosy.'

'How often will I need to feed them and how much milk should they take?'

'I would say they should be given three to four ounces of milk every three to four hours. That's an easy formula to remember and should see them right, but if they appear to want less or more, want it more or less often then be guided by them for tonight. But be very careful not to overdo it – little and often is by far the best rule when they have been deprived of food for so long. I'll have a good look at them tomorrow when, hopefully they will have survived the night, and that should tell us more. Will you be able to cope – it's a huge commitment taking on three such tiny puppies?'

'I'll manage – I feel someone has to make it up to them for the terrible start they've had, a few sleepless nights will be nothing if I can save them.'

'What about your work though?'

'Fortunately I have my own business so I can take them to work with me by day.'

The tea was made and very welcome. Barry's mouth had become dreadfully dry, but whether it was due to his earlier shock at being stopped by Tim or the realisation of what he was taking on he didn't know. Two rapidly drunk mugs of tea later he reluctantly rose and prepared to leave this warm cosy haven to begin the responsibility of caring for those three poor little scraps – whose lives were now, quite literally, in his hands.

Thanking Sue and Tim effusively, exchanging telephone numbers and promising to ring if he was in doubt about anything he took up the box Sue had prepared for him and left with Tim who was to take him back to his own car which they had left in the pub's car park.

Chapter 3

No sooner was Barry home, and without even taking off his coat, he went to check on the pups. They seemed a little livelier now that they had access to warmth and air which they could breathe, but they were whimpering piteously.

'O.K pups,' Barry said 'just give me a minute or two to sort this lot out and I'll feed you – you'll have to help me out here though I'm as new to this as you are.'

The first thing Barry did was to warm the milk which was fortunately pre-mixed and not in powder form. While it was heating gently he found some coloured tape and stuck a red, yellow and blue band around each bottle, then he tested the milk as Sue had advised, poured some into each tiny bottle put an old towel on his lap and began to feed each one in turn.

The smell of milk must have excited them as they all began to scramble blindly yet furiously to its source. Torn about which to feed first Barry picked up the smallest one, reasoning that the other slightly larger ones might be able to wait a little longer. At first the tiny pup seemed confused and unsure how to take the milk but after Barry had gently opened its mouth and wiggled the teat around in its mouth, as Sue had suggested, it soon got the idea and sucked frantically until all the milk was gone. Barry remembered too what Sue had said about the importance of stimulating their need to defecate and urinate, but decided for this first feed to leave that until all their tummies were full. There was no knowing how long they had been without food and sating their appetites, to Barry, seemed the most important task. The indignity of toileting could wait until they were all full and content.

As Barry had hoped would be the case, the first feed went very well, the pups were all extremely hungry, in fact he surmised that they wouldn't have survived much longer without milk. Rather than find the small doll-sized feeding bottles strange and repellent after the warmth and softness of their mother's teats they latched on immediately and sucked ravenously until each of their bottles was dry, such was their need for urgent feeding. Now as he looked at them with their newly rounded fat little tummies, it was evident to Barry once again how near starvation they must have been. For their tummies had shown no signs of roundness before their feed - in fact he recognised now just how emaciated they had looked.

Toileting the pups was not something he had been looking forward to. Surprisingly though Barry found this task both satisfying and even pleasurable knowing, as he did, how vital it was to the health and well being of the tiny creatures. Once cleaned up Barry set to making their bed even more comfortable by placing the heat pad under a soft mock cashmere sweater he had been given one Christmas. He had never really liked it, as he could not think himself a cashmere, even of the mock variety, sort of chap; and he definitely fought against baby pink! The puppies however had no such prejudices and happily snuggled into its soft pink depths curling themselves up so tightly together that it became almost impossible to see where one began and the others ended. Before many seconds had passed there were all fast asleep.

By now it was past midnight and Barry realised that he'd had nothing to eat since lunchtime which seemed an eternity ago. It was too late for a full meal but he quickly scrambled an egg and toasted two slices of bread before sitting down to his long overdue supper. Chastising himself for his slovenliness he nevertheless left the few dishes he had used in the sink and climbed the stairs wearily, but not before rousing each sleepy pup once more to give them each a fill of re-hydration liquid as Sue had advised. He then set his alarm clock for three o'clock the following morning, before collapsing onto the bed still fully dressed and instantly falling into a deep, deep sleep.

It seemed to Barry as if he had only just closed his eyes when they were jerked open once more by the alarm clock ringing imperiously in his ear. At first he couldn't work out why the alarm should be ringing at such an ungodly hour, when the world beyond his window was still heavily cloaked in darkness. But then with sudden clarity he remembered the pups and dragged himself from his warm comfortable bed to once again play foster father.

As he made his way down the stairs Barry was filled with sudden apprehension as to what he would find. Would the puppies still be alive or had they been neglected for so long that all his recent efforts would have proved futile? Worse still had he himself done something wrong which would have brought about their deaths? He felt himself utter a silent uncharacteristic prayer that they would all be alive and well.

Any resentment he might have felt at being wrenched from slumber, evaporated like morning mist when he went into the kitchen and heard the pitiful squeaking of the pups desperate once again for food. As he warmed the milk and filled the tiny bottles he marvelled at how much more lively they had become in the few hours since food, hydration and warmth had been restored to them. The biggest one whom he instantly christened Butch was even trying to crawl over the top of the box to get at the sweet smelling milk before any of his litter mates, thus proclaiming his dominance.

Once again feeding went without a hitch, as all three seemed just as frantic for their feed as they had been the first time he had fed them. He was getting the hang of the toileting business too now and so before long all three were tucked up warm and snug in the bed once more.

By the time the third feed and rehydration session at half past six had been accomplished, Barry recognised that Sue had been right when she had warned him about the enormity of the task before him. He was already exhausted after just one night's disturbed sleep and now he had a day's work to face as well as the continuing cycle of three to four hourly feeds. As he gently placed the box with his charges on the back seat of his car, however the smallest and weakest of the puppies crawled over its siblings and licked Barry's finger with its tiny bright pink tongue. It was enough to spur

Barry on and he knew that whatever the cost to himself, it was insignificant compared with the responsibility he felt towards these three tiny creatures. Silently he raised the tiniest pup to his face and nuzzled it close, promising them all that he would raise them and find them wonderful kind and loving owners and safe forever homes.

With typical perverseness the shop was constantly busy that morning. More customers demanded attention than Barry could remember for a long time and it was gone twelve o'clock before he had a minute spare in which to make himself a much wanted mug of coffee. He had fed the puppies during the one quiet spell – just after he had opened the shop and now they were clamouring for their next one. Sighing Barry took a sip of his coffee desperate to assuage his thirst only to burn his mouth in the process.

He was just in the midst of making up the puppies' next feeds when he heard the shop bell tinkle, 'Damn and blast it,' he swore to himself. 'I thought I'd locked the door and put the closed sign up.'

Tiredness was making him bad tempered and although he recognised this, he still felt unable to rise above the black mood into which he had plunged - until he heard a welcome voice calling him.

'Barry are you there? I've been trying to ring you at home since yesterday lunchtime but there was never a reply.'

'Oh Peggy,' he said, relief that she wasn't yet another customer, along with sheer joy at seeing, her making him act in an uncharacteristically demonstrative way by hugging her warmly as he came into the shop from the back room.

'Well that's a nice welcome I must say – what have I done to deserve it?'

'Just being you and being here is enough – just let me lock the shop door and then I'll bring you up to date with what's been going on.'

'What's that strange noise I can hear?' asked Peggy heading toward the sound which was coming from the back room.

'Ah well - that's why you haven't been able to get hold of me. Come on through to the back room and I'll introduce you,' he said smiling widely.

Peggy's response on seeing the tiny scraps was typical of her warm compassionate nature. She immediately bent down to their improvised bed, picking them up one by one to be cuddled and caressed while all the time firing questions at Barry. She demanded to know how he came to have them at his shop, where he had found them and what he was intending to do with them. When at last he was able to get a word in between the torrent of questions, he told her the whole story.

'I'm determined to raise them, if it's at all possible. They obviously knew nothing but unkindness and abuse, before I found them. It is vital to me that they learn not all humans are cruel or callous. I have made a pledge that they will all be in my care, until loving new homes can be found for them.'

'But you can't do all that on your own and run the shop as well you'll be on your knees with exhaustion before the week is out!'

'Never mind before the week is out! I'm pretty much there already after just a day and a night. They have to be fed every three to four hours and have a drink of re-hydration fluid in between. It seems that as soon as you have finished one feed it's time to start the next.'

'Pretty much like caring for a newborn human baby then.' she smiled. 'But seriously you do look fit to drop. Why don't you sit down and drink your coffee while I see to these little ones?'

'Well alright - you've talked me into it,' replied Barry gratefully. 'You feed them and I'll take over once they are fed, as you have to encourage them to go to the toilet.'

'If you talk me through it I'm sure I will be able to cope with that as well, it can't be all that different from changing a baby's nappy surely. But first things first, let's get them fed.'

For the next three quarters of an hour they talked quietly about everything and nothing as Peggy fed and toileted the pups and all the time Barry watched her entranced. She made it look so effortless, her actions smooth and practised as if she had been hand rearing baby animals all her life. It must be that she has brought up her own babies thought Barry, and she is adapting all that expertise to the puppies.

'I think what you are doing for these puppies is wonderful,' Peggy said as she laid the last now replete and sleepy animal back into its cardboard box haven. 'But I still think it's too much for you to take on all by yourself. It might work if you had retired or if you had someone else to share the load, but as it is, I'm sure you will struggle. Have you thought that it might be better to take them to a rescue centre where there are professionals who would take over their care.'

'It has occurred to me yes, but – and this may sound stupid - but when I found them I made them a promise. I promised that I wouldn't let them down as their previous owners had so callously done with such evil disregard for their lives; and I want to keep that promise. They have already been severely let down by mankind - just literally thrown out with the rubbish - and although they are only tiny I want to show them that we are not all uncaring, irresponsible, wicked creatures. I know what you're probably thinking, but it is really important to me.'

'I don't think you do know; because what I am actually thinking is what a thoroughly decent and wonderful man you are. No don't contradict me and please don't take what I am about to say the wrong way. But if you are going to do this on your own, how about I come and stay at your house until they are weaned and re-homed. I am not propositioning you - it would just be another pair of hands; one friend helping another in time of need.'

'I would really like that in fact I was trying to pluck up the courage to invite you for a meal, but I was afraid you would be put off by the state of the house. You see I've done nothing to it since Meg died, I couldn't find the incentive, even though she was so proud of the house but now I feel as if I've let her down. But now it is in a right state, I have sorted out someone to come and refurbish the kitchen and bathroom and then decorate but until then it's truly a sorry mess.'

'I don't care what state your house is in - you silly man. By nature I'm not a bit house-proud, the only reason my own home is so tidy and clean is because housework gives me something with which to fill the long, lonely hours of each and every day, when I am not at work. At times I've been so desperate to fill the lonely hours that I've even asked for more hours at the café.'

So with a smile and a hug the deal was sealed. Peggy went home to collect everything she thought she might need but not before picking up Barry's house keys along with a scrap of paper on which Barry had written his address. They had decided that, in that way, she could take her things straight there and make up the bed in the spare room. She left the shop promising him again that she would not think badly of him because of the state of his house.

Two days after moving into Barry's house, Peggy felt as if she had lived there for ever. They had established a comfortable routine and atmosphere without even trying; Barry was far less tired and the puppies were thriving. Their eyes were now open for most of the time and they were even trying to lap although more milk landed on their fur and the floor than ever reached their tummies. It was hilarious to watch though and usually Peggy and Barry ended up crying with laughter.

Tim and Sue had become regular visitors too and the four of them had become close friends. Sue was delighted with the progress of the puppies and gave ongoing advice as to their care.

'You have done a really good job with these little ones.' Sue had told them on one of those visits. 'You both should be proud of yourselves.'

'I'm not sure I would have managed so well without Peggy's help though. As you told me when we first met it's more than one person can cope with, especially with work as well. Still they are thriving and growing so quickly that I can see a real difference in them even from the time I leave for work and when I come home.'

Work had started on Barry's house too and progress was much quicker than he had imagined it would be. Secretly he wondered if this was because Peggy was now in residence and could chivvy the workmen along, effectively acting as project manager. If they were tempted to take too many tea breaks, she soon sorted them out and they all quickly discovered that she knew exactly what she wanted. Perhaps the work was progressing with speed and efficiency too, because she was on hand to answer any queries they may have. But for whatever reason the kitchen was nearing completion and the bathroom only needed tiling and a few cosmetic finishing touches.

As he looked around him that evening at the almost finished jobs Barry could almost hear Meg telling him how much nicer the house looked. Never a fanciful man he wondered too what she would say about his deepening feelings for Peggy. Neither of them had talked about their relationship since she had moved in to help take care of the puppies, but there seemed to be an unspoken feeling between them that it was becoming a permanent thing. For himself Barry knew he would like to marry Peggy, but it was almost as if he was waiting for a sign of approval from Meg.

Telling himself he was being extremely foolish and that his thoughts were taking him into the realms of the bizarre he squared his shoulders as if to rid himself of his foolishness.

He didn't have to wait long for his sign however, for when he returned home from work that night and, after he had fed the puppies and spent some time playing with them, he went into the sitting room to be greeted by a picture of Meg on the mantelpiece. It was a picture he had put away in a cupboard immediately after her funeral, as he could not bear to look at it. But now lovingly dusted and polished it was back on display. Barry went into the kitchen where Peggy was preparing their meal and asked her how it had come to reappear.

'I found it in the sideboard under a pile of old papers,' she said somewhat sheepishly - avoiding eye contact as she spoke. 'I thought she deserved better than that. I know you put the photograph away because you were hurting so much, but I thought that if you could bear to look at it now, then maybe most of the pain would have gone - and there might even be a chance for us.'

Barry was amazed on many levels ... amazed by her intuition, her courage in confronting the issue, but most of all amazed because she appeared to want a future together for them as much as he did. He found that, for the moment he was unable to speak though and turning on his heel he returned to the sitting room to gaze at this, his favourite photograph of his beloved, long dead wife. And there he had his sign because as he looked at it the image, one which he had always considered serene if not a tiny bit serious, the face in the photograph appeared to smile at him. The sensation was fleeting, but he was sure it had been there - a small contented happy smile which lit up her face and brought a twinkle to her eyes.

    A part of Barry knew he was being ridiculous and fanciful, but nevertheless he felt released. It was as if Meg was smiling on his relationship with Peggy, as if she approved of it and was giving it her blessing. So he went back to Peggy who was standing in front of the cooker, put his arms around her waist and said 'Shall we get married then?' Her response was so joyful that no words of consent were needed.

    By the time the wedding was planned and due to take place, the puppies had long since been weaned and two had found happy caring homes with two of Barry's best customers. These people were more like old friends than customers and had been as incensed by the puppies' wicked treatment and abandonment as Barry had. These kind folks had avidly followed their progress ever since Barry had first brought them into the shop. One of the pups would never be rehomed however. Peggy and Barry had decided to keep the third pup Butch, who having been renamed by Peggy, was now

Liquorice. And although Barry had initially argued that this was a stupid name for a dog, reluctantly accepted it when the puppy refused to respond to any of the alternatives he had come up with. Peggy had chosen the name, not only because his coat was predominantly black but because when they had taken all three to the vet for their first inoculations Barry had asked the young man what mixture of breeds they might be. The vet had looked at the puppies, then at Barry before looking down at the puppies once more and bursting into laughter. 'Heaven only knows', he had replied. 'They look as if they have got allsorts in them!' The name had soon been shortened to Riss however and the compromise suited everyone. Barry was no longer embarrassed to call his now six month old puppy when they went to the park. Peggy had the satisfaction of having named him, and Riss – well he was just happy – purely and simply the happiest dog either of them had ever known.

They were married in a simple but moving civil ceremony twelve months to the day they had first met, Peggy's daughter and her family had flown over from New Zealand to be with her on her special day, thereby adding to Peggy's joy because she had had the opportunity to hug and get to know her grandchildren in person for the first time. Tim and Sue, along with a few other relatives and good friends, made up the wedding party who all later gathered at the best hotel in town for a small but sumptuous reception. After a joyful day Peggy and Barry returned to Barry's house, which was now both of theirs, to begin their lives together.

As they relaxed with an unromantic but warming mug of cocoa neither of them could believe their good fortune in finding each other such a random way.

It was an act of kindness which had brought them together a haphazard gesture of one stranger to another, but it had led them to new happiness and an unexpected second chance of love for both of them.

Tim's Story

Chapter 1

Tim loved his job, he loved the feeling that he was a vital part of the local community. He loved going in to schools to talk to the children, some of whom had real reason to fear the uniform, about his job in the hope that this might allay some of their suspicions. Rather like a well established vicar with his personal catalogue of sermons Tim had his own collection of talks on a wide range of subjects form "Stranger Danger," "Cycling Proficiency" and "Staying Safe" to "Helping others" and "If You Find it Hand It In."

He also enjoyed getting around and meeting people, listening to their concerns, checking the security of their homes and businesses even helping to resolve disputes between neighbours. He had lived locally all his life, except when away for his several training courses, and was proud to say that he knew at least 90% of the locals by name. He knew where the various family members worked and often even the names of their family pets. And if he was ever asked to compile their family trees, he could make a good attempt to go back at least two or sometimes three generations. But despite all this, or maybe even because of it, he was considered something of an oddity at the station. Unlike his colleagues Tim had no ambition to gain promotion after promotion, or move into C.I.D. nor to solve drug related crimes, assaults or even murders. He was perfectly content to stay as he was, a lowly constable, serving the community he loved. The only reason he could foresee him wanting or needing his sergeant's stripes would be if his present position was threatened and then perhaps a promotion might help to secure it.

Having been brought up solely by his Mum since his father had left them when he was only six, Tim recognised and appreciated the value of family. Perhaps simply because it had only been the two of them since then, or perhaps because he personally knew the pain apparent rejection had caused, he was fiercely family oriented. This made him all the more determined to support those families, on his beat, whom he knew to be in crisis or at least experiencing difficulties. In some ways he considered himself to be man wearing many hats; police officer of course but also social worker, confidante, counsellor, and many others.

Although many of his bosses were unaware of his many efforts to help, Tim was continually ribbed about his altruistic approach to community policing by his colleagues – but he took it all on the chin. He only had to remind himself how his mother would have valued help, advice and support when his father left home so suddenly, so unexpectedly and without apparent reason.

Tim had learned many years after his father's sudden disappearance that he had had a complete nervous breakdown brought on by the enormous pressure he was under at his work. So severe was the breakdown that he had simply got up one morning, got dressed and walked away "Reggie Perrin" style from his home, his work, his whole life. The only difference being that Tim's father had left no enigmatic clues to his disappearance – no clothes left lying on a deserted beach, like Reggie – nothing.

  Learning about his father's complete and catastrophic breakdown had made Tim feel better about it somehow. Until that moment he had always carried the guilt of his parent's separation inside himself, thinking that it had somehow been his fault. When he was eighteen, driven by his all-consuming need for answers, he had traced his father, who had spent many of the intervening years in a succession of mental hospitals. Seeing the frail, barely lucid man who was supposedly his father had an enormous effect on Tim and, as he stood looking down on this shrunken figure slumped in an arm chair, all resentment had left him to be replaced by an overwhelming sense of pity.

  The realities of the situation, when his father had first left them however, remained the same. Sue had still needed help and support to see her through those dark days and there had been no-one around to help her.

  Having been a stay at home mother until then, she was forced to find ways of supporting herself and Tim, and was catapulted into a life she had not known since her marriage. One of having to apply for any jobs which became available, only to be turned down time after time due to lack of experience. After many months of applications and rejections, she was forced to lower her expectations and apply for jobs for which she was now, ironically, told she was over qualified. Stuck in this dead end cycle Sue had drifted from one job paying minimum wages to another, in the hope that the next one would lead to advancement and higher wages – but they never had. Things had been so dire Sue had been forced into thinking about selling their beloved pet as a way to save money until one day at the supermarket, where she was working, a notice advertising pedigree puppies for sale caught her eye.

The rest, as they say, is history their pet had been a beautiful beardie bitch and, having meticulously researched breeding processes and ethics, she had contacted an owner with a stud dog and nine weeks later seven adorable little pups entered the world with only minimal help from Sue.

It had not always gone as smoothly and there were many times when Sue wished she had listened to the dire warning of professional breeders. Warnings that responsible breeding was not for the amateur or the devoted pet owner. But for her the triumphs had out weighed the tragedies and although not as lucrative as might generally be thought, in their case the income from selling the pups as pets to good homes made a considerable difference to their way of life. And a lot of the pressure to pay bills on time had been lifted. Sue had been lucky - she knew that - and had never regretted her decision to breed on a small scale. She had even established a reputation for being able to bring on weak or sickly puppies and was often called upon to do just that for larger scale breeders who had neither the time, nor occasionally, the inclination to spend hours on what some of them considered hopeless cases. An added bonus had been that these breeders had passed over the sickly pups legally to Sue, who having reared them could sell them on to good homes.

Tim knew of all his mother's trials and triumphs of course having lived with her through them all, doing whatever he was able in his boyish way to help her. It was this which now drove him to try and help others in a similar position. He had known honest, devoted husbands and fathers driven to petty theft after being made redundant in a desperate attempt to keep their families together, well fed and with a roof over their heads. In these circumstances he had quietly asked around, called in a few favours and even resorted to a spot of mild coercion in his efforts to secure them a job and prevent them being caught up in a cycle of crime. A result which would have been the death knell to the family he was trying to keep together.

All in all Tim was content with his life he had a nice home, a great relationship with his mum, a job he loved and was well liked and respected in the small town in which he lived. What he didn't have was a girlfriend, and this was another reason why he was the subject of needling and risqué comments at the station. There had been girls before, of course there had, but for one reason or another, the relationships had never lasted long. Some girlfriends had been scared off by the uniform and the fact that long hours or unsocial duties ruined dates, leading to disappointment when long awaited arrangements were cancelled. Others thought he was not enough of a mover and shaker for them or that he was too involved, too soft with the people he looked out for, while with others it had just been a case of simple incompatibility.

Typically though, Tim was less concerned about his romantic life – or rather his lack of it - than his mother was. It was she who longed for him to meet a "nice girl" and to settle down happily; quickly producing a healthy brood of grandchildren for her to adore and spoil into her later years and old age. She was also concerned that each time a relationship ended Tim was less willing to start again. Each time he was a little bit more introspective, quieter; more reluctant to go out. She also knew her son well enough to know that none of his previous girlfriends had broken his heart, but some had severely bruised it. His pain, as with all mothers, became hers, because more than anything else she longed for him to be happy.

Sue was wise enough not to mention any of this to Tim though, but she kept a close eye on him. She had a wide repertoire of comforting words, positive optimistic comments and motherly advice, suitable for any occasion should he ever need it.

The way his father had left them also concerned Tim in another way for he wondered if he might react in the same way or experience the same kind of mental meltdown which had precipitated the desertion. Certainly he had never shown any signs of collapse when under severe pressure, but what would happen if he did experience the same thing and ended up leaving another family, his own, to suffer as he and his mother had done.

These dark thoughts only raised their ugly heads during night time periods when Tim was unable to sleep, but they were there, especially when he had met someone new and was in the "beginning to become fond of them" stage. Generally though he thought of himself as fairly responsible and level headed so why these doubts plagued him, when he was normally the sort of man to push worries aside, was a mystery to him. If there was nothing he could do about them, why did they haunt him so? He couldn't explain it - all he knew was that, for the last few nights, he had been lying awake stupidly worrying about problems which didn't exist and might never exist. Angry and annoyed with himself he nevertheless tossed and turned his way through the hours of darkness. When morning finally came he was only too glad to get up, shower and chase the demons away with the prospect of a good hard day's work.

* * * * *

Tim's mood became even more despondent when he checked in to the station for his call list later that morning. There at the top of the sheet was the name Kyle Hickman written in bold red capitals and deeply underlined with three exclamation marks after it. The colour, and the manner the note was written in, saying more about the situation than anything else could.

'Sorry Tim I don't think you are in for a good day,' said his sergeant as he passed over the piece of paper. 'It looks as if your old adversary has been up to new and even more inventive tricks. You'd better get yourself over there and see what's afoot.'

Kyle was a constant problem to his own long suffering and despairing mother who had tried to do her best by him and to bring him up to be an honest, reliable young man. But in all fairness, this Kyle was not, although Tim had long held the belief that Kyle was capable of it. He had caused great trouble at his school, from which he was regularly suspended, trouble to the neighbours, the police and their small town in general. If there was ever trouble to be found then Kyle would be at the centre of it. He was not a hardened criminal: he didn't deal drugs or even use them, he didn't break in to people's houses, or steal cars. Nonetheless he was always in trouble. Nicking push bikes or babies' prams from outside the local shops, before dumping them far enough away to inconvenience and annoy the owners. He enjoyed plastering newly painted walls with amateurish graffiti, letting car tyres down, and throwing bricks through windows of empty properties. He was also well known for taking anything he fancied from the shops which lined the High Street on both sides, while laughing in the face of the shopkeepers, before running away faster than they were able to follow him. These were all parts of Kyle's modus operandi. His one redeeming feature was that he was totally non-violent, but Tim, Kyle's mother and the rest of the small town were now seriously fed up with his antics. The good, but Kyle weary, people of the town were demanding some sort of action which would resolve the matter once and for all.

Tim had tried taking the boy in hand talking to him offering him advice and warnings in equal measure, finding positive activities which might capture his interest and deflect him away from his on the cusp criminality. Tim had tried enrolling him in youth clubs, with football teams, swimming and diving clubs and even for a conservation project run by their local branch of the environment agency. His attempts to find Kyle a more positive outlet for his energy and positive role models to influence him had, however, had not even left first gear. Now it seemed as if Kyle had moved up a notch by becoming involved with a gang who were notorious for much more serious crimes.

Assaults, robbery with violence, car theft with the added menaces of drugs and knife crimes were parts of their portfolios. If Kyle was not prised away from them soon he was looking at a future littered with court appearances as well as spells in young offenders centres or even prison.

It was now imperative that Tim visited Kyle again to try and find some way of capturing his interests and enthusiasm in a positive way. The most frustrating thing was that Tim was convinced, that behind the surly couldn't care less attitude, there lurked a warm, honest, decent and intelligent lad.

Chapter 2

The red rimmed eyes, the harassed, drawn features and the fear in her eyes as Kyle's mother opened the door to Tim told their own story; much more eloquently than mere words could ever do. This woman – prematurely aged by overwork, privation and constant worry was clearly at the end of her tether.

'What's he done now?' was her usual greeting and she spoke the words now as her eyes filled with new, yet to be shed, tears while she clung to the door frame for support, terrified of the news Tim might be bringing.

'Nothing Mary, it's okay, but I did want a word with him if he's around he's got into bad company and I wanted to warn him what the consequences could be of mixing with them.'

'I know, it's been worrying me to death – not that I've ever been free of worry since his dad died, but it just seems to get worse and worse. And the worries just get bigger and bigger if you know what I mean.'

'He's not a bad lad, you know that better than anyone – that's the tragedy of it - he just needs to be in with a better crowd and find something worthwhile to do. I'm sure if that happened he'd come right and be the credit to you we both know he could be.'

'Well come in, you can hear from the music that he's in his room, go on up and I'll get a cup of tea ready for you when you come down. Perhaps he will listen to you, I hope so anyway. God knows I've tried warning him about those thugs, but it's a long time since he listened to anything I had to say.'

Tim took off his Police cap and took the well trodden path to Kyle's room. He had paid numerous visits to the house and to Kyle's personal space over the years and he knew that once the truculence and surliness, born of fear and lack of confidence, had been overcome Kyle would be his usual friendly self. Just as he was, whenever he and Tim were alone together. This more than anything else was what gave Tim the most hope, he felt he saw a side to Kyle which nobody else, not even his own mother, ever saw. Kyle was so determined to project an antagonistic, aggressive image that he hardly ever let the illusion slip. Yet Tim was convinced this act was obscuring a decent young man with the potential to make something truly great of his life.

Their conversations in the past, once Kyle had let his defences drop had shown Tim just how bright and knowledgeable the lad was on a wide number of subjects. It was just that he didn't seem to feel deeply enough about anything to really care – to commit himself wholeheartedly to any cause. Tim was convinced that if Kyle did find such a passion, it would be the complete incentive the young lad needed to stand against the gang of lads he went around with, and who were such a destructive, controlling influence on him.

Halfway up the stairs it was as if a blinding light of inspiration lit up the shabby stairwell. Pulling out his mobile phone he quickly sent a text to his mother, secure in the knowledge that she would respond and play along as he had requested. With a new spring to his step he ran up the rest of the stairs two at a time and knocked on Kyle's bedroom door loudly enough to be heard over the blaring rap music – if you could call it music - thought Tim whose own tastes ran more towards country and western.

Sure enough after ten minutes of chat during which defences had been breached and amicable relations resumed, Tim's mobile started to ring to the plaintive tones of Dolly Parton's "Jolene." He answered it knowing that it would be his mother as it was the special ring tone he had chosen for her calls. Smiling to himself he put the phone to his ear – 'let the show begin' he thought to himself.

'Hi Mum, what do you want - I'm at work,' he began, then changed his tone to a worried 'Oh my God are you alright? Do you need me to come home and what about the puppies, how are you going to manage with them?'

There was a long pause during which Tim listened to what his mother was apparently saying, while concentrating on maintaining his worried look even pushing his hand through his hair as if he was at a complete loss.

'Well try not to worry and I'll get home as soon as I can. In the meantime try to keep off it as much as possible and make sure you strap it up with a bandage. I'll look at it when I get there and if necessary take you to A&E for an x-ray. Bye Mum look after yourself.' Tim closed his small phone with an exaggerated sigh and a anxious look worthy of an Oscar.

'What's up?' Kyle asked after a few minutes of watching Tim pacing up and down the small bedroom.

'Oh sorry Kyle, I should be concentrating on you, but I've just had some bad news. My mum has hurt her ankle – it could be broken although hopefully it is just badly sprained, but the problem is we have a new litter of puppies. Their mother hasn't got enough milk to satisfy them all, so at least some of them need supplementary feeding and other basic care. Now Mum might be too laid up to care for them and I haven't got any holiday owing to me. Oh God what a mess,' said Tim pretending to brush his own troubles away and to concentrate on the matter in hand. 'Anyway Kyle, that's not your problem but if you don't mind I'll get off home, but I promise I'll come back to see you once everything is sorted out at home.'

'Would you mind if I came with you,' Kyle asked with a new hesitancy and hope in his voice. Gone was the brash, cocky bravado and false aggression which had been one of his characteristics and it was then that Tim knew his rash gamble had paid off.

'Well you can if you want to I suppose, but it won't be very exciting – just my invalid Mum - a few bundles of fluff and me. But if it's ok with your mum then by all means tag along, although I really don't understand why you would want to.'

'Well I thought I might be able to do somefink to help,' was the lads reply but the words were like music to Tim's ears.

It was nowhere near the end of Tim's shift but he knew he would need time to put his plan into action effectively, so had to square it with his superiors. He phoned the station while Kyle was for the first time in a long while, asking his mother's permission to do something. He outlined his scheme knowing the sarge would be fine with his plans. Kyle had been a constantly irritating itch which nobody had been able to satisfactorily scratch for as long as the sergeant could remember, and any plan which might get the lad sorted out and the itch soothed was just fine with him.

Tim had no opportunity however to phone his Mum to tell her that he was on his way home with the main character in this little drama he had dreamed up. On reaching his home therefore and in order to keep up the subterfuge, he called loudly from the hallway as soon as he had opened the front door. 'I'm home Mum and I've brought someone with me.'

This gave Sue just enough time to throw herself onto the settee and lift her totally undamaged ankle onto a cushioned stool in front of her as well as arrange her features into what she hoped were expressions of both dismay and pain.

'Oh Tim, I'm so glad you're home,' she called back with a very convincing wobble in her voice. 'This ankle of mine is killing me and before you shout at me I haven't managed to get it strapped up as I couldn't make it up the stairs to get a bandage from the bathroom. In fact I can't do anything very much at all - it hurts so much. I can't even bear to put my foot to the floor, and I'm really worried. The puppies need seeing to, Sasha needs feeding and taking out into the garden to do her business, and I'm stuck on this sofa as useless as a beached whale. However are we going to manage while I'm like this?'

If not quite worthy of another Oscar it was nonetheless a convincing performance and Tim had to hurriedly turn away in order to conceal a smile.

'Don't worry Mum I'm here now and I've brought reinforcements,' Tim replied as he opened the door to the sitting room while ushering Kyle in before him. 'Mum I'd like to introduce you to Kyle, he wanted to see the puppies and has offered to help out a bit while you are off your feet – haven't you Kyle?'

'If you think I can, though I don't know nuffin 'bout dogs we could never 'ave one see,' the lad said trying to maintain his tough don't care attitude to the last, while all the time shuffling about on his feet nervously.

Sue wasn't fooled. One glance at this lad with his "don't cross me" attitude, his shaved head and his multiple facial piercings was enough to convince her that Tim's interest in and hopes for the lad had not been misplaced. It's all window dressing she thought to herself. Or better still it's a kind of armour – he thinks if he projects a fierce "don't mess with me" aura it will protect him.

'Well that's very kind of you Kyle I must say, as you can see I can do with all the help I can get at the moment. There isn't anything too complicated in it – nothing a clever looking young lad like you wouldn't be capable of anyway. Go with Tim to see Sasha and the puppies, but don't try to pick them up just yet. Like any Mum she is very protective of her babies. She will need time to get to know you before she learns to trust you. Only when she is sure of you will she allow you to have anything to do with them. After that perhaps you could take her for a walk, just up and down the garden will be enough, but she hasn't been out all day poor thing and while you're out Tim could strap up my ankle.'

'Come on then Kyle, this way,' said Tim leading the way to a kind of utility area off the kitchen where a large whelping box was placed near a warm heater and surrounded by newspapers half an inch thick. 'Say hello to Sasha first,' encouraged Tim. 'Hold your hand out to her first so she can sniff you - that way she will assess whether you're a friend or a foe. Then the next time you come, if you do the same again, she will recognize your scent.'

Kyle did as he was instructed and was almost overcome when Sasha wagged her tail and licked his hand in greeting. 'There you see she likes you already,' said Tim. 'Good girl, now can we see your puppies please; we aren't going to take them away we just want to look at them.' He spoke in a soft lilting way as he put his had under the bitch gently moving her to one side of the box revealing eight sparsely furred puppies. Six of them were just beginning to sprout back and white fur – the last two would be and two brown and white.

Turning to Kyle, Tim watched him closely for a reaction to see if his gamble was to pay off. One furtive glance was enough to tell him that it had. The surly don't-mess-with-me-I-hate-the-whole-world expression was gone to be replaced by one of tenderness, joy and wonder. Kyle's face was alight with happiness, his eyes no longer held his usual guarded or aggressive expression and his smile brought a new warmth to the small room. Just as importantly Sasha, although understandably wary of strangers and on high alert to guard her babies, as any new mother would be, sealed her approval of Kyle. She had taken to him with unprecedented readiness, her tail thumping loudly and vigorously against the side of the whelping box. Not only did she appear to welcome him as a long lost friend but she actively pushed the smallest of her puppies gently but firmly towards his waiting hands in a gesture of complete trust. Kyle, after looking to Tim for approval and getting it, gathered the puppy in his arms instinctively supporting it under it's chest and bottom. Folding his arms protectively around the tiny body Kyle was almost overcome and Tim considerately looked away before Kyle realised he had seen the lone tear coursing down his unlined young face.

'Well I must say I'm amazed Kyle! Sasha has never before allowed a stranger to touch her babies when they are as young as these are. You must have a magic touch!'

'They and Sasha know I won't hurt them is all,' the boy answered so quietly that Tim had to strain to hear him. 'I could never have a dog of me own, Mum said it weren't fair as she was out working all day and I couldn't be trusted to care for it and walk it. She said I'd soon get bored with it, but I would have looked after it. I really would - if she'd given me the chance.'

'Well if you want a chance now, my Mum and I would be very grateful for your help with this little lot while she is semi laid up with her bad leg. Eight puppies make for a lot of work even when they have such an attentive mother as theirs, and of course there's Sasha herself to look after. As the pups grow and become more boisterous she will need time out from them and a gentle walk in the park would be a real treat for her then.'

'Would your Mum trust me to do it right though, nobody's ever trusted me with nuffink before they just thinks I'll cock up all the time.'

'Mum will trust you and so do I,' replied Tim thinking that to be trusted and given some responsibility was probably all Kyle had ever needed. He had never had the chance to prove himself capable of anything to anyone, or even to himself, and so he had given up trying and become surly and irresponsible as if to prove a point to the world. Rejecting it as it had appeared to reject him.

Chapter 3

And so it was that working with Sue, whose only problem all the time Kyle was with her was remembering to limp on the correct leg, turned the boy's life around to the amazement of everyone who had known his previous wild behaviour. He began to work harder at school, gave up going around with the gang which had been such a negative influence upon him, and for the first time he relaxed sufficiently around people to allow himself to show the sunny, friendly nature his former belligerence had been hiding. Even the aggressive looking piercings and shaven head soon became things of the past.

He was the very best helper Sue had ever had or could have wished for. Nothing was too much trouble; no job too hard or too messy for him, and before long, rather than waiting for instructions, was using his own initiative which proved to be both accurate and intuitive.

The dogs all loved him and their greeting every morning was noisy and rapturous. In his care they blossomed and Sue found that within a few days of his arrival she could virtually leave everything to him. Moreover he could do anything with the puppies, who all gave the impression that their only desire in life was to please him and because of this they were both weaned and paper trained more easily and more quickly than usual.

The only problem Sue foresaw was that, understandably, Kyle had become too attached to the puppies who were all booked and were due to go to their new loving and well respected owners very soon. Owners who met Sue's high standards and had proved themselves worthy to receive a puppy. They had all shown themselves to be responsible in the past and many of them had had previous puppies from Sue so they had experience of Beardies and the trials of grooming.

In Sue's opinion the long amount of time needed for the weekly grooming session was the only drawback to owning a Beardie. They were the nicest of dogs, kind, loyal, gentle and usually eager to please, but their long thick coats were a real struggle to keep matt free and were often a challenge to even the most responsible and dedicated owner. Some solved the problem by having the coat cut very short. But Sue herself still preferred to see them as they were intended to be, just as she preferred to see certain breeds of dogs with their proper tails rather than seeing them cruelly docked.

Tim meanwhile was delighted that his gamble had paid off, not for any kudos it might bring him, but for the lad himself as well as any relief it might bring Kyle's mother Mary. He knew from personal experience how easy it was for lads without a positive and supportive father figure to get in with the wrong crowd. They could often be embroiled in severe trouble, often before it became too obvious where they were headed. By that time it was often too late to reverse the process. Tim had seen something of himself in Kyle, although he had never gone that way himself. For that he had to thank his mother who had been both father and mother to him and had taught him right from wrong and respect of others and their property. Rather he had seen in Kyle what he himself might have become if he had not been given the right boundaries, the right directions to follow. So his motives were not totally altruistic – it was more complicated than that, it was as if he felt he had a debt of gratitude to repay. Kyle's mother Mary had tried her very best to give Kyle good principles on which to live, and needed to be given credit for that. Kyle though had been more wilful, stubborn and verbally aggressive that Tim himself had been and so Mary had been fighting a losing battle.

Tim was only too aware that his scheme was merely temporary however. All too soon the puppies would be fully weaned, house trained and ready to go to the eager new owners who had proved themselves worthy in Sue's eyes. What would happen to Kyle then? Tim knew that he was to finish school in a matter of weeks and although he had worked harder in the last few months could never hope to make up for all the time he had wasted at school or the many days during which he had perfected his truancy skills. Therefore any qualifications would be few and far between or even non existent.

Tim knew he had to come up with another plan, or at least help Kyle formulate his own, otherwise the advances he had made would melt as effectively as snowflakes on a wet pavement. He spent his lunch hour ringing around contacts who might be able to help, but with the recession he was invariably met with negative responses. Most of the people he spoke to expressed their regret at being unable to help, but just could not afford to take on any extra staff - even at the minimum wage level.

However at the very last place on his list he was given some hope. When he spoke to the lady at this, his last hope, she had suggested that he should bring Kyle around to get a look at the place. They would then take it from there, but first she suggested that he should meet her for a drink to talk over his plans more fully. Tim replaced the receiver with excitement coursing through him, but it was not just excitement on Kyle's behalf. The strangest thing had happened to him during the course of their conversation and it had left him with a weird fizzing feeling in his stomach; but it seemed too ridiculous to even allow it to crystallise into a rational thought. As he couldn't stop thinking about it, however, he realised he would be forced to evaluate the conversation and the effect it had had on him; but not now as his lunch break was over and he was back on duty.

As Tim sat in the Dog and Whistle that evening waiting for the person he had spoken to on the phone that day to join him he was filled with trepidation and not only on Kyle's behalf. Never before had a disembodied voice had such an effect on him. His mum had noticed how withdrawn and occupied he had been at supper time, which in itself wasn't normal. Tim invariably brought worries or anxieties home with him – but this unusual reticence was both strange and slightly worrying. Normally they could talk about virtually anything but tonight her gentle prodding went unnoticed.

In fact Tim had noticed his Mum's gentle but insistent hints and queries, but didn't know what to say. How could he explain to her, or to anyone what had happened to him – it was just too ridiculous. He didn't understand it himself so how could he expect anyone else to. How could he look his mum in the eye and say "I fell in love with a voice today!" But crazy as it was - that seemed to be just what had happened. The woman he had spoken to had the most musical, bubbly, joyous voice he had ever heard. It had sounded like some weird combination of a blackbird's song, a rippling brook, and a baby's delighted laughter and he had quite literally fallen in love with the sound. Tim knew he could listen to that voice for ever and never get bored with it – but as far as meeting its owner was concerned he was terrified. After all she could be wizened old hag with a witch's hooked nose, a cold callous person with a face like an ice sculpture and eyes which could freeze hell. She could even be someone who had merely perfected a charming telephone voice or she could be 93! It was hard, however, to imagine that she could be any of the above.

    He had tried not to imagine what she might look like, but his imagination wouldn't be stilled; it had conjured up an image of a tall willowy figure with legs like Julia Roberts and a face resembling that of Claudia Schiffer and what, he told himself, severely, was the likelihood of that happening! As it happened no likelihood at all - because the woman who entered the bar and looked around her searching for a possible candidate for her meeting was older than his mum, as wide as she was tall and walked leaning heavily on a stick.

'Hi I'm Jan and you must be Tim,' she had said introducing herself as Jan the owner of the boarding/rescue kennels he had contacted. But the voice was one he had never heard before. She then apologised that the person he had spoken to earlier was unfortunately unable to come as she was caught up at work. But before long, Jan too had totally charmed him with her sense of humour and her positive optimistic outlook – but she was most definitely not the owner of his mystery voice.

'The dogs are my life now you see,' she said smiling such a broad infectious smile that it was impossible not to return it. 'I ran the kennels with my husband at first – we both loved dogs and wanted to rescue all the poor abused or neglected ones we could. It soon became obvious though that we had to find extra ways to finance our mission, hence the boarding side of the kennels. Honourable decent owners leave their dogs in our care while they holiday or whatever, and their fees help to pay for food, veterinary bills and staff costs for the rescue dogs. The dogs have always been important to me but since I lost Bill, my husband, they really are the most important things in my life,'

'That would explain why the person I spoke to on the phone was so keen on getting cheap or even free help in your kennels I suppose.'

'Oh yes, we are always on the lookout for extra help, we can't afford to pay all our kennel staff even the minimum wage unfortunately, but we operate as a training establishment. So trainees do at least leave us with one or more qualification, which helps if they want to stay in our kind of work. We do courses in animal husbandry, dog training and dog grooming, so it can be a good start for a young person who is willing and able. We might not pay much in ready cash, not much more than pocket money really, but I like to think we pay them in education. We liaise with the local college who assess the students and set the content of the courses for us, but one day we hope to be an accredited training centre as an extension of the college. Then the college would then pay us a small fee to take students for work experience and this in turn would help with our staffing problems.'

'That sounds as if it might suit Kyle,' responded Tim with a smile before going on to give Jan a potted history of his dealings with Kyle over the years. Culminating in the story of his Damascus road experience after seeing and caring for Sasha and her puppies. 'It was as if he had become a different lad, almost instantly,' continued Tim. 'There was suddenly no surliness, no belligerence - just this willing cheerful lad for whom nothing to do with the dogs was too much trouble and no job too unpleasant or arduous. He has never had the opportunity to shine or to take responsibility for anything before you see, and he just blossomed when he was given the chance.'

'He sounds just the kind of lad I need,' Jan said clapping her hands in delight like a small child. 'I've seen animals have the same effect on another young person only once before. This time it was a girl, but working with them, learning respect for them and caring for them turned my life around completely,' she added laughing uproariously at Tim's stunned expression. 'If you really think he'll be interested bring him along tomorrow afternoon at three – you are not on duty then are you?'

'No I'm not - but if we could make it a little later I could pick him up from school and bring him along then.'

So it was agreed - all Tim had to do now was put it to Kyle and hopefully elicit a positive response. And in the event Kyle, depressed and miserable as the pups had started to go to their new homes, jumped at the chance so enthusiastically that he didn't want to wait until the next day but wanted to go immediately. But wait he had to, and the hours between hearing about the kennels and half past three the next day passed excruciatingly slowly for poor Kyle. But eventually it was time for Tim to drive him to see the kennels and to meet Jan.

'Hello Kyle, you look as if you might be the answer to all my prayers,' Jan said grasping his hand between both of hers and eliciting a beaming smile in response. 'Let me show you around and then we'll sit down with a warm drink and really get to know each other properly.'

They began in the section where happy dogs, secure in the knowledge that they were loved and that their owners would return for them barked confidently and approached the front of their runs with an orgy of tail wagging and licking tongues. Kyle was excited and enchanted by the dogs with their myriad sizes and shapes. He asked many questions ranging from the dogs ages to their breed names and characteristics - as thirsty for knowledge as a man lost in a desert was for water. He enquired about the daily routine and how they were cared for on a daily basis. Then as he bent to greet a small, pretty mongrel Jan looked over him at Tim, smiled and winked as if to seal the deal.

The contrast between the boarding runs and the rescue runs could not have been more marked in both the dog's behaviour or Kyle's manner. Most of the dogs were wary and much more nervous than the boarders had been. Each one looking at them with sad troubled eyes as if terrified about what might be about to happen to them next. With each dog Kyle drew quieter, more reflective and sadder with each run they passed. Several times he reached out to an animal which looked utterly terrified as if the hand offered in friendship would become a weapon with which to beat it.

'What happened with this one?' Kyle asked his voice thick with emotion, as he looked into the shadows at the back of the run where a small terrified white dog was cowering and whining quietly as if all the hounds of hell were after him.

'A cruelty case as you've probably guessed. The previous owners have been prosecuted and the dog confiscated. We took him on in the hope of rehoming him but he is so scared no one can get near him. When we clean out his run or put food down for him he cowers in the very back of the kennel like he is now, trembling and crying. He only cautiously creeps out again when he is sure we've gone and he knows it is safe to do so. No-one had been able to get anywhere near him and we have all tried our best.'

'Can I go in and try?' Kyle asked surprising himself as well as them.

'If you really want to, he's not at all aggressive so he won't bite or anything, but please don't be upset when he still cowers away from you.'

Jan opened the run's door and sure enough the little dog slunk to the farthest corner of the run, his belly almost dragging along the ground. Then when he could go no further he forced his back right up against the back wall as if trying to push himself as far from the perceived danger as he could, even through the very wall itself if he could. Kyle sat down on the concrete floor and crossed his legs without even looking at the dog. He sat with his back toward the dog his head bowed and began to quietly hum soft lilting tunes, which may have been those of the lullabies his mother had once sung to him.

Many minutes passed as Jan and Tim held their collective breath. They were both transfixed by the scene before them, frozen to the spot and almost afraid to breathe. Slowly, after many long minutes had passed, the terrified dog began to raise its head, each minute movement so slight that the onlookers couldn't even be sure it had happened - and still Kyle sat unmoving. More time passed until at last Jan nudged Tim gently and pointed to the dog, who had begun to lose some of the tension in his body and peel himself away from the wall. Slowly oh so very slowly the poor little dog began the huge journey toward the boy. In reality and in practical terms, it was only a matter of ten feet or so. But in terms of what it meant to the dog and the courage it took him to take, it was a marathon. Still Kyle sat as still as a statue, but he seemed to be aware that the dog was inching cautiously towards him, at last the dog was in sniffing distance and stretching his neck as long as he could - beginning a thorough nasal examination of this strange statue which had invaded his sanctuary. And still Kyle didn't move until he slowly, and with infinite care, he placed a hand on his thigh before sliding the hand slowly, oh so slowly down his leg until his wrist was resting on the very edge of his knee and his fingers outstretched as if in welcome.

    Having completed his thorough nasal examination of the thing in his run, the little dog began inching his way around Kyle until he found the outspread hand. Still looking like a coiled spring ready to flee at a seconds notice he sniffed the hand with infinite care before placing his head under it. Then and only then did Kyle respond by gently fondling the dogs silky ears. This seemed to seal the pact and for the first time, the little dog really began to relax. After several more minutes of being fondled he trotted around to stand at Kyle's side, then the miracle was complete. Before Tim or Jan had time to let out the breaths they had been unconsciously holding, for what seemed like hours, the dog climbed onto Kyle's lap with soft contented sounds. Kyle's arms then gently enfolded the dog and he buried his face in the soft fur of the brave little dog, who had taken the first bold steps towards trusting a human again.

'Well I've never seen anything like that before! It was truly miraculous' whispered Jan in wonder. 'That lad has a magic touch.'

'Perhaps they instinctively recognised something in each other,' said Tim. 'Kyle has had a rough time learning how to trust – even who to trust come to that.'

'Well whatever the reason I want him to come and work here more than ever, he would be a wonderful asset to the kennels – let's face it he's proved that to us in no uncertain terms.'

After leaving Kyle and the dog to bond for another half hour or so during which time they continued to watch the process in awe and wonder, they all made their way back to the reception area cum office. Even Bob the little dog after much whining and clawing at the front of his pen was allowed to accompany them.

'He's obviously decided you're going nowhere without him,' said Jan with a laugh. 'I can't believe the change in him after such a short time,' she said watching Bob dance around Kyle's legs with obvious joy and adoration.

Once in the office Jan made them all tea, and they sat around chatting. Jan immediately offered Kyle a place on their team and explained about the training courses. A delighted Kyle responded as quickly, saying he would work at the kennels for whatever Jan could afford to give him and would do any and every course available to him.

'I never knew I could feel so good about meself,' he explained, constantly stroking an adoring Bob as he spoke. 'Just knowing that I can make the dogs lives a bit better makes me own life better an all – do you know what I mean?'

'I do' said Jan. 'I have always found that doing a kindness for someone or something else has a way of improving your own life as if by reward.'

'Good heavens what's going on here? Do my eyes deceive me or is that Bob sitting on that young man's lap?'

The sound of the female voice confirmed that someone else had entered the already crowded room and her first few words were enough for Tim to realise it was "THE" voice and immediately tensed on hearing it. He was afraid to turn around, afraid that the reality of her would be a disappointment after all his imaginings. So he sat completely still until forced to acknowledge the newcomer when Jan introduced them.

Rising and turning to greet the person he had fantasised about was not easy, but although once again nothing like his imagination had conjured up, the young woman standing smiling at him matched her voice totally. Bearing no resemblance to either Julia Roberts or Claudia Schiffer she was nonetheless as captivating as her voice. Of medium height with coppery brown curly hair which bounced as she talked and eyes the colour of newly opened conkers she smiled up at him and held out her hand.

Tim had heard people talk about electric sensations caused by the first touch of someone to whom you were attracted. But he had dismissed it a romantic twaddle – until now. As he reached out for her hand and held it in greeting, pins and needle like sensations shot up his arm so strongly that his eyes involuntarily opened wide. Even more surprising was that he witnessed his own reaction mirrored on her face.

'Hi, I'm Lizzie, Jan's vet – well vet in progress, so to speak. Did we speak on the phone the other day?'

'I believe we did, I was asking if you needed any help at the kennels – I didn't realise you were not actually employed here.'

'You couldn't be more accurate,' laughed Jan. 'Poor Lizzie comes here to check out the dogs and generally do any veterinary work we need, but without being paid a penny for it. She is a qualified veterinary nurse, and is over half way through her training to be fully fledged vet. I really don't know how we would manage without her.'

'Hey, that's quite enough about me. Tell me what's happened with Bob here, has some kind of miracle taken place?'

'It has and its name is Kyle, and here's the man himself,' answered Jan enigmatically. 'Make yourself a cup of tea and I'll tell you all about it.'

It didn't take long for Kyle to prove his worth. Over the following weeks and months he became an invaluable member of the kennel staff. He proved to be as willing and hard working as he had been with Sue, but the special needs of the rescue dogs added a new dimension to his skill and aptitude. After winning Bob over so effectively any abused and terrified animal brought in was given the 'Kyle treatment' and most were soon happier and ready to, at least begin, to trust humans again.

Having been coerced into meeting Bob and seeing how keen and responsible her son had become Kyle's mum happily agreed that he should be allowed to adopt the little dog. This was a great relief for everyone as Bob grieved and pined when Kyle was forced to leave him. Apart from those times he followed Kyle around the kennels like a shadow, which in turn made many of the more nervous new rescue dogs trust Kyle more readily. Once Kyle had officially adopted little Bob though, the dog's joy was complete as he never again needed to be parted from his beloved human. So Bob now went everywhere that Kyle did.

Kyle had enrolled at night school to begin the first of his training courses which was to be linked to his work at the kennels. As the practical aspects of his course were to performed at he kennels, this in turn was another boost for the kennel's reputation. After being approached by the course tutors, Jan and her establishment were to become an accredited training centre. This had long been an aim of Jan's as it gave them greater stature. It also meant that they would be paid a welcome annual fee in return for monitoring and providing training placements for students. The centre might even be able to attract more donations as well, because sponsors would now see that it was helping both animals and young people.

Of course Tim was anxious to keep up to date with Kyle's progress and so became a regular visitor – where he just happened to run into Lizzie on several occasions and before long he had plucked up the courage to ask her out.

The only sadness that both Tim and Lizzie confided to each other was that they had noticed a gradual but marked deterioration in Jan's health. Lizzie, as one of her oldest friends, had expressed her concern but typically Jan had laughed it off.

'Don't you worry about me lass,' she had said. 'I've had a good life and when the time comes I'll go willingly. The only worry I've had for years is who I could leave the kennels to and know they would be kept running as they are now. I had thought of leaving them to you, but you've more than enough on your hands as it is, and now it looks as if you might have a husband and family to factor into the equation shortly,' she teased. 'Now though my prayers have been answered. I know I can leave the whole thing to Kyle. Oh, I know he's only a lad right now, but that boy has been a godsend in more ways than one. I feel as if I've been waiting for him to come along for a long time. Now I know I can leave my life's work in safe hands knowing he will take good care of it. I can begin to take things more easily now and give him more responsibility. And when I finally go, which hopefully won't be for some time yet, I know he will be able and willing to take over.'

Part Nine

Full Circle

Two years later Kyle was the owner of the kennels. Thankfully Jan was still alive, although in all honestly, no longer kicking, as life had become a permanent struggle for her. The arthritis with which she had battled for so long had finally made it impossible for her to work on a daily basis. Her life now comprised of severely restricted movements, constant pain and frustration that the simplest of tasks was now beyond her. Her spirit and her determination remained indomitable though, as she faced each new day with a resolve resembling that of the "spirit of the blitz."

As soon as it became obvious that managing the kennels single handed was now beyond her, she contacted her solicitor and had the business transferred, lock stock and barrel, to Kyle. He had objected strongly saying that he was too young for such a responsibility, that he was not experienced enough and that he certainly didn't deserve it. When these arguments fell on deaf ears he tried taking the tack that, although dealing with the dogs was fine, the account books and office side were another matter – one which was way beyond him. Resistance proved useless however as Jan, always one to gently get her own way in the end, made him see that he would be doing her a favour by keeping her life's work alive.

'Don't worry about the books or the other office work though,' she had said. 'The very last decision I will make about the active running of the centre will be the appointment of someone willing to do all that. In fact I have someone in mind.'

'Who is it?'

'A lady who over the years has adopted two of my rescue dogs. They are both gone to the great kennels in the sky now and because she is no longer as fit as she was she is afraid of taking on another dog. She has helped me out in the office before though, and I know she will do a great job. Being around the other dogs will help take off the sense of loss she is feeling at the moment too.'

And so it was decided.

Kyle had learned from the mistress, over the years though, and knew resistance was useless once her mind was made up. So, having no other choice, he replied that he would only agree if she continued to live there as long as she wanted – advising where necessary. So it was agreed. Kyle and his mum Mary left their council house and moved in to the house attached to the kennels, where Mary took on the role of housekeeper without even having to be asked. She could also help Jan with her day to day needs if necessary and just as importantly there was always someone on hand to act as carer – as long as Jan was not made aware of it! Mary, herself being a quick learner, soon learned that the trick with Jan was to make her think she was doing them the favour, in this way masking her own need of Mary's help. So she made the point of often thanking Jan for all she had done for them both and in particular for Kyle. But then this was no more than the truth and was just how she felt.

Having Mary there on hand, in turn meant there was even less for Jan to do, leaving her, when she felt well enough, to happily potter about the kennels doing what she could. Even on days when her arthritis was so painful that she could hardly move she was able to pass on her experience and knowledge to Kyle who was always willing to gain new knowledge and insight; apparently soaking them up like a sponge. And in this way Jan still felt as if she was playing a vital part in the work of the kennels.

Kyle had not only passed all the qualifications Jan had suggested he should take but, under Lizzie's tutelage had learned animal first aid, meaning he could stitch wounds, dress cuts, lance boils and cysts and many more of the simpler veterinary tasks. He had also opened a very popular dog grooming parlour, puppy socialisation and training centre, agility field and even had plans to build a hydro-therapy pool; and he had never been happier or more fulfilled.

Mary often said she dreaded to think how differently his life might have turned out if it were not for Tim's kindness and patronage. She was also eternally grateful to Jan as well of course. But she knew Kyle would never have met Jan if it hadn't been for Tim's initial subterfuge when he had hatched his scheme to introduce them. Unlike others who had tried to set Kyle on a better path before, Tim hadn't given up on him. Like Mary he had looked beyond the wall of resentment and aggression, Kyle had built up around himself, and seen the lad's true nature and potential.

Mary, Jan and Sue had also become great friends and usually met up most mornings for a coffee and a chat in the warm kitchen of the rescue centre's house. Sasha, Sue and Tim's beloved Beardie was getting on in years now having reached the age of ten but was still lively and healthy. She very much enjoyed her visits to the kennels too where she was often to be found happily playing with the other dogs, giving the impression that she was still in her puppy hood.

One of the other most incredible changes though had been in Tim. He and Lizzie were now firmly 'an item' and everyone noticed how happy he was these days. He was going out more now that he had someone he wanted to go out with, and had a constant spring to his step. Although he had thought himself, if not exactly happy, at least contented enough in the past, he now seemed to have a smile permanently glued to his face.

Although his story was somewhat different to the others in as much as he had been the one offering the kindnesses to both Barry and Kyle, without appearing to receive anything back. In fact he felt he had been given the greatest gift of all. He had met a very special person in Lizzie who was, she assured him, happy to share the rest of her life with him. Sue of course was over the moon embracing Lizzie into their small, but close, family with an eagerness which bordered on the embarrassing. She had already bought herself a wonderfully outrageous hat for the wedding although it was not planned to take place for a few months yet. She was permanently found talking about the wedding to friends and neighbours ending each conversation with 'you must come along if you can.'

So it seemed that the whole of their small town might be destined to turn out to what locals were calling " the wedding of the decade" if Sue had her wish. Certainly in the way of villages and small towns the round-robin effect of news and gossip circulating from person to person was well underway. Discoveries of how Tim and Lizzie had come to meet and the tales of the others involved in the circle of kindnesses, given and received, buzzed from ear to ear.

Sue and Tim had naturally invited Barry and Peggy who were themselves married now and living in happy contentment in Barry's old house. As well as its occupants, the house itself had in turn been happily transformed by an ocean of emulsion, acres of new carpet and an army of workmen. Peggy's own house had been rented out and the money they made from it each month went into a special "New Zealand account." This meant that regular visits to her family on the other side of the world could be eagerly anticipated without financial burden. With Barry to accompany her they were not a physical or emotional strain either, she felt safe as long as he was with her. His natural organisational skills meaning that checking in to airports, handling baggage and arranging transport to and from their airport of choice went both smoothly and effortlessly.

Sue and Tim also took in Riss, the puppy they had rescued along with his litter mates, whenever Barry and

Peggy were away on their extended visits and in this way they had, as Barry was wont to say "all our bases are covered,"

Barry still owned the computer store but he had taken on a reliable and trustworthy manager – another of those who had fallen on hard times and whom Tim was desperate to help. Vikram was a technological wizard who had been tossed aside by his previous employer when the company's profits started to fall. It had been a rash and deeply regretted move on the part of the company but stubbornness and unwillingness to admit any error on the part of the managing director, meant that poor Vikram had continued to swell the ranks of the unemployed. He had tried repeatedly to find work in his specialist field but when this had been fruitless had tried any and all opportunities of which he had become aware - all without success.

Then in desperation he had walked in to Barry's shop on the off chance that a job might be on offer. He had a wife and a young baby to support and being a proud, honourable man wanted to be the one to do the supporting, rather than relying on the country which had given his great grandfather sanctuary in the early part of the 1950's.

It had not only been a meeting of minds but an instant liking of one another and a short trial period had resulted in Vikram becoming manager which was a blessing for them both as the young man now had a job, a salary and his pride restored to him. In turn Barry now had time on his hands, time he had craved to spend with Peggy, visiting places they had never been or re-visiting old haunts. So it was a win-win situation for them all and it meant that when extended holidays to New Zealand were planned Barry could relax knowing the shop and his loyal customers were in good hands.

Peggy was still seeing Patrick on a regular basis, but now more out of habit and true friendship than necessity. Patrick through gentle encouragement had learned to open his heart to Peggy pouring out all the bitterness, anger, resentment and even hatred which his mother's desertion had fostered within him. Patrick now accepted that there must have been reasons, other than those he had previously considered, which had prompted her to leave him cold, alone and starving at such a tender age. But as yet he had not been able to ask her the questions he had longed to phrase throughout all of his life, since all efforts to trace her had as yet proved fruitless. He now accepted though, that her desertion was nothing to do with him – that he was in no way to blame for it. Previously he had always thought that it must have been his fault - that he was a wicked, naughty child or that he was so unlovable that she could not bear to be around him.

For as long as he could remember her desertion had made his grandfather feel the need to redress this balance. He had been well aware of Patrick's feelings, and had tried to compensate by constantly praising Patrick - telling him that he was sure he was capable of anything; reassuring him that he was neither unloved nor worthless.

Patrick could hear the much loved and greatly missed voice even now, telling him that nothing was impossible to a boy – then a man as good or as worthy as Patrick. "You can do whatever you set your heart on my lad," or " you are clever enough to achieve anything you want to, but kind and honourable enough not to stamp on others as you are doing it," or even "the way you live your life, respecting all living things, marks you out to be among the finest of men and don't you ever forget it." These had been a few of his grandfather's wise and encouraging words all of which he had said with impeccable confidence. Patrick had wanted so much to believe it, but his mother's abandonment had generated such a lack of self-worth in him, that no such praise could completely eradicate it.

    Many quiet contemplative talks with Peggy later he had begun to accept that whatever had led his mother to take such drastic action – none if it had been caused by him. As a young child of eighteen months there was no way the blame could be laid at his door. Perhaps if he had cried incessantly day and night, his mother's nerves might have been so stretched to breaking point that she would leave him for a short while in order to get a little peace and perspective. But this had not been the case! Neighbours had stated that he was normally a happy child who cried only rarely until the last few days before his rescue. So whatever had driven her, he now accepted that the fault , most likely the result of an illness, must be have been hers and hers alone.

    There had been no trace of her since the search by the Salvation Army had begun but Patrick was assured that there were still one or two channels to be explored before the case was closed. And as no evidence of her death had been discovered the hope of finding her still existed.

The main thing Patrick now felt was that, although he would never be able to condone or completely forgive her actions, he could at least understand them. He could now consider possible situations, which might have resulted in her need to take such drastic measures. He acknowledged that she might have been so desperate that she thought complete escape might be thought her only option; maybe had even begin to understand what desperation had driven her to take the course she had.

During one of their many chats Peggy had talked about Tim and Lizzie's wedding and Patrick had said he and his family would love to come to the church to wish them well, although he would not expect them to be officially invited.

Patrick told Trish about the wedding too when she came on one of her regular visits to the respite home where her mother, Fiona, was spending more and more time. Both Patrick and Trish were aware that the stage where Fiona needed more specialist, permanent residential care had been reached or at the very least was fast approaching. But Trish was still reluctant to permanently pass the burden of care over to strangers. Her mother had been wonderful, in Trish's eyes the best of mothers, friends, confidantes and supporters. She had cared for her family with selfless devotion and Trish felt very strongly that now the tables had turned it was her duty and her indeed her joy to care for her mother.

With the respite care Patrick's home offered she felt she could cope for some time yet. Just the thought of passing her mother's care to strangers who, although they might see to her every need, would never love her was anathema to her. While she was still able to hold her down her part time job at the library, which Trish still found such a welcome respite for herself; and with Patrick's constant support she knew she could cope. At the library, although never able to forget her mother's plight she could at least lock it away in the deepest recesses of her mind; she could chat happily to colleagues and customers alike and bury herself in her work. She found the very order of the library with its Dewey system soothing. With a place for everything and everything in its place she found a calm and a predictability she could never experience at home, because life with her mother could by no means be described as calm. With Fiona's every increasing mental fragility, one never knew what to expect next and " the phrase living on a knife's edge" took on new meaning.

Often Trish found herself greeting visitors to the library as firm friends now, rather than mere customers. Her network of friends and acquaintances had expanded, not only though her work but also through her involvement with Patrick's centre. One of her very favourite friendly faces though was Sam for whom she felt the greatest affection.

Sam had "graduated" from his adult literacy class with honours. Due in part to being the student who had taken the least time to complete the course, and to become a competent and confident reader. The change in his fortunes and lifestyle as a result was nothing short of amazing. He was still employed as a crossing patrol officer, as he enjoyed the job too much to give it up. In a startling turn around though he had taken, and passed, courses to become a classroom assistant at the school. He now worked there five mornings a week.

The duties he loved the most were those where he worked with individual children or with groups who were experiencing difficulties with their own reading. With his background he was an ideal teacher for he understood their frustrations and hardships. He could confide in them about his own experiences and difficulties like nobody else could. He could empathise with them, as well as making practical suggestions which could improve their lives, until the time they had mastered reading. He could also point out to them the very real practical and emotional problems being unable to read would create for them as they grew to adulthood and how their inability would curtail every aspect of their lives He explained how everything would be more difficult, from finding jobs and understanding partners to having to deal with the perception many unenlightened people would have that because they were unable to read they must be mentally retarded.

Becoming one of the literate majority had been the start of a whole new life for Sam as he now thought of himself as whole a real complete person for the first time. He felt he could hold his head high, that he was entitled to hold and voice opinions on a wide variety of subjects and that those opinions would be not only listened to but respected even if others did not agree with them.

He had also shared his secret with his wife and daughter as he arrived home one day with his certificate clutched in his hand. For the first time he felt guilt free because no longer did he have to lie or deceive them with excuses, subterfuge or half truths. But best of all because he was now earning more money by having the two secure jobs he and Lisa had discussed expanding their family. They had always wanted a brother or sister for Emily, but they had depended on Lisa's wage to survive which meant leaving her job to have another baby had been totally impracticable. Now it was at least a possibility and one they could anticipate with joy.

As well as keeping in touch with Trish, Sam often met up with Sharon for a coffee or just a chat on "their" park bench. She was so much happier now that she and Steve were officially a couple. They were living together but had decided that they would not marry until both the children had left home to begin their own lives and become independent. Both Katy and Adam loved Steve though. They recognised that he was a genuine guy who was obviously devoted to their mum – which was a refreshing change after the treatment meted out to her by their father. They had both been forced to re-evaluate their opinions on their father and had simultaneously reached the conclusion that it was he who had, in fact, been the cause of the marriage breakdown, rather that Sharon. As a result and also as a direct reaction to Sam's stern words on the night of Sharon's attack they had both become much more helpful around the house, they had both gained jobs and appreciated their mother more than they ever had.

This was wonderful and Sharon thoroughly appreciated the turn around in her fortunes, there were no hostile comments or resentful glances now and their home was filled with mutual respect, laughter and love rather than bitterness and anger. There was no longer any animosity or strained silences and they no longer took their mother for granted.

Steve had, by example, shown how they ought to be treating their mother. He demonstrated that he had the utmost respect for Sharon and showed his love for her in many ways, by offering to help do tasks around the house even by taking over the cooking sometimes. He would often buy her silly little gifts, leave jokey affectionate notes for her to find as well as demonstrating his love in a hundred other ways. Because of this Katy and Adam were forced to recognise the difference between how Steve behaved toward their mother and how their father had treated her. He had shown her only such callous disdain – selfishly pursuing his own pleasures with neither a thought nor a care for how it affected his family.

Katy summed it up one evening as they sat listening to music when Steve and Sharon had gone to the pictures. She had laughed about it saying 'Surely this should be the other way round and we should have a better social life than them. Or at the very least the oldies should be paying for us to go the cinema to give them time alone!'

'Parents eh - what can you do with them!' responded Adam grinning wickedly. 'They just don't make them like they used to!'

'It's good to see Mum so happy though isn't it? I know it's an out dated term now but Steve is a really *good* bloke isn't he?'

'He is – he's great and nothing like that tosser we are forced to call Dad. In many ways I just wish Steve had been our Dad all along.'

Strange as it seemed Sharon put her change of fortune down to being mugged. She knew many people would consider this irrational but everything had improved from that moment. Although she would never go as far as thanking her mugger – she had been too badly injured for that, she was perversely thankful that it happened. The event had changed so much for her, it had given her back her children. Coming so close to losing her had given them both a severe shock to the system, making them realise how much they loved her. In that moment when they had first seen her injuries for themselves they had changed from sullen, resentful children to the loving, caring ones they had been before the divorce. But more than that the mugging, horrible though it had been, had given her Steve. Sharon doubted that without those traumatic events either of them would have found the courage to reveal their feelings for each other.

Sam and Sharon still met up every week or so for a coffee and a chat. It was Sam, while sitting and enjoying one of these get-togethers, drinking their coffee in a pavement café on a gloriously warm day who finally put the whole story together and completed the circle. Sharon had been talking about Lizzie, who was now over half way to being qualified as a vet and working part time at the surgery to gain extra practical experience. When she happened to mention that Lizzie was getting married a few months later to a policeman called Tim, a bell had rung in Sam's head. He had always been a good listener and had heard through Trish about the circle of people connected by a thread of kindnesses as tenuous yet as strong as spider silk. Kyle's mum had naturally become good friends with Tim, but a friendship had also blossomed between her and Barry and Peggy through Kyle and the work at the dog sanctuary. They had met when Barry had sorted out a second hand computer for them to use at a knock down price. Barry had also by coincidence been approached by Patrick to service his computers at the centre and in conversation Trish's name had been mentioned as Barry and Peggy were regulars at the library. As they chatted about these people something clicked in Sam's mind and he realised how all of them were inter-connected by this circle of kindness. Sharon was amazed when he told her about his theories. She told him about how Lizzie had become part of the veterinary surgery's family revealing a strand of the story which led them full circle back to the Lizzie they had talked about earlier and whose wedding was forthcoming.

    Everything gelled for them in seconds. Between them they knew all the participants in the story which had started with one act of generosity and kindness.

Kindnesses which had spread out like ripples on water to touch so many lives.

'I wish I was able to write' said Sharon jokingly. 'This would make a good subject for a novel.'

But Sam had other ideas – he suggested that all those involved, apart from Tim and Lizzie, should meet at a local pub one night. There they could chat and either prove or disprove this theory and discover whether their suspicions were correct. Sam thought how lovely it would be if they all – together with their families - turned up at the church to give their blessings and good wishes to the two people who were at both the beginning and end of their amazing journey.

So almost like Chinese Whispers each of the characters in our story told those nearest to them about Sam's ideas and his plan to meet up. It took some time to find a night when all of them would be free but eventually a date was decided upon and the evening of their first meeting dawned. Some were excited at the thought of meeting each other for the first time while others were a little nervous at the prospect of being thrown into a group of folk they didn't know. They need not have worried though. Sharon clapped her hands, after the drinks had been brought, before rising to introduce herself to any of the others who didn't know her. She briefly told them about Lizzie and how she had met the young girl, but modestly played down her part in turning the teenager's life around – giving most of the credit to Steve who in turn made them all laugh by telling his own version of events in which Sharon had been the main protagonist and he a mere bystander.

Then she introduced Sam telling them all how he had been her rescuer and encouraged him to tell his own story. So the evening passed with each of them adding their own particular story in this incredible chain of events until at last they got to young Kyle who had come with his mum and Jan. It was Kyle himself who, showing more maturity than anyone knowing him in the past would ever have expected, remarked how amazing it was that so many situations and indeed whole lives had been transformed for the better by one initial and simple act of kindness from a stranger.

They were all agreed that it would be a wonderful idea to present themselves at the wedding – few of them expected to be sent official invitations, but all of them wanted to be there, hoping nevertheless that they might find the opportunity to introduce themselves and reveal their own part in the story.

Standing and raising his glass, Steve proposed a toast. 'To the Kindness of Strangers, and all those whose lives have been enriched by it,' he said as loud applause and cheers bounced off the walls of the small room.

If you enjoyed this book , please share on Facebook or Twitter.

It would be great too 'like' my 'Tina Cox – books' page on Facebook, and even review this book on Amazon.

Have you read my other books on Kindle?

'Sanctuary'

'Table for Eight'

'One man and his dog … came to tune a piano'

'Christmas Presence'

'Dream Doorway'

'Laying the Ghosts'

Also in print:

'Table for Eight'

'Christmas Presence'

'Sanctuary'

Enjoy!

Made in the USA
Charleston, SC
14 October 2015